WHERE
THE
TREES
WERE

WHERE THE TREES WERE

INGA SIMPSON

B
BLACKFRIARS

BLACKFRIARS

First published in Australia and New Zealand in 2016 by Hachette Australia
First published in Great Britain in 2016 by Blackfriars

1 3 4 5 7 9 10 8 6 4 2

ISBN 978-0-349-13441-3

Typeset in Adobe Garamond Pro by Bookhouse, Sydney
Printed and bound in Great Britain by
Clays Ltd, St Ives plc

Blackfriars
An imprint of
Little, Brown Book Group
Carmelite House
50 Victoria Embankment
London EC4Y 0DZ

An Hachette UK Company
www.hachette.co.uk

www.blackfriarsbooks.co.uk

Lachlan Valley, 1987

WE FLOATED DOWNRIVER. Stringybarks and red gums leaned over the water, throwing shade too thin for the heat. The boys were ahead of me, in formation. I had missed the start and given up, let them go. It was quieter on my own. Sometimes it was as if the water was talking and I liked to listen.

There were four of us. Five, counting Matty. We left Kieran's little brother at home when we could, but during the holidays it was difficult to get away without him.

I drifted past the swinging tree, with its knotted rope, waiting. Ahead, Kieran paddled towards the beach, wanting to win, although it wasn't really a race. I paddled, too, now, to catch up. Kieran was out, on the scoop of pale sand and gathering up his lilo. The back of his calves were burnt brown, disappearing up the bank. Ian was out next, then Josh, then Matty and me. We pelted along the path, well worn by us and stock coming down to drink. Our bare feet gripped the earth, impervious to rocks and roots. On land I was quicker, more certain, even dragging the lilo, and left Matty behind.

From a high point on the bank – the launching pad – we threw ourselves into the water all over again, rubber slapping on water and skin slapping on rubber. This time I got myself into a better position, where the river was deep and ran more swiftly, helping me move in front of Kieran. I was lighter and, if I kept my balance, would reach the shore first this time.

'No paddling!' he said.

'I'm not.' I pulled in my arms, tucked them by my sides, and lay my cheek on the pillow of the lilo. Once red and navy, it was now more pink and grey, from the sun. My swimmers top itched where I was peeling and I wished, not for the first time, that I could still take it off the way I used to, and go bare-chested with the boys. Mum had put an end to that last summer – saying I was too old.

Ian and Josh floated out either side. Our wingmen. Matty called from behind, which we ignored, although Kieran did glance over his shoulder to make sure he wasn't drowning.

'What time do you reckon it is?' Ian squinted into the sun.

'Not even close to lunch, yet,' Josh said.

Ian was always most concerned with time, for fear of missing a meal. Fear of his dad, too. His mum worked, so he had as many chores as us even though they lived in town, and was always in trouble for getting home late or messing them up.

Matty paddled to catch up, his splashes getting closer. 'I'm hungry, too,' he said.

Dragonflies flitted and dipped between us. We drifted around the bend in a languid line, as if the river was ours, as if it always would be.

Afternoons were for swinging.

We climbed up the tree and onto the horizontal branch, waiting our turn to place our feet on the knot, grip the rope and throw ourselves out into midair, to freefall into the river. If the timing was right, the arc perfect, we would reach the middle and touch the bottom with our feet or our hands, depending how we had left the rope.

The water was cold down there, brown and quiet. Things brushed against my skin. I felt a pull, not just of the river, the current wanting to carry me. When I looked up to the surface, the world was strange and far away, as if perhaps I was no longer part of it. But I always needed breath and had to return to the surface, and then it seemed that I belonged after all.

Matty couldn't get his swing right, lacking the strength to push out far enough, and often hesitating before jumping. So one of us would push him and tell him when to let go, or jump with him.

It was all easy for Kieran. He was getting muscles and moods and had started wearing board shorts over his Speedos. He did somersaults and dives and bombs to impress us, sending up great fountains of water. Sometimes he would climb to the top of the tree and dive from there. I held my breath when he did that, even though I wasn't underwater, because I knew that he was too high and, with the summer we'd had, the river too low.

We had been at it for an hour or so when we found ourselves up the tree without Kieran. For a while it was fun. I could keep up with Ian and Josh and we jumped in pairs, taking turns with Matty.

Then we found ourselves all in, treading water. Waiting for Kieran. Even the cockatoos had gone quiet.

'I'm tired,' Matty said. I let him grab my shoulders, although it nearly sent me under.

Ian looked towards the shore. 'Maybe he's started on the food already.'

Josh's hair was sticking straight up on top, like wet straw. 'Should we go look for him?'

'There he is,' I said.

Kieran was high on the bank, gesturing for us to follow, as if we weren't already on our way. The look on his face was enough. The promise of something new – an adventure.

Canberra, 2004

SHE SHIVERED. THE basement was kept at a constant temperature – twenty degrees – but always felt colder at night. She had been sitting still too long.

The few times she had worked into the night, prepping for a big exhibition, had been with others, the place alive with movement and noise. In the low fluorescent light, and the quiet, the room most resembled a morgue, its walls lined with specimen jars and stuffed animals, the tables littered with dismembered and decaying objects, some being prepared for display, others for storage or disposal. Until recently, there had been human remains, too. They were hidden away now, off site, awaiting identification and repatriation. The knowledge of them lingered in the room.

She stretched one leg and then the other, closed her hands into fists and released them. Upstairs, the night guard would be completing another circuit, around the great masters and the other pieces deemed of significant cultural value. Frank always did

Wednesday nights. Unless he was sick, which had only happened once in five years. Or when he was on leave. He took his four weeks all at once, over Christmas, every year. He was one of those guys counting down the remaining workdays until retirement, actually crossing them off the calendar with a red texta. He was old enough to be in the original super scheme, which through some drafting glitch, gave a financial return so good, if retiring at age fifty-four years and eleven months – rather than fifty-five – that you had to work for another ten years to match it. 'Fifty-four eleven', they called it. Or they used to, before September Eleven.

They had shut that scheme down before her time. It was another of the baby boomer booms she was paying for. Like the rest of her generation, she would have to work until she was sixty. In theory, anyway. It could all be over tonight.

Her stomach growled. Being alone with her thoughts had been peaceful at first but now those thoughts kept coming back to food – the pasta she might have had for dinner, the pear she had forgotten to eat for afternoon tea, the sushi she could have packed in her pockets. The emergency power bar still in her pannier.

She checked her watch again. Frank would be in the tearoom, his two-minute noodles turning in the microwave. She could almost smell them. Right on midnight, he sat down at the square table, with a detective novel – it was always a detective novel – and slurped and read for fifteen minutes. The monitors allowed him to keep one eye on things. Or they would, but he sat with his back to them, listening to jazz through his earphones. It was always jazz.

They had been installing an exhibition around the clock, trying to make the opening on time after a customs delay, when she had first seen him. The presence of five senior conservationists scoffing Turkish pizza at the tearoom counter hadn't disturbed his routine in the slightest. She should have reported him. Someone should have. It was a major security flaw: a ten-minute window. Just what she had been looking for.

She moved now, a shadow in the shadows, to deactivate the alarms, disarm the outer cameras, and open the gate. The loading dock camera was out of order. A stroke of luck she had taken for a good sign.

The driver backed in: lights off, plates and brakelights covered, reversing alarm disconnected. The truck was gunmetal grey and immaculate.

The exhibit was waiting. Like a prisoner, it had been prepped for transfer tomorrow, back out to the Mitchell storage facility. Laid out and bubble-wrapped. *Bubble wrap* for fuck's sake. But all that plastic would help it travel safe now. It was worth a hell of a lot to the right people.

The truck's tray crept closer to the ramp. She held up a gloved hand, signalling stop. His face, like hers, was hidden beneath a cheap black balaclava, but his eyes shone in the side mirror. She started the forklift, eased forward. Its modified prongs were more used to paintings, busts and sculptures, but it took the package in a familiar embrace. She raised it slow and steady, just one finger on the hydraulic lever, as she had practised, keeping the package balanced.

They were almost out of time.

He tapped his hands on the wheel, watching the clock. He could still take off, fly free, if something went wrong; that was their agreement. She drove to the edge of the ramp and lowered the forks onto the truck's tray.

He climbed out of the cab and onto the back, gripping the tree as she reversed. He rolled it into the middle of the tray, spun it lengthways, and covered it with a soft tarp while she parked the forklift and cut the motor. In the quiet, she could breathe again.

She caught one end of each strap, looped it under the rail, and threw it back. He tightened the fasteners.

She climbed into the passenger seat, shut the door. Thirty seconds. He was up and in, all in one smooth movement. Twenty seconds. They drove out the gate and into the lane, into the night, and along streets still damp from the afternoon's late shower. It was windy on the bridge, the water choppy in yellow lamplight, and then they looped away via the off ramp. There were few cars on the Parkway, and lights twinkled in the satellite city centre in the valley. She kept one eye on the lanes behind them in her side mirror. He watched the road ahead. 'So far, so good,' he said.

They were already pulling into the warehouse by the time the automated message alerting her to the security breach flashed on her pager.

Their footsteps were loud on the concrete, the space inside vast and empty around the truck. They bumped fists for a job well done before slipping out the side door. He locked it behind them.

They walked in opposite directions without looking back.

It was cold, even in her fleece and jacket. Even with her blood still pumping. She walked to the car park of the nearby club, fished her keys from her pocket and unlocked her bike. There was already a crust of frost on the grass.

She cut across the club's service road to the bike path. Her headlight showed the way around the curves and through dips, up that last steep rise. Back past the empty city centre. It was the ghost town everyone said it was. She saw no one.

The sky was so clear she could see the pits on the moon. Her legs had found a rhythm; she was part of the bike, and together they were part of the universe. The stars looked on, guiding her home through the empty streets and around the back of her local shops. She threw the balaclava and gloves into the cafe's skip, which would be emptied in three hours. She shook out her hair, ran her fingers through it.

There should have been a further message on her pager by now but the screen was blank.

The carport light didn't flicker on. She had remembered to cut the switch when she left this morning. Yesterday morning. She locked her bike and slipped up the back steps in the dark. Something stirred in the hedge. She removed her shoes, opened the door, and padded to her bedroom without turning on the lights. She stripped, left her clothes on the floor in a neat pile, and slid between cold sheets.

She went back over every detail, every moment. No one had seen them, nothing had gone wrong. There had been no mistakes. On the road home she had just been a cyclist. It was done.

IT WAS KIERAN who found the trees.

We swam and then ran, still dripping, behind him. It was hot away from the water, and the path dusty. My skin dried and began to itch. I was imagining a calf stuck in the mud, needing rescue, or an old vehicle for playing in. A raft or even a pirate ship. A body, perhaps.

We entered a kind of grove further up the bank of the river, the sort that is quiet inside, and makes you feel quiet inside yourself. There was a covering of fine grass underfoot, still green, despite the season. Kieran stopped, turned and crossed his arms.

'What?' Josh craned his neck to see what was behind Kieran's back.

'Turn around,' he said.

So we did.

It was a tree. Or rather, a series of trees. The largest of them, a big old yellow box, was long dead. A great grey ghost. The other four, still slender and youthful, staggered back either side of the clearing. They leaned over the raised mound of earth, as if protecting it. A section of each trunk had been cut away, in the shape of a shield. There were designs carved inside, curved and straight lines that were not quite pictures and not quite words but told some sort of story. They had been there a long time. You could still see rough tool marks, and where the trees had kept on growing, bulging out over the carvings.

We had only ever approached from the other side, marching past without looking back. Without noticing. As if the trees didn't want to be seen. Or we hadn't been ready to see them.

Now we couldn't look away.

There was one tree for each of us. As if they were *for* us. What breeze there had been stilled. The birds and insects paused. For a moment, there was no sound. Even Matty had nothing to say.

I pushed past the others, to touch the ledge between the bark and the carved surface of the largest tree. The cuts were deep and wide, right into the heartwood, like fingers making a river. Scrolls and diamonds filled the space around it. It all meant something. It meant a lot. We knew that straight away. We didn't quite understand, the way we didn't fully understand a lot of things. At the same time we almost did, although it was more than we could have explained. And we knew that we all felt the same, without having to speak. It was as if the trees said everything for us.

Although dead, the timber was warm. It might just have been the afternoon sun, but it felt magical.

Only when a peewee called and all the sounds started up again was the spell broken.

'Far out,' Josh said.

I turned to look at Ian. We were all looking at him. But his face wasn't telling us anything.

'What is it?' Kieran said.

Ian shrugged. 'I don't know. An important place, for sure. I could ask Mum?'

We walked the tree circle before stepping inside. It was another time, out of the world. We were younger, we were older – we were together. We heard the wind, the sky, the leaves, the earth, and all of the birds and creatures who lived there. And we were part of it.

Afterwards, we lay on the grassy mound, looking up at the roof of the world through the tips of our trees, until our stomachs were growling and I thought Ian would remind us of lunch.

It was Kieran who first sat up. 'This is our secret, right? Our secret place.'

I frowned. I had started to imagine telling my father at dinner, triumphant. Finding something on our farm that even he didn't know about.

'For sure,' said Josh.

Ian said nothing. I couldn't tell if his eyes were open or shut behind his dark curls.

'Jay?' Kieran stood over me, blocking the sun.

'Okay,' I said.

'All in?' Kieran pulled me up, and the others followed. We gathered around the bigger tree. No one asked Matty – he just reached up and put his right hand on the trunk with ours. I put my left arm around Josh, and he put his around Ian, and Ian put his around Kieran, and Kieran hugged Matty, until we were a circle around the tree.

Kieran cleared his throat. 'We swear, on these trees, to always be friends. To protect each other – and this place.'

———

'Jay, did you even wear blockout today?'

'*Yes.*'

Mum was serving dinner but looking at me instead, spilling peas over the edge of the plate and onto the bench. 'You have to reapply it when you've been in the water,' she said. 'Look at your poor nose.'

Dad took off his boots at the back door and washed his hands in the laundry. 'How was it down there today, love?'

'Tell her, David. I'm not going to agree to them spending the day outside if she comes back looking like a lobster.'

I carried the meals to the table, sliding two slices of pork from my plate onto Dad's. He winked.

It was too hot in the house for roast, too hot for anything. I poured two glasses of cordial and fetched Dad's beer from the freezer.

'Someone should be supervising them,' Mum said. 'Or their parents will be ringing to complain that we burn their children.'

I put the beer bottle down on the table harder than I meant to. The last thing we wanted was some grown-up putting the brakes on our days.

'Smells great,' Dad said, and for a minute I thought he meant burning children, but he was leaning over his vegetables. 'I don't have time to spend all afternoon down there, do you? We were both let run wild at their age.'

My parents running wild, or even running, was hard to imagine but it was a better direction of conversation. Mum finally sat down, as pink in the face as she said I was.

'Maybe on Sunday we can all go?' he said. 'So they can use the swing.'

I chewed my potato slowly, even though it was burning the roof of my mouth.

Mum gave me a look, as if she knew we had already broken that rule, but I just took a long drink of my cordial and refilled my glass from the jug.

'Good girl,' Mum said. 'Keep your fluids up.'

FOG CLOAKED THE city. It had been a cold and damp ride in. By now, the tree would be on the highway. She showered and changed in the basement, hung her towel over her locker door.

She blow-dried her hair, although she hated the noise of the machine, and the heat. It was not something she had bothered with, until a senior staff member had commented, as she was bent over the paper in the library one morning, about the connotations of arriving at work with still wet hair. He was a sexist arse, from last century, and didn't realise that she rode to work, but she didn't need him thinking about her in bed. Or to attract any attention.

She carried her pannier by her side, took the stairs up to the meeting room. 'Morning,' she said, taking her place at the brush box table. Keeping her head still and her face expressionless took some work – but then it always had.

The head of security was already there, along with the head of public relations and the director-general herself, a triumvirate she had only seen assembled once before. They were just waiting on Geoff, her boss, head of collections.

The director-general, Noni, checked her watch. 'Let's start. Max, can you give us a run-down on what happened last night?'

Max touched his hands on the lapels of his jacket. 'Right on midnight, we had a security breach. The alarms and cameras were disabled, and a vehicle appears to have accessed the loading dock.'

'Was there no guard on duty?'

Max coughed. 'He was on his meal break.'

Noni lifted one pencilled eyebrow. 'I beg your pardon?'

'If you'll remember, in the last round of budget cuts, we reduced our security staff, leaving only one guard on duty at night. It's an eight-hour shift. They have to take a break.'

'But we placed monitors in the lunch room at that time, did we not?'

'I have spoken with the officer. One of our most experienced. It's all in my report,' Max said, tapping a manila folder.

'I don't understand,' Noni said.

Max sighed. 'Unfortunately, when the officer conducted his security check, he found nothing amiss and just reset the alarm. While the duty officer – Jayne – and myself were automatically notified, we thought it was a false alarm until I checked the camera logs this morning.'

The look on Noni's face suggested Frank might be taking retirement earlier than he had expected. 'But you said nothing was stolen?'

'Actually, it appears that we may have lost one item.' Geoff had appeared in the doorway, clutching a handful of pages. 'Sorry I'm late, everyone. Our printer is on the fritz.'

Noni waited for him to sit down, touching the table with a pink nail. 'What is it?'

'We did an inventory,' Geoff said. It would have been Marnie and Dan who had actually done it, but they didn't get to come to meetings. 'An arborglyph,' he said. 'It had just been returned from the Tweed Gallery.' He passed around printouts of the summary notes from the database.

Noni blinked. It was likely she hadn't known they had the piece, let alone what it was. 'Could it have been taken by mistake?'

'Looks like a professional job to me,' Max said.

Noni leaned forward, so as to better see down the table. 'Jayne?'

She had long imagined this moment, being asked for her opinion, consulted for her expertise. 'It's a Wiradjuri arborglyph – or dendroglyph – from the Central West, a carved tree marking the grave of a significant male elder. It's a practice particular to New South Wales. Each design is unique to the individual, and is thought to map his way to the Dreamtime. There were probably thousands at the time of white settlement, but today there are only a handful left intact in their original locations. While there are a number in public collections,' she said, 'for obvious reasons, they're not on display.'

Noni sipped her water, leaving a pink lipstick print on the edge of the glass. 'Yes, I mean, seven metres . . .' She ran her nails down the database notes. 'It's a tree?'

It was more than a tree, or they wouldn't be sitting around the table discussing it: artefact, artwork, sacred object, part of a sacred site. It was worth a hell of a lot to the right people. 'Just the trunk, yes.'

'Is it registered?'

Noni had come to them from the Mint, and sometimes it showed. The National Registry was for paintings, and voluntary. 'I don't believe so, no,' Jayne said.

'What are our options?'

Jayne leaned back in her chair. 'It's hard to imagine it being moved through traditional channels. It's difficult to hide, and very distinctive. We could get some pictures in the mainstream media, flush it out. Report the theft to the police. Place it on the Art Loss Register – then it's almost impossible to sell on, at least.'

Tamsin, with her brand-new public relations degree from Monash, shook her pretty bobbed head. 'We can't go to the press with this. Or the police.'

'You're right,' Noni said. 'This is a publicity disaster. There are plenty these days who'd argue we shouldn't even have the thing. And now we've lost it.'

Max examined the laces of his combat boots.

Noni nodded. 'We keep a lid on this for now. But Max, I want a thorough internal investigation and report. And have a look at that regional gallery – it seems a coincidence that the tree had just come back from its first exhibition in fifteen years.'

Max was already half up, keen to get out of the chair and the room. 'On it.'

Jayne covered a yawn with her hand. It had been almost dawn before she had fallen asleep, and she hadn't slept much the night before, either. A wind had picked up outside, toying with the bare branches of the plane trees.

She should be surprised but she wasn't. Procedures weren't always followed, and things went missing all the time. Like the Christmas someone hadn't emptied a packing case properly and a certain 1920s masterpiece had gone off to the tip. Whether it was lying in landfill or hanging on someone's wall, they had no idea. There wasn't much they could do about it either – except try to keep it quiet.

Noni made eye contact with each staff member. 'I don't need to tell any of you how sensitive this is. Quite apart from what the arts and Indigenous communities would say, we're facing another round of cuts this budget. We don't need any bad news stories. This incident stays in this room. Agreed?'

DAD WAS ALREADY on his way out the door by the time I sat down for breakfast the next morning. 'I can give you a lift down to the river later if you like,' he said.

'Okay.'

'Say ten?'

I nodded, my mouth full of pancake, golden syrup and lemon. Mum didn't say anything about reading at the table, since I was the only one at it. It was like sitting with someone, enjoying a good book while eating – like sitting with lots of people. I was with the characters from *Treasure Island* again. We were old friends. Dad's copy had colour plates, which helped me imagine boarding a ship and walking the plank and Billy Bones and Black Dog with his missing fingers, though what I really wanted was a picture of the black spot. That had kept me up at night when I was younger. Especially when a mole appeared on my leg that was kind of dark, like someone had stuck it on.

'I have to go into town,' Mum said. 'But there are sandwiches, cake and fruit in the fridge.'

'Thanks.'

'Don't forget—'

'I know. Sunscreen.'

'And a hat.'

'Got it.'

After four pancakes I was heavy, and felt like going back to bed. I cleared the table and washed up. The sink water was only just warm and a line of ants filed in through the window to drink. Black spots.

I rang the boys after eight. That was a rule. Kieran's mum liked quiet in the mornings while she read her romances. I'd loaned her *Kidnapped* once, thinking she would have to like it much better than all that soppy stuff. When she finally returned it, she smiled and said it was 'a bit old-fashioned' for her. It made no sense at all since she was old-fashioned by the fact of her birthdate. I figured it was more about not accounting for bad taste, which was what Mum was always saying about people who lived in town.

Kieran answered the phone.

'We'll pick you up after ten,' I said.

Ian was already at Josh's, and his mother would drop them over, Kieran said.

I put on my swimmers, fetched my towel from the line, and packed my canvas knapsack. It was my old schoolbag, signed with everyone's names from primary. Kieran, Josh, Ian – they were all there. Mum said she went to boarding school, which was way different, and Dad went to school down the road in the one room with the same ten people his whole life. One of them was Josh's dad. He took over the farm, like Dad did, when his father died. Kieran's dad was there, too, but he was two years younger, and only had the farm because his older brother died.

I wouldn't be taking over our place, though sometimes, like when I helped with the cattle, Mum said I was a farm girl, or a cowgirl. Dad said I could be anything I wanted. That times were changing, real fast. Maybe they were, but where we lived nothing much ever seemed to change, or go fast, except the holidays.

I piled my things next to the lilo at the back door and sat on the step to wait. A willy wagtail showed off to his own reflection in the kitchen window. They were vain birds, Mum said, fighting and flirting with themselves.

Dad beeped the horn and pulled up in a cloud of dust. I ran across the lawn, under the clothes line, and threw everything in the back of the ute.

'We saw your dad in the lane, so Mum dropped us off there instead,' Josh said, and gave me a hand up. A stock route threaded behind our properties, connecting them – and us. When the creek was up, the school bus had to go that way, too. Then we could cut home across the paddocks instead of going right round by the main road.

We pulled up at Kieran's mailbox: an old four-gallon drum. They were our neighbours on the other side, the river side. Josh threw his head back at Matty standing there, but Kieran shrugged. It was what it was. We took their esky and lilos, and they climbed on.

We rode the bumps together, wind in our hair, grinning with the secret between us. We were bigger for it, and the world had expanded to accommodate us. Even Matty didn't look quite so lost in Kieran's old shorts.

On the main road, we crouched down behind the cab, hanging onto the grille. Once we were back on our property and Dad leaned his arm out the window, we could stand up again. It was my job to hop off to open and shut the gates. Things like that went without saying.

I knew the trick of lifting the first gate with my boot to loosen the chain, so I could get it off the catch. I knew which way each gate swung and which ones it was okay to ride on, their hinges strong. And which ones you had to drag through the dirt.

Dad dropped us at the top of the track. He got out and waited until we all put on our hats and sunscreen. Even Ian, who never really burned. When I hugged Dad goodbye, he smelled of wheat dust as well as himself, and I knew he had taken a break from the header just to drop us down here. 'Thanks, Dad.'

'Try and stay out of the sun during the middle of the day, okay?'

I nodded.

'You right to walk home?'

'Yep.'

'Before sundown, please.'

We were already running towards the water. Only a small stretch of the river was part of our farm, one extra snaky bend. It was just on our land, not Kieran or Josh's places either side. We were the lucky ones. But it gave us all access, the right to treat the whole river as if it was ours. I didn't know then where it came from or where it went or what had happened there – and what would happen yet.

HER WHOLE DAY had been pushed back by the meeting, and all of the mini-meetings since, in the corridors and tearooms. The story was off and running like stubble fire. Even the database upgrade training had taken twice as long as it should have, with everyone talking all the way through and lingering outside in the break. It was a nice idea to keep the theft in house – but impossible. Everyone in cultural management knew each other and opportunities for promotion were scarce. Their loyalty was to art, and their allegiance to their friends, rather than their employer. One of her uni buddies, Tanya, was in charge of acquisitions at the National Gallery and another, Rob, ran exhibitions at the National Library. Jayne would have to avoid having lunch with either of them for a while or face twenty questions.

Max hadn't helped, patrolling the corridors with his file and making interview times with staff. It was a giveaway something was up. Her own interview was first thing tomorrow morning, which she was not looking forward to.

By the time she had answered her urgent email and finished a briefing note for the upcoming exhibition on Canberra's history, Jayne had missed her normal yoga class. The next one wasn't until seven.

She bought a special Tour de France edition of *Cyclist* and messaged Sarah while waiting for a veggie burger. The route for the Tour was to be a tough one, deep in the mountains of Massif Central – all grassy craters, wooded peaks and plunging gorges. It was the birthplace of four of France's major rivers, the geological heart of the nation. Her perfect holiday would be to follow the race around, staying in villages perched on the mountainside and exploring the landscape between stages. It might be one she would have to do alone, though; Sarah wasn't much into cycling.

Sarah hadn't replied to her message, either. She was probably stuck working late again. The new job, up at Russell, was proving even more consuming than Foreign Affairs. At least she had been able to contact Sarah there, even if everyone did have a plum in their mouth.

The burger repeated on her right through the yoga session and all she really wanted to do was lie down on the mat. She should have gone straight home. It was like the aftermath of winning a big race, when the adrenaline ran out and left you empty. Except that she couldn't tell anyone she had won, and wasn't even sure that she had. By the end of the class she had gained a little extra movement in her spine and restored her breathing to normal levels. Far from calm, but better.

Some of her energy was back when she mounted the bike. Her limbs worked on muscle memory, and the night air bit her cheeks.

After she'd showered and packed her clothes for tomorrow it was almost ten. She zipped up her coat, fastened her shoes and headed back out into the cold.

She waited to cross Northbourne Avenue in starting position: her hands gripping the bars, legs poised, anticipating the green light. Even with her head down and racing she was still in stealth mode, scanning the streets, taking in every detail – watching cars. Her heart still lived in childish stories, and her conscience nagged.

She circled the car park of Sarah's apartment, in a new complex near the O'Connor shops. Her lungs ached from the cold air. There would be another frost for sure. It was as if there was nothing between her and the stars. She imagined she could hear them vibrating, singing almost, but it was more likely the powerlines, or a faulty streetlight.

Jayne released her shoes from the pedals, dismounted, and locked her bike beneath the green exit sign. She took the stairs to the second floor in socks, carrying her shoes. The glow of a television seeped under the door of the apartment opposite. The young couple who had moved down from Sydney were still suffering from climatic and cultural shock. Sarah said she slipped them pamphlets, of exhibition openings and book launches, to help them find their way. Canberra was a city it was hard to get past the surface of until you found your people.

She let herself in and locked the door behind her with the slightest click. Sarah's apartment was dark but her satchel was on the kitchen bench and the dishwasher was running. Jayne undressed in the bathroom, the tiles cold even on her socked feet, and left her cycling gear folded in a rough pile. She felt her way along the hall to the bedroom and slipped under the doona. She warmed her hands under her arms, and then wrapped herself around Sarah, pushing her breasts flat against Sarah's back. The tension she had been holding began to flow out of her at last.

'Hey.' Sarah's voice was blurry.

'Hey, love.'

'What time is it?'

'Late. Shhh.' She kissed Sarah's shoulder, breathed in the smell of her hair, and held her until she fell back to sleep.

IT WAS ONLY one day later, but it was as if we were looking forward now, to high school, rather than back to primary. Our little bend in the river was part of a wider world.

We carried our gear down to the beach, and we did swim and make a couple of lilo runs, but it was all about the trees.

Kieran wanted a game of brandings and we gave in, dodging through the trunks as cover. I managed not to get hit for once and to hit Josh *and* Ian, leaving red welts on their bare backs, but it all ended in tears when Matty copped a ball to the back of the head.

'Sorry, mate,' Josh said. His hand was nearly as big as a man's on Matty's thin shoulder.

'Like you didn't mean it,' Matty said, shrugging him off.

Josh gave Matty his slice of chocolate cake and they called it a truce.

It was too hot for running around anyway. We started making a magical land on a flat patch between the biggest tree and the one closest to it. Ian scratched in tracks and Josh dug a dam in the middle, ferrying water up from the river in the plastic cup-lid of his drink cooler. Kieran built houses out of sticks and bark and I worked beside him, marking out our world's perimeter with gumnuts.

'What about a shop?' Ian said.

We smiled at that, because we only imagined farms and houses but he thought differently because his parents ran the service station. We set up a kind of market in the middle of the land, under a stick and leaf cover, and stocked it with blossoms and seeds.

Mum's blockout stung my nose, even though it said it was for sensitive skin. We swam again, across the river and back, to cool off. Kieran won and I only beat Matty – that much hadn't changed.

We set up a picnic lunch in our grove. Ian had cans of lemonade, still cold, for each of us. We always pooled our supplies although it didn't work out even. Josh's mum was the best cook, and once she figured out that Josh was sharing what she packed for him, she just made extra. Today he had roast chicken and potato salad in a square container, and what was left of the chocolate cake. Kieran and Matty had sandwiches, like me, though theirs were beef and chutney rather than ham and cheese.

We laid everything out on the blanket and lounged around the edges to eat. I positioned myself so that I could see the biggest carved tree and study its design. It was starting to feel like good company, like a book I had already read and knew I would read again. Sometimes it spoke to me, like the river. Even though the other trees were still alive, they didn't say as much. I didn't mention any of that to the others. If they didn't feel the same, I would never hear the end of it.

Ian wiped his mouth with the back of his hand. 'Mum and Dad said okay to the video night on Friday.'

'Yes!' I said.

Ian lived in town and was the only one with a video player. We bumped fists.

'What about something scary?' Kieran said.

'Or funny,' Josh said. 'Nothing like a good comedy.'

'We have you for that,' Kieran said.

'Ha ha.' Josh flicked a piece of eggwhite from his potato salad but Kieran swayed out of the way and it landed in the dust.

'We can walk up to the store when you get there,' Ian said. 'That way Mum won't have a hand in it. And we can pick up chips and drinks from the service station. Dad will be working.'

'Can I come?' Matty said.

Kieran and Ian exchanged a look.

Ian shrugged. 'Kylie will be home anyway.' Ian's little sister was only six. Cute, but annoying when she was tired.

'But you'll have to ask Mum,' Kieran said. 'And no kiddy movies.'

Matty kicked Kieran's foot. 'Shut up. I'm not a baby. And you'd better be nice to me. I've seen all those notes you've been writing.'

Kieran made a grab for him but Matty was already off and running. Josh and Ian were covering their mouths, trying not to laugh.

I frowned. 'What's so funny?'

JAYNE SCANNED THE media clippings for any mention of the carved tree. Nothing. The Fairfax papers were still going on about whether or not Ruddy's Archibald-winning portrait of David Gulpilil was a painting. Serial and unsuccessful entrant, Johansen, was arguing that it was a drawing, taking it all the way to the Supreme Court. Talk about a sore loser.

The Murdoch press was revelling in the ongoing saga of the Cézanne caught up in the middle of a police investigation. When twenty works were stolen from John Opit's Murwillumbah home, he claimed he had lost Cézanne's *Son in a High Chair*, worth fifty million. During the investigation, police experts had pronounced it a fake – and Opit a silly hippy. Now he was offering up his inheritance as a reward for the painting's return, angering police. Opit argued that the police should concentrate on catching the criminals rather than discrediting the Cézanne's provenance. It must be the paint fumes that sent men's egos into overdrive.

She looked up at a knock on her office door. 'Max. Come in.'

'Morning.' He stepped over piles of paper and wedged himself into the red visitor's chair.

'Sorry. Filing. I always put it off until it's completely out of control.'

'You should get the EA to do it. Or an intern,' he said.

'I do my own shitwork. It's a thing.' After too many years of doing other people's.

He pulled his notebook and silver pen from his top shirt pocket. 'Thanks for meeting me so early,' he said. 'Just some questions about the other night. Routine. I'm talking to everyone.'

She smiled. 'Sure.' Max had been in army intelligence – if that wasn't an oxymoron – and prided himself on his 'investigations'.

'You exited the building from the basement at 18.15?'

It all rested on this. She had swiped her card and opened the door, but not left the building. The car park was covered only by sweeping cameras, making it possible to walk from the exit door to the bike racks without appearing on film. 'Sounds right.'

'Why the basement?'

'I was working down there. I try and take the stairs rather than the lift, and keep my bike on that level.'

'The tapes don't show you riding in that day.'

She blinked. 'I had breakfast up the road. Left the bike there – just forgot. Creature of habit.'

'Right.'

There was nothing to prove she had left the building. It was a problem. But there was nothing to prove she hadn't either. Or so she hoped.

'When the log came back from Tweed Heads, you checked it in?'

'I did a condition assessment. We do that for everything coming back. In case it's been damaged in transit,' she said. 'Paperwork, you know.'

'Was there anything to note when you assessed the log?'

She would have liked to pull him up on his description, but it was probably better if he didn't value the tree. Or perhaps he was trying to irritate her, army style. To establish if she had an emotional attachment to the stolen item. She shrugged. 'Some light scratches, a patch of sticky film.'

'So that's why you marked it as in conservation?'

'I cleaned off the film then and there. That's minor. And the scratches . . . there's nothing we can do. It's the cost of showing an item sometimes,' she said. 'We mark anything going back into storage as in conservation.'

'Why is that?'

'It looks better than "in remote storage". We wouldn't want people to think we didn't value an item. Especially if it has been donated. It sounds more . . . cared for.' She smiled.

'Do you have any contacts at Tweed? Know any of the staff?'

'The curator. Karen Glynn,' she said.

'Anything stand out there?'

'We're a pretty mundane lot, really. Like librarians.'

Max snorted. 'Can't see you as a librarian, mate.'

'Thanks.'

'I understand that they obtained permission from the local land council to include it in their exhibition,' he said. 'Is that unusual?'

Jayne scratched the back of her wrist. 'A bit.'

'Any thoughts on why this was a special case?'

'You'd have to ask them.'

Max scribbled a question mark next to that one. 'What's the log worth, do you think?'

'A monetary value?'

'Yeah.'

'I'm not an assessor,' she said. 'But it's rare, unique. Culturally significant.'

'Sensitive?'

She nodded. 'Very – it's a burial tree.'

'So no gallery is going to buy it – if they can't display it.'

'Exactly. At the end of the day, I guess it's worth the price someone is prepared to pay.'

'A private collector, then?'

She sipped from her water glass, which needed a wash. A film of lip balm had built up around the rim. 'It's possible.'

'Right. Well, I think that's it for now,' he said. 'Thank you, Ms Jayne.'

She shut the door behind him and sat on the windowsill. There was a fresh dusting of snow on the Brindabellas and the wind coming off them flurried brown leaves around the empty park below.

I TIED STRING around the last bit of meat and tossed the line out into the dam. It was hot already, a glare reflecting off the pump shed. I pushed the stake down into the mud, rinsed my hands and retreated to the shade of the willow. 'What's Matty doing?'

Kieran shrugged. 'He has to go to drama class with Mum. He got sunburnt yesterday at the pool. As red as these yabbies will be coming out of the pot.' He rubbed his belly.

Kieran's mum was in the dramatic society and always had a leading role in the play they put on over the October long weekend. Kieran carried on like it was the most embarrassing thing in the world, but she was really funny and could sing, too.

One of the lines tugged. Kieran raced to the water and held the chicken wire net poised while I pulled the line in between my thumbs and two fingers, as slow as I dared. As soon as we saw the aqua and white pattern of the yabby's claws, Kieran scooped it up.

'What a beauty!' Its joints were blood red, always shocking at first. Too real, too raw. Kieran dropped it in the bucket of water.

I pointed. 'They're all going!'

Six of the eight lines were pulled tight, as if by one giant creature. We ran along the dam's edge, pulling them in one by one. Cool mud squished between my toes.

'This one has eggs,' Kieran said. He threw it out into the middle of the dam.

'And this one's too small?'

'Yep.'

I tossed it back, tail flicking through the hot air.

The others were all good-sized, going into the bucket with a plop. The lines kept going one or two at a time.

'Look at the markings on this one,' I said, grabbing it behind wide, blue-swirled claws.

'Older, maybe?'

Crayfish scrabbled in the bucket behind us. A white car slowed as it went by up on the road.

'The others are missing out,' I said. Ian was stuck working at the service station, and Josh's sister was home from university. Their whole family was in Orange for the day while his dad had some test.

'Reckon.' Kieran threw back another mother with eggs. 'Do you think all those babies survive? There were dozens there.'

'Maybe not, or the dam would be overflowing with crayfish.' Dad said that they did walk between dams sometimes, when one place was no good anymore, or overcrowded. But he had never seen it. Maybe they walked overnight. Under the cover of darkness.

We raced to the far end, where the line was tugging so hard, the stake was coming free of the mud.

'It's a monster!'

I pulled it in, hand over hand. One massive claw gripped on to what was left of the meat. It didn't let go when Kieran scooped it out of the water.

'Grab it,' he said.

'You grab it.'

He tried to get his fingers in behind its head, but its free claw was nipping. 'Ow!'

The cray almost flipped out of the net, but Kieran was quicker, and then it was in the bucket, causing a great skirmish. Hopefully it wouldn't eat all the others.

Kieran sucked the webbing between his finger and thumb. 'Geez. Strong.'

The lines had all gone slack, as if that had been the last great cray, and anyone left had lost their appetite.

Kieran wiped his hand on his shorts, leaving a bloody trail. 'I didn't really get the ending of that last video. Did you?'

The Mosquito Coast had been my choice, because River Phoenix was in it. 'The father lied to them when he said America had been destroyed,' I said. 'To get them to stay in the jungle with him. When he gets shot, the mother lies to him, too. She says they were heading upstream, but they were really going downstream, going home.'

'And the father dies.'

'But the rest of the family are okay. Better.'

Kieran nodded. 'Cool,' he said. 'I liked it – it was just a bit complicated.'

He had been too busy throwing Maltesers at Kylie through that part of the film.

Crayfish feelers and claws poked out of the bucket water, and their feet scrabbled around underneath.

'What do you think it will be like at high school?'

'I don't want to think about it yet,' Kieran said.

'I've heard everyone gets their heads flushed the first week.'

'That's not going to happen to me,' he said. 'Or you, if I can help it.'

I smiled. 'Okay.'

'Let's put on the fresh meat.'

'I'll start at this end.'

Kieran took four cubes of fatty beef from the plastic bag and handed me the rest. I worked along the row, pulling free what was left of the old bait, pale and soggy, and flinging it out into the water. One line had nothing left on it at all; someone had had a good feed. As soon as I had finished baiting the fourth line, the first was taut again. Kieran was still tying up his last, so I ran back and pulled the string in with one hand and scooped with the other. It was a female, loaded with eggs. 'I think we've seen this one before,' I said.

'Maybe she's figured out she's not going to end up in the bucket.'

I laughed. 'Free feed.'

'Free ride,' he said. We stood close, watching her arc through the air, tail curled, and land with a splash. Kieran put his arm around my waist. It wasn't new – we all hugged each other all the time – but this felt different.

———

Dad shook his head. 'I don't understand why you'll catch them, but not eat them.'

I shrugged. I had eaten a couple. It was the sound they made scratching at the sides of the old boiler. It took too long for them to die. I didn't like the muddy smell, either, or their empty shells in the compost bucket afterwards.

Dad was shifting crayfish from my plate to his. 'You ate them when you were little.'

They used to just appear on my plate then, in a pretty pile between the lemon, mayonnaise and potato salad. Somehow I'd never seen them for the living creatures they were.

When I had first caught them, with Dad, I didn't know to throw back the females carrying eggs, and he hadn't said anything, so they cooked up pinky-orange under their tails – all those babies.

'How's Kieran?' Dad said. 'He'll be eating plenty, I bet.'

'Good,' I said. It was true, Kieran loved crayfish. He'd be gutsing up more than his share over at their place. It was one of the many ways Dad wished I was more like Kieran.

'Got any plans for tomorrow?'

'The river. I'll ring the others in the morning.' Kieran and I hadn't really organised anything; I had run off as soon as his dad pulled up, after the weird moment by the dam. But it sounded like Dad needed help with something, and it was best not to be caught at a loose end.

'I thought we'd play a game tonight,' Mum said. 'We haven't seen much of you over the holidays.'

'Which game?'

'Scrabble?'

'Okay.' I forked up the last of my potato salad. It wasn't much fun playing on my own with them – they knew more words and how to get massive scores – but it wasn't often they felt like games. I cleared the table and ran to fetch the box from the spare room before they changed their minds.

'IS SOMETHING GOING on at work?'

Jayne swirled wine in her glass. She had been expecting the question, but still hadn't figured out an answer. 'Why?'

'Oh, the late-night arrival, early departure. I wasn't sure it was really you, except for a hair on the pillow,' Sarah said. 'It was like a fairytale.'

'Sorry.'

'You haven't answered.'

This was the moment, time to bite the bullet. She swallowed another mouthful of wine. 'I can't talk about it yet,' she said. 'I had to go in early this morning for an executive meeting.'

Sarah stopped chopping. 'Everything okay?'

Jayne nodded. 'What are you making?'

'Just a quick pasta. Salmon, dill, preserved lemon.'

'Yum.' There was something indulgent about someone preparing a meal for you in your own kitchen. She was trying to pace herself, but her glass was empty already. She walked behind Sarah to look for the open bottle in the fridge. 'I like this,' she said, examining the label. One of their local vineyards.

Sarah smiled. 'I know you don't like riesling much, but this is a good one. I had a glass at lunch, and thought it would suit the dish.'

Jayne kissed the back of Sarah's neck, bent over the chopping board. 'It's perfect. I wish you were on my side of the lake, so we could have lunch together sometimes.'

'There's talk of us moving,' Sarah said. 'Somewhere in the triangle.'

'Well, that would be good,' she said. 'How was the Ottoman? Did you have the zucchini balls?'

'Yes, but I only had one.'

'Garfish?'

'Two.'

Jayne pulled a sad face. 'Turkish coffee?'

Sarah laughed. 'Stop it. I can't help it that we have all of our office lunches there.'

'Whose farewell?'

'Leo,' Sarah said. 'I don't think I've mentioned him. He was our transnational analyst.'

'What does that even mean? *Transnational*. It's like another language.'

Sarah pushed over the jar of preserved lemons. 'Open this for me?'

Jayne tapped the lid on the breadboard, listened for the pop, and twisted it free. She held out the jar but pulled it back when Sarah reached for it. 'Transnational?'

'They deal with international terrorism, trafficking, that sort of thing.'

Jayne handed over the lemons. 'Isn't Law of the Sea international?'

'Yes. But it's not one of our priorities. I'm with Pacific branch because of some specific issues at the moment. But I'm consulted by other sections, too.'

'That must be nice.' Jayne pinched a slice of smoked salmon from the cutting board. 'You never tell me anything, you know.'

'There are reasons for that.'

'I can keep secrets,' Jayne said.

Sarah shook her head.

'I'm sure there's banal stuff, funny things that you could tell me without any great threat to *national security*.'

Sarah shelled peas, popping the empty pods in her mouth. She crunched and then smiled. A hint of mischief smile. 'All right. Today, when I got to the restaurant, I was the first there.'

'Okay.'

'We don't name the agency when we book. Or any senior staff. I had to give the name Pushkin, to find our table,' she said. 'I felt pretty silly.'

'Pushkin?'

'Alexander. He was a Russian writer. One of the guys from the Middle East section made the booking.'

'Like a secret password? That sounds fun.'

'It's a wank, really. Those old guys think it's still last century. "Our man in Moscow", and so on. It's a kind of showing off. Letting everyone know they read Russian poetry – *in Russian*.'

Jayne smiled. 'I get that shit from acquisitions. They make a point of saying the name of a work in a language other than English, so you have to ask what they're talking about.'

'Exactly.'

'What else?'

'Laurie Oakes was having lunch behind us.'

'So you had to watch your conversation?'

'He was with one of the foreign minister's advisers, so probably more interested in him.'

'Journalists always have their ears open.'

'True.'

Jayne took napkins from the linen cupboard and cutlery from the drawer. She pushed the spread of magazines, brochures and paint swatches to one end of the table.

'I like that oven you've picked out,' Sarah said. 'It would look great.'

Jayne leaned over the pictures. She hadn't exactly picked it out; the magazine was open at that page for the cupboards in the feature kitchen. 'Not too big?'

'You have plenty of room in here.' Sarah fried off the leek and poured the rest of her glass of wine in the pan. She called her own kitchen a galley, which was about right; it was only a single bench. 'When will you start?'

'I don't know,' Jayne said. 'Everything would be ripped apart for a month.' And she might well have lost her job by then.

'You can stay at my place.'

She smiled. 'I know.' A few days would be nice, but weeks crowded in together at Sarah's might be a bit much. Surely it would only be the kitchen out of action most of the time. She watched Sarah add the cream and then the dill fronds – it was nearly ready. 'Smells great,' she said. She fetched the wine and their glasses and sat in the chair opposite her usual spot, so as to better consider the kitchen.

Sarah set down their plates.

'Thank you.' Jayne twirled her fork in the creamy pasta. 'It's all the decisions, too: benches, cupboards, splashback – oven.'

'The oven is *hot*. I love it.'

Jayne smiled. 'Well, that's a start.'

KIERAN PULLED DOWN the ladder to the top storey of the hay shed with an old pitchfork. He no longer had to jump or even stretch to reach it. Sometimes I wished I was tallest, fastest, strongest. Out front. The best at something.

As soon as the others had arrived, Dad had called Kieran over to help him lift the new pump out of the ute and set it up next to the underground tank. Josh and Ian handed over tools and washers. I folded up the packaging and took it to the bin. It was how it was.

We climbed up, hand over hand, as we had dozens of times before. The rails were worn smooth in the middle, but if you grabbed the outside, you could still feel the rough grain. It was the way life seemed then. Things were easy, familiar, like a worn path – but there was so much more out past the edges.

From the top platform, a kind of mezzanine, we could see out over the house and surrounding paddocks. Josh sneezed and blew his nose on a man's blue handkerchief.

Kieran threw himself over the edge onto the bales below, whooping all the way down. I would never have admitted it but I didn't really like the hay shed. Up close, straw was much more prickly than it looked, especially when cut and packed in square bales, but I didn't want to be left until last, with everyone looking at me.

I manoeuvred myself over the highest part of the stack, where the fall was only a few feet, and stepped off, prompting cries of 'Girl!' from Josh and Ian. It was stupid really, given I *was* a girl, but it stung.

We clambered up to do it all again. Matty grinned. He was good at hay jumping. It was one of the few things we did together where it helped to be small.

My next jump, I went off backwards, landing next to Kieran in the lowest point of the stack, where Dad had been loading feed into the ute. Loose hay scattered about us. I punched Kieran in the stomach and sat on top of him. He pretended to be winded but then flipped me off and tickled me under the arms.

The afternoon passed like that, like so many others, until Josh's eyes were streaming, and Matty accidentally kicked Ian in the face and his lip blew up like a heifer's.

———

The next time in the hay shed that holidays it was just me and Kieran. His dad came over to help rebuild the ramp in our cattle yards. There was a whole lot of talking first, something about the local election, and we took the opportunity to run off before we could be enlisted to hold nails or planks.

Hay jumping was a little flat with only us, and maybe Kieran knew it wasn't my thing. We lay around up top talking, throwing the apricots we had picked from the orchard back and forth before eventually eating them. They were still too sharp and firm.

We got into a wrestle about the last apricot, which was nothing new. The kiss was, though. At first I wanted his tongue out of my mouth but then it was kind of nice. Warm. It made my tummy upset but in a good way. I didn't know then how to breathe while kissing, and I guess neither did he because it didn't last long.

I couldn't look at him afterwards, and when he tried to grab my hand, I froze up. The wall of the hay shed was swaying and the crows were calling too loud outside.

'That was real nice,' Kieran said.

I nodded.

His dad saved the day, calling out that it was time to go home for lunch. Kieran said, 'See you later,' and hurried down the ladder and across the orchard to the ute. When they were gone I came down and walked back to the house with Dad.

'What did you two scamps get up to?' he said.

I felt my face get hot and turned to watch a mother quail and her chicks scurry off the side of the track into the wheat stubble. 'Hung out in the hay shed. Ate some apricots.'

'Are they ripe?'

'Not quite,' I said.

'That tree has been turning out fruit like that since I was a kid.'

I nodded. The tree was old.

He took the path through the garden rather than the driveway. 'Me and Craig made ourselves sick on them every summer. Used to have to pick them in the mornings, for my old man. One for the bucket, one for us,' he said. 'We figured it was our payment.'

Craig was Josh's dad. I smiled but wasn't really listening; I'd heard enough stories about how hard things were and how kids worked for nothing back then.

'Kieran's growing up fast all of a sudden, isn't he?'

Sometimes Dad's timing was so bad it was hard to know if it was on purpose or not. I leapt from one stepping stone to the next, making sure not to crush Mum's violets crowding around their edges. 'I hadn't noticed.'

Dad put his hand on the back of my head. 'I'm glad you two are close. He's going to be a great young man – he'll always look out for you, you know?'

———

The second last day of the holidays was all about the trees. I drew a map of the grove, with an inset of each tree showing its design. For something so simple, they sure were hard to copy. Then I sketched a larger map of that part of our farm and marked in the grove, along with the river and the road in. The fences were easy but the hills and where the trees were thick was more difficult. I tried shading but ended up drawing tiny individual trees close together, as if from above. It was not a treasure map but it did hold secrets. I would have to think of a new hiding place for my sketchbook once school started.

When the sun was overhead, I stopped to eat my sandwiches and found that Mum had tucked a Milky Way in my lunchbox, which just about made it a perfect day. I sat in the shade to eat, with my back against the smallest tree, and watched honeyeaters feasting on blossom. It was like chocolate to them.

Mum always made us wait half an hour after lunch before swimming and even though I didn't really believe stomach cramps could make you drown, I took my time stripping down to my swimmers and walking down to the river. Instead of diving in and splashing around the way I would with the boys, I lowered myself under the water's surface with hardly a sound, as if I was half platypus. I breaststroked downstream, the water slicking off my face and arms as the birds and insects carried on around me, like I wasn't there.

So much had happened that summer. It was like a good story I had read over and over, and knew I would read again.

———

I spent the last day of the holidays reading in my room, trying to make time pass as slow as possible. Mum had bought me new books when she was shopping in Orange. She always bought Australian stories. They were good to read, more familiar than snow or tropical islands but not so much like escaping into a different world. Except for *The Nargun and the Stars*. For a while I was hoping that the tree people might give me some answers about our trees, but now I just wanted the kids to stop the developers.

Dad had already pinched *I Can Jump Puddles* to read himself. He liked stories like that, people battling the odds. His biggest compliment was saying that someone 'showed a lot of courage'.

Each time I turned a page, I popped another bullet in my mouth, sucked the chocolate off and chewed the liquorice. Trouble was, the Nargun had gotten cranky, and I was starting to turn the pages faster, before I had quite sucked the last of each bullet out of my teeth. I wasn't allowed lollies, but Ian sometimes sneaked me packets from the service station that were out of date or too smashed up. Bullets went to me, raspberries or frogs to Josh, and teeth or spearmint leaves to Kieran. I liked those, too, but we had our preferences and no one else ate liquorice.

Mum popped her head in. 'It's good, then?'

I nodded, mouth closed. My teeth were sure to be black.

'I'm just ducking into town to pick up something for your father. Be back for lunch.'

I'd known that already. She had her hair done and her town dress on, the one with the blue and green swirls. Dad had taught me how to refine my peripheral vision. If you kept looking straight ahead but kind of relaxed, and didn't focus on what was right in front of you, you could see more at the sides. I could smell the roast chicken in the oven, too. My favourite.

There was another flavour intruding. New and plastic. The smell of tomorrow. The holidays had gone too fast. At the beginning, high school had seemed a world away. Now it was almost here. My books were piled up on my desk, all covered with Contact. I'd chosen treasure map paper for underneath and done the best job yet. But I still needed Mum to do the hard part. The plastic was so sticky, if you set it in the wrong place there was no getting it off without wrecking the paper.

My new bag sat by the door in a shaft of sunlight, as if seeking my attention. After my satchel, the suitcase was too big and square – too serious. I rolled over to face the wall.

JAYNE STOPPED AT the phone booth at the Acton Peninsula tourist centre. Buses were already pulling in, unloading schoolchildren and geriatrics. It was all colour and noise, her own blue and red lycra outfit lost in the mix. According to the radio news blaring from one of the coaches, Tour favourite Lance Armstrong was suing the authors of a new book accusing him of doping, and the French papers that had quoted from it. The mud was starting to stick.

She waited until five past the hour and dropped her coins into the slot, pressed the numbers with gloved fingers. He answered after the second ring.

'Hey. Parcel arrive okay?'

'All good,' Ian said. 'What about your end?'

She gripped the booth's graffitied perspex frame, rocking her bike back and forth. Ready to race. 'So far, so good,' she said.

'We'll lay low for a few weeks. Just in case.'

'How are the kids?'

'Good. Holidays here at the moment. It's hard to keep coming up with things for them to do.'

Jayne laughed. 'We always managed well enough.'

'It's different now. They need scheduled outings. Constant excitement,' he said. 'If I was a cynic about it, I'd say they're not happy unless my hand goes into the wallet.'

'That is cynical.'

'Well, I don't remember much being spent in our day.'

'I don't suppose there was much around.' Jayne heard a small impatient voice in the background.

'Gotta go,' he said. 'Breakfast, then we're off to the park. Soccer, Kane reckons.'

'Cheap at least.'

'It's a ploy,' he said. 'Ice-cream shop's nearby.'

Jayne smiled into the phone. 'Have a choc mint for me?'

'Ha. That's still my favourite, too.'

She returned the receiver to its cradle and picked up her takeaway latte. It was cold but she swallowed the last of it. Caffeine made the world go round.

The fountain had started for the day, shooting lake water high in the sky. The breeze sent a drift of fine spray over her face. Traffic streamed across Commonwealth Bridge and up the ramp to Parliament House. The nation's giant flag flapped at half-mast, for the death of Tasmania's former premier, Jim Bacon – and so many other things.

She rode one-handed to the bike path, dropped her empty cup in the bin, and took off downhill, leaning into the bend. Life was much more simple on wheels. Move forward, go faster, stay streamlined.

I DIDN'T GET my head flushed the first day of high school. None of us did. A couple of the year nine girls held me up on the library stairs, laughing and teasing me about how long Mum had hemmed my uniform. I had figured that out as soon as I got off the bus; only the minister's daughter's was longer.

After assembly the first thing they did was split us into houses. The deputy principal read out names and we had to reassemble in four groups. In primary we had all been in Bradman and won the athletics and swimming carnivals during our last year. Now Josh, Kieran, Ian and I all ended up in separate houses, which we took pretty hard. It had to be deliberate. I was in Lachlan. The others were in Murrumbidgee, Murray and Molonglo.

We were in the same class for English, maths and science, but split up again for electives. They weren't really electives, not yet. We had to try everything so we could make better choices later on.

The day was divided into eight periods. Some of them were doubles but it all meant a whole lot of packing up and moving around and you had to carry everything with you, like a snail, and pay attention to your timetable.

Josh and I found ourselves in Japanese and sat together up the back before there could be any more splitting up. When Mr Nixon started drawing kanji on the board, Josh put on his 'you've got to be joking' face and it stayed there until the bell rang.

We sat under the blue gum in the middle courtyard to eat our packed lunches. The boys took in the tuckshop queue, and what groups sat where, getting their bearings. I watched a magpie diving for crumbs, imagining we were still picnicking at the river – but it was hard with all the noise.

'You should see Ian's apron,' Kieran said.

Ian frowned. 'Shut up.'

'C'mon, it's real pretty.' Kieran made a grab for Ian's bag but Ian was quicker, scooting it under the seat.

'It's Mum's, all right,' Ian said. 'She hasn't had time to get me one.'

'Let's see yours, Kieran,' I said.

'It's a butcher's apron,' Kieran said, holding it up. It was striped navy and white, still creased from the packet.

I shrugged. 'Did you cook anything?'

'Not yet.'

'We're making hamburgers next week,' Ian said.

Josh's head went back. 'That's not fair!'

I took a corn chip from the packet Ian offered. 'We're going to make Japanese food later in the term,' I said. We would get our turn at home science later in the year.

'I'll take the burger any day,' Josh said.

———

Josh was happier in metalwork. We spent most of the lesson learning about all the machines and safety rules before the teacher gave us our instructions for building a metal pencil box. Mr Triffitt treated us girls the same as the boys, so I made sure he didn't catch me yawning.

I didn't see how it would take all term to make one box, but we did only have two hours a week. The room overlooked the ovals, all three of them. The main one had running tracks marked out already. There were netball and basketball courts, too, but they were around the side, next to the hall. Below the ovals I could see the town football and cricket fields and the tree-covered hills towards home. For a moment I missed the holidays and the grove, and everything was moving so fast I had to sit down on a stool. Mr Triffitt patted me on the shoulder and said to take a breath, which was what teachers usually said about me talking too much, but he meant it in a nice way.

We had to wear white coats when we were in the workshop, like doctors. They had a pocket for your pencil. Mr Triffitt kept his glasses in his, and was always taking them on and off. I had to roll my sleeves up; there weren't enough small sizes to go around.

Josh's gear soon spread all over my side of our bench, he was that keen to get started. We had to share the square rule between us, and cooperate, which we weren't too good at. But he helped me mark out the pattern on the metal with a special man-sized pencil, using the square rule for corners, before we had to pack up. Cutting it out was going to be much more difficult.

We were out the door the minute the bell went, and in trouble for running down the stairs. That was going to be hard to get used to – walking everywhere. Like running was kids' stuff. It was hard to pick out our bus in the crowd, and the year twelves had already filled the back seat. They weren't only bigger but bossy. Mean sometimes. Mum said we would be the little fish in the big pond all over again and she was right.

Josh and I sat behind the back door, the next best spot. Josh opened the window and threw himself back in the seat. 'Far out.' It was the same way his dad always said, 'What a day.'

'Reckon.' I gulped cordial from my water cooler, which Mum had frozen so that it would still be cold for the trip home, and offered it to Josh.

'Thanks.'

The doors closed and we lurched off, fourth in a line of buses heading out of town in different directions. 'Where's Kieran?'

'His mum was picking them up, to help her with all the bags at Grogan's.'

'Oh.' Grogan's was the farm supplies store, at the top end of the main street. I couldn't lift the big bags yet – twenty kilos – but I was practising. Dad said twenty push-ups and fifty sit-ups every night was enough to stay in shape. He had been doing them since he was my age. He showed me how to do push-ups properly, not like the girls' ones they taught us at school. Sometimes he showed off, too, and did his one-handed, or flexed his arms and chest up if he wasn't wearing a shirt.

I was up to thirteen a night and getting stronger every week. The boys had a head start but there was no way I was going to be left behind.

Josh was watching me, smirking. 'When are you two going to get it together?'

'What?'

'C'mon. Everyone can see it.'

He meant Kieran, and he was probably right, but it was still annoying. 'Shut up. He's my best friend. You all are.'

SHE TRIED TO make every Wednesday and Friday basement days, breaking the back of the week and ending it more quickly. The practical tasks, and lack of view to the outside, saw time fly past. There was always a backlog of acquisitions to work through. It was like detective work: examining the pieces, gathering evidence, chasing up leads.

She took a brown cardboard box – box one of three – from the shelf, ran the scanner over the barcode at the desk to check it out, and carried it to her bench. There was always the promise of a discovery, something everyone else had missed – like cracking a cold case. She tried to remember that, even on the worst days, when all the boxes and the emails, meetings and internal politics were overwhelming, threatening to turn the whole world mundane. It was the opposite to Sarah's work, where everything was top secret, caveated, and urgent.

She pulled up the record on her screen, and scanned the acquisition notes while she snapped on a fresh set of blue gloves. A donation from a private collection: prints, letters, documents and journals – what they called a dirty mix. Donations were the most likely to contain surprises, potential gold to unearth, unlike planned – and previously assessed – acquisitions. There was also a lot of dross.

Dross didn't come her way as often these days. Marnie had flagged these boxes for her because the prints offered promise. Drawings were always interesting, not only for their own sake, but the stories behind them.

Jayne paused, hand on the lid. An urgent all-staff email from Noni, about the budget cuts, had just popped up on her screen. It was nicely worded, padded with obtuse phrases in passive voice, but publications was to go, and the acquisitions budget had been halved. Security would be taken over by a private firm that would manage all of the arts institutions.

They were also offering redundancy packages, asking for volunteers, particularly from collections. There was to be an all staff meeting at three.

She stared at the screen. It was terrible, but this might be the way out she needed. Even if she wasn't caught, she wasn't sure she could stay. Or if she should.

———

She pulled the first package from the box. The items had already been sorted into bundles, listed, labelled and a few basic details entered by Marnie or Dan, their new temps. He had archaeology honours and she was the latest museum studies graduate. Both were hoping for something permanent – and more exciting than the registrations desk. They were good, and worked together to make the most of their collective experience, but it paid to check their entries. They made mistakes, pushed for time or fooled by a piece out of place or out of the ordinary. There was the occasional fake, too, even from acquisitions, who were supposed to check the provenance before even considering a purchase. The Art Loss Register was a wonderful initiative, but institutions now seemed to believe that if an item wasn't listed as stolen, it had therefore been obtained legally, which was not the same thing at all. Only recently, a gallery had purchased a set of Indian seals that turned out to have been looted from a temple.

She was the last line of defence. That was where experience counted. Dealing with each piece, getting it right. Not that the real work was valued anymore. It was all management skills and small talk and sucking up to potential sponsors at cocktail parties.

Not for much longer, perhaps. If she applied for a package she had a good chance. Anyone too close to retirement wouldn't be chosen. They would cost the organisation too much, and soon go out on their own steam. With only a decade of service, she was a cheap option. And, of the senior conservationists, she was the most superfluous: no European language, no masters, no doctorate, no management aspirations. Also the only Australian specialist, but that didn't appear to matter.

The trick was not to seem too keen.

Convincing Sarah might not be as straightforward. But the more she thought about it, the more it felt right. She had gone over to the other side, like a double agent. And what sort of system was it anyway, that she had taken such pride in defending?

She slipped the letters out of their plastic sheath, an exchange between the original sponsor of the collection and another natural history collector about a particular set of wildflower drawings. Replicating collections had been common in the early days of New South Wales, when natural history was all the rage. Acquiring images – and specimens – of the plants and animals of the colonies was a way of cataloguing knowledge, taking possession. It was also part of selling the colonies to the world.

She spread the letters' pages over the bench in order and checked off each date, name and place, before updating the summary screen. It wasn't thrilling, in itself, but these were the details that mattered. They would help establish provenance for the drawings.

Last, she photographed the pages, uploaded the images, and attached them to the file. People thought they knew history, what had happened. But it was the gaps, the untold stories, which revealed what had really gone on. You just had to know how to look.

Dan popped his head over the cubicle. 'Coming up for lunch, boss?'

'Yeah. Give me a sec.'

———

Jayne pulled a drawing from the box. A watercolour, and a familiar image, of a grass tree. It was a copy, with the inevitable loss of detail and quality. When artists copied other artists' work, it was often without the same skill base and without sighting the actual plant or animal – and certainly not a live animal. It was part of learning, like an art school in the old-fashioned sense – just made up of a motley crew of forgers and naval officers rather than old masters. But there were a handful of artists among them.

What was interesting was the inclusion of the local name for the grass tree: *goo-rung-arra*. Today's books and databases were far less progressive.

The Indigenous collection had been all the talk at lunch. Word was out that something had been 'misplaced', fuelled by her presence at the executive meeting. It had been one of the maintenance men who noticed that the tree was not on the dock that morning and he must have been bragging. It was hard to keep a good story down.

Things went missing all the time, of course, especially small pieces, with staff the main culprits. It was an accepted problem across cultural institutions. This was different; it wasn't as if someone could have slipped an arborglyph in their handbag.

There was no signature or date on the goo-rung-arra, common practice at the time. The patron owned a convict's time and labour, and therefore their work, and few collections were the work of a single artist. It made establishing any sort of chronology difficult.

She flicked on her light box to examine the paper stock. There was no watermark, which should put it before 1794, when watermarks were introduced. The trouble was, some artists, especially those with few resources, stockpiled the non-watermarked paper, using it for decades. She couldn't be sure of anything based on this piece alone.

If she packed up now, she would be home before dark, but the next item had caught her attention. A familiar-looking fish. Even through the plastic, she could see that it was no copy. It was too clear, its lines too sharp, its scales still wet, as if it might leap off the page.

She slipped the print free of its protective cover, holding it in the fingertips of both hands. Again, it was unsigned, undated. What had been glinting appeared to be metal leaf, used to capture the iridescent patterning on its belly. It was not a common technique among early Australian collections, suggesting a piece intended for a patron or for sale. Drawings of fish were also far less common than birds, flowers and mammals.

Jayne pulled up the acquisition notes again. The dates were all over the place, without clear connections; all that sharing and copying, buying and selling, muddied the trails. She searched the donor's surname, producing some hits. She was from a significant family, with a pedigree dating back to the time of the Second Fleet. Interesting. She'd have to examine the other letters and paperwork accompanying the pictures, find the catalogues of sale, and follow the trail backwards. It was time-consuming, but answers were almost always there to be found.

It was a skill she had honed over the years, hunting down the trees.

WE SET OUT on our expedition early, equipped with ice-cream buckets and two pairs of gloves between us. The best blackberries always hung over the water, full and plump.

We headed upriver, lilos under our arms, looking for a long, straight stick that we could use as a pole to steady ourselves along the way. I was sorry to go past the grove. It called me in. I'd been dreaming about the trees, and a forest of tree people beneath the stars.

We walked until spiky blackberry bushes blocked our path along the bank, then it was a slide down to the water, gripping on to a tumbledown fence.

Kieran and I were first in, baggsing the north side. It was in shade longer and grew the bigger berries. We rode our lilos like river horses, keeping to the edges, and letting the current take us. When we spotted a good patch, we'd ease in underneath and use the stick to stop. After a lifetime of summers, we were expert pickers.

We could grab hold of a cane with one gloved hand and pick with the other. The first dozen went straight into our mouths, the rest into the bucket in our laps.

There was a window of a few days when the bulk of the berries were at their ripest before the birds found them. I had been checking for weeks, determined to get a good harvest, and for once everything lined up with a weekend and we could all make it. It helped drag out our summer. It had only been a short week back at school, but there was already too much to take in. Here we could still pretend it wasn't real.

On the water, in the shade of the blackberries, with birds calling and insects buzzing all around, I could be Huck Finn or Jo March or whoever I wanted to be. The boys were always close but we worked separately. I found a bird's nest in my first bush, lined with brown string – possibly ours left behind after some game – and a clump of fat berries too good for the bottom of the bucket. They were cool on my tongue, and sweet. I squashed them into the roof of my mouth and let their juice run down my throat. It was like crayfishing, gathering food for free, only blackberries tasted better.

Mum preferred us picking on the river. We washed most of the mess off ourselves, she said, rather than bringing it home. I loved blackberrying on land, too. Dad would tie a board in the back of the ute, and when we found a good spot, he'd throw it out into the thick of the bushes. It squashed a path through the prickles, giving us access to all the best berries. It was like walking the plank; you were never quite sure what was at the end. I'd seen a brown snake slither away, giant spiders, a nest full of eggs, and once, a football, which I brought home and kicked around until it went flat.

Councils were starting to spray the blackberries. Mum said it had to be done, that they were taking over the state and a terrible menace. Dad had got rid of all the bushes on our place, but none of us minded that our neighbour across the river hadn't. He wouldn't spray near the water.

'Found some beauties over here,' Ian said. The banks were high, and his voice echoed. It had grown deeper, too. Overnight, it seemed, or I hadn't noticed until now.

Josh was the slowest picker, less able to focus on the job at hand. 'What's the story with Scott, Jay?'

Kieran looked over his shoulder, as if to see my response.

I shrugged. Sometimes I preferred Matty being there, because they didn't go on with crap like that in front of him.

'I heard he asked you out.' In one week Josh had turned into some sort of mad matchmaker, only interested in who liked who.

'Nope,' I said. Scott Grady *had* left a note on my desk, but I'd gotten rid of it quick smart.

'Do you like him?' Kieran said.

'As if,' I said. 'You picking any, or what?'

Kieran smiled and turned back to the berries. I pushed off for the next bush. Something had changed once Josh started with that stuff. Like it was them and me now, not us. I knew they talked differently when I wasn't around, too. Especially at school.

The next bush, all tangled in on itself, was alive with yellow butterflies. They landed in my hair and on my face, tickling while I worked. My container was half-full, the day warming. Cockatoos sang out from the treetops. We were not yet back at our beach, where we would stop for morning tea and a swim. The thought of plunging into the cool water kept me going.

We were due home for Sunday lunch. There would be baking this afternoon, with the berries. Josh's mum was going to help – and pick us up on the way.

Kieran didn't seem in a rush for once, his lilo drifting into mine. We were pulling blackberries from the same bush. He could reach a little higher, so I pulled in closer to the bank to find those hidden by long grass. Something slithered, slow in the heat.

When Kieran's leg touched mine, I didn't move away. This time, if he kissed me, I'd be ready.

'Did you hear Josh's dad is sick?' Kieran said.

'What?'

'I heard Mum and Dad talking.'

Across the river, Ian and Josh had drifted closer together, too. 'Shit.'

'I know,' he said.

'He hasn't said anything?'

'Nuh.'

I popped a blackberry in my mouth. 'What do we do?'

'Just be normal, I guess.'

SHE HAD FOUND the arborglyph leaning in a corner. Fresh out of uni, she had been one of three temporary staff employed to conduct an assets check at the Mitchell storage facility. It was dusty and dull work, punctuated only by morning coffee, lunch and afternoon tea. She had stepped into a new room and flicked on the lights to reveal the tree growing out of the concrete, minus its roots and crown. Its glyphs faced the wall.

Martin, an officer who'd just returned after a round of redundancies at the War Memorial, trod on the back of her boot. She was still rooted in the doorway.

'Sorry,' he said. She had thought he was talking about the tree.

They worked clockwise, Martin checking items off the list while she stuck on barcodes from her roll. After four years of study, first-class honours and an internship with the British Museum, placing stickers on every single item in a warehouse was frustrating enough. But as the afternoon went on, she felt the rage building inside her. It came from somewhere so far down she wasn't sure what would happen if it got out.

The tree, on the other hand, was like an older person in the room; its stillness held a quiet certainty. It had known she would come.

When she had backed out of the storeroom, at four-fifteen that Thursday, she promised the tree she would be back. She hadn't even had access to the database then, but how that tree had ended up topped and tailed in storage, and who was responsible, were questions she intended to answer.

When she took the contract at the gallery, building a CD-rom of their Australian collection with a team of other ambitious young things, the tree was rarely out of her mind. With licence to search databases and catalogues, she found her tree was not alone. During morning tea and lunchtimes, before and after work, she began to compile a dossier of arborglyphs held in public institutions around the country.

———

Jayne stared at the screen. She knew the fish. It was a silver perch, endemic to the Murray-Darling basin. The Lachlan had been full of them, reaching monster – and sometimes mythical – proportions. Now they barely made plate-size and were listed as vulnerable. The artist had again included the fish's local name, its Wiradjuri name: *baawan*. In a turnaround for the books, its Latin name was not that of some white English male who 'discovered' it, but *Bidyanus bidyanus*, both species and genus taking its Wathaurong name, as first recorded by Major Mitchell, on the Barwon River.

But it was the metallic paint that held all the clues. Laying down gold leaf beneath watercolour to create iridescent highlights was a technique that had been in use at least since the Middle Ages. Artists applied adhesive gum to attach the leaf to the paper and, once dry, coated the area with ox gall to receive the colour and hold it in. Instructions were included in artists' manuals at the time of settlement, but how would they have obtained the materials – and who would have had the skills? There were only a dozen other pieces featuring metallic media listed in cultural institution catalogues, all dated between 1789 and 1794.

The paper stock for the fish was watermarked 1794, which dated the work no earlier than 1795, when the paper would have first reached the colonies, and probably before 1798, when paper bearing the next watermark, 1797, arrived. She was starting to narrow the window.

The composition of the metallic leaf and pigments would unlock more of the drawing's secrets, but she couldn't touch its surface. It was too delicate, too precious. It was a job for the big microscope.

She pushed her chair away from the bench and spun over the concrete floor to the phone. Marnie answered on the first ring.

'Can you and Dan come down? I've found something interesting I need your help with.'

ONCE WE SETTLED into high school, everything began to change. Kieran, Josh and I saw each other on the bus every morning and afternoon, and Ian at school. We were all still friends, but the boys did more of their thing, and I did mine. It wasn't the done thing for boys and girls to sit together at recess and lunch – unless they were going out. I could have been going out with Kieran but I felt too pressured about the whole thing, like it was something inevitable that I had no say in. So I tried to make friends with some of the girls who played handball.

I had homework after school. More and more of it, it seemed. Projects and assignments for every subject, and textbooks instead of real books. We had to write essays instead of stories. Sometimes I was so tired of words when I went to bed, I didn't even read.

Mum always sat with me while I had my breakfast, usually muesli with fruit and yoghurt during the week. 'It will get easier, kiddo,' she said. 'Just do your best.' She made my sandwiches every day, and a snack for the week, like passionfruit slice or chocolate cake. And Dad only asked me to help out with the cattle on the weekends. The boys didn't seem to worry as much, mucking around in class and making jokes about everything. My marks, when they started to come back, were better than theirs but not as good as I would have liked. I had come first or second in most things in primary but now I was always in the middle. It looked like I had peaked too early.

The boys still had cricket on Saturdays. Once we hit high school, girls were no longer allowed on the team. They reckoned it was about safety, but boys were more easily damaged by a cricket ball than girls. I went along for a while, to watch, before giving that up, too. It had been hard enough to kid Dad to take me when I was playing, and I couldn't help feeling cranky when I heard leather on willow from up in the stand. Ian was really good – a natural at batting, bowling and fielding – and Kieran, of course, but I should have been playing instead of Josh. I was the better batter.

I didn't say so, though. He was worried about his dad and turning up to cricket and scoring a few runs was probably the only time he forgot about it.

As soon as cricket season ended, football started, and my weekends were mostly without the boys. Sometimes I walked down to the river on my own, and read under the trees, or took pictures with Mum's camera. I expanded our magical land, building a road in, and new huts, while tractors hummed all around the district, putting in the crops.

Josh and I did art instead of metalwork in second term and it was my turn to help him with brushes and colours and ideas. I decided to sketch the designs on our trees for our term project but it turned out to be much harder than I thought. I tried drawing the whole grove but couldn't get it right, and one tree on its own didn't work. In the end I did a shading of part of the largest carving by holding paper against the tree and rubbing over it with charcoal. It didn't look much, only the river and scrolls and diamonds, but Mrs Milligan helped me turn it into a linocut, which I printed in three different colours on proper paper and got my first A.

Those carvings were like a code I needed to crack. I lay inside the grove looking up at the sky and listening to all the sounds – the birds and animals and insects and the wind in the leaves and the whispering the world makes. I walked around and around each tree and put my palms on them. I stood at a distance to see them together, and considered each one on its own. I daydreamed in their shade. I was trying to find the answers but I didn't really know the question. It wasn't just another language but a whole different alphabet, like the kanji we learned in Japanese that were sounds and pictures with stories behind them rather than letters.

Stories filled my head whenever I was with the trees, but they were of pirates and islands and river journeys and forests, and I always saved the day, girl or not.

JAYNE LIFTED THE salmon fillets from the hotplate and placed them on oversized white plates. An ordinary-looking meal – compared to Sarah's, at least. Her breath already made fog in the night air. It was too cold for barbecuing, but she always did her best cooking outside. She stepped over the belt sander and yellow extension cord and wiped wood dust from her socks on the mat.

Sarah opened the door for her and the room's warmth rushed out. 'Looks great,' she said.

Jayne put the plates down on the table and hung her jacket on the back of a kitchen stool. 'How was work?'

'Uneventful, which is a rare and good thing,' Sarah said. 'You?'

'The DG announced some pretty serious budget cuts. They're offering packages.'

'Really?' Sarah carried their wineglasses, and the bottle, to the table.

'We're always the first to be hit. Unlike you lot.'

'Are you worried?'

'I thought I might apply.'

Sarah turned. 'Are you kidding?'

'No.' She paused in the doorway to dim the lights.

'Where has this come from?' Sarah said. 'I thought you liked your job?'

'I do.'

'Then why? It's crazy at your age. You have a mortgage.'

Jayne slid into her chair, and found Sarah's socked feet beneath the table. Here it was: another opportunity, a second chance to come clean. But how to say it? And what would happen afterwards?

'Is there something you're not telling me?' Sarah ground pepper over her salmon.

'It was just a thought,' she said. 'The salad looks great, thank you.'

'Will you explain? You don't tell me enough about your work.'

A piece of cane poked through Jayne's jeans. The new chairs she had ordered could not come soon enough. 'You can talk.'

'That's hardly fair.' Sarah piled salad on Jayne's plate.

'I don't even know what you do,' Jayne said. 'And when I ask, I get stories about lunch.'

Sarah picked out a snow pea and crunched it. 'I'm not sure I know what you do either,' she said.

'That's not true.'

Sarah sighed, cut into her salmon.

'Is it okay?'

'Perfect,' Sarah said.

One of the tea lights flickered inside the green glass. She had meant to replace it before dinner. She had meant to do a lot of things.

'I can't really talk about the details of work – it's part of it. What I signed up for,' Sarah said.

Jayne swallowed, sipped her wine. What they had both signed up for, it seemed. 'You used to tell me things when you were at Foreign Affairs, like when you heard gunfire on the tarmac during the evacuation from the Solomons, or that woman who was posted to Iraq because she was having an affair with a director's wife. And that big report you were working on about illegal logging and orangutans.'

'I probably shouldn't have,' Sarah said. 'And this is different.'

Jayne pushed a bone to the edge of the plate with her fork.

Sarah cut a neat slice of salmon and placed a salad leaf on top. 'Okay. Today I helped write a report on the Patagonian toothfish.'

'What?'

'The Patagonian toothfish.'

'You're teasing.'

Sarah shook her head, mouth full.

Here they were eating fish, and both working on them, too. 'A fish is a security issue now?'

'More of an economic issue. And foreign relations,' Sarah said. 'They're highly sought after – and there's illegal fishing in Australian waters.'

'Which is where you come in.'

'Correct,' Sarah said. 'It's a Southern Ocean fish. The pirates operate off the Antarctic coast, which is complicated. Territorially.'

'Toothfish pirates?'

Sarah laughed. 'Ridiculous, right? And it's the ugliest fish you ever saw. This huge bottom-dweller that lives for decades.

Prehistoric-looking. But it's a major export earner for Australian fishers. They call it white gold.'

'Sustainable?'

'Well, the legal catch is certainly *more* sustainable. And there are moves afoot to ensure the industry takes steps. There's a commission now, for the conservation of Antarctic marine resources.'

'Sounds more exciting than sifting through dusty boxes.'

Sarah smiled. 'I envy you your job. The clarity of it.'

'Clarity?'

'It's much less complicated – clearer you're working for the greater good.'

Jayne gave up pushing the last of her salad around the plate and put down her cutlery. Things always seemed simple from the outside. It wasn't the time to raise the ethics of past collection practices, their dubious legacies. Let alone her own. The candle went out, and a thread of smoke drifted across the table between them.

'Do you even like this job?'

Sarah frowned and emptied her glass. 'You know, that's a good question,' she said. 'I'm not sure.'

IN THE WINTER holidays we didn't go down to the river as much, and if we did it wasn't to swim. We sailed Josh's model sailing ship, a gift from his grandfather, making up stories about who was on board, the treasure they were carrying, and where they were going – until it ran aground on a branch or on the opposite bank and we fought about who should fetch it. Sometimes we threw rocks as far as we could into the water or tried to hit a target. Kieran always wanted to play those games because he usually won.

More and more often, we would lie in the grove, just talking. Gossip from school and the court case about the man who had held up the State Bank and the policeman – Damian Whitlock's father – who had shot him. There was so much going on in the real world that we didn't need to create our own adventures as much anymore.

It was harder to get together, too. Ian and Kieran made it into the district rugby semifinals and had away games and a training camp, and I had started Little Athletics. The days were shorter.

For once, our parents had planned something for all of us. Dad had been piling up dead trees, branches and rubbish in the house paddock for weeks. Every other day he would add another ute-load. Mum was barrowing all her garden prunings out there, too. It was going to be the bonfire of all bonfires.

Dad and I had gone into town the week before and bought a twenty-dollar and thirty-dollar pack of fireworks – the thirty-dollar pack was a special one, mainly parachutes. The bags had been on top of the fridge, out of my reach, but now they were waiting on the washing machine and I had already counted every item twice.

Mum was making salads and my only jobs were to ice the chocolate patty cakes and then put on clean clothes but it was hard to concentrate. It had looked like it might rain early in the day, and I was doing half-hourly checks from the back step. Josh's mum had come over early to help, with Josh's sister, Megan, who was home again for a few days. She was studying to be a teacher at Wagga, and called Mum Deidre now, which took some getting used to. I hoped she would come back and teach at our school because she was nicer than most of the teachers who came from the city and smarter, too. She had been dux of the school the year she finished. Josh had a lot to live up to.

When Josh burst into the kitchen it was with a *fifty*-dollar bag of fireworks. There were things inside I had never seen before and we started yelling out all of the different crackers we could identify through the plastic until Mum pointed out that the icing was starting to melt and the ants were on their way to the cooling rack and there would not be any patty cakes unless I settled down.

Our dads already had the fire going when we carried everything out to the back of the orchard. It was all roar and flames, with the dry fuel and a bit of a breeze still around. It would be better when it died down. The clouds had cleared off; we would not only stay dry, but have stars as well as fireworks.

Ian and Kieran arrived at sunset with their parents and Kylie and Matty. The sky was all swirls of mauve and orangey pink, as if it was getting in on the act, and we stood around feeling pretty good about everything. Our dads drank Tooheys and talked about the crops and stock, with one hand in their jeans pockets. Kieran's dad was always trying to get the others into sheep. He had never even wanted to be a farmer, Dad said. He had almost finished teachers' college when his brother didn't come back from Vietnam. Then Ian's dad said something about their service station and the big BP that was setting up on the road into town and they all shook their heads.

Mum had bought a cask of moselle for her and the other mums – and Megan. We had cans of soft drink. I hadn't even had to campaign for that. Mum just said, 'It's not every day we have a party.' It would have been more correct to say we didn't have parties every year but I wasn't going to quibble.

As soon as it was dark we started with the pinwheels and tom thumbs. Dad showed Kieran how to light them and then they left us to it. Dad and Josh's dad let off a couple of fountains and four rockets at the same time. Almost the same time, anyway. Mum said they were like schoolboys, and I could almost see it with their matching jumpers, checked shirts and jeans, and when their shoulders touched as they lit the fuses. Having whet our appetites – another of Mum's weird expressions – we stopped to pile our plates with sausages and salads and sat by the fire.

There was dessert as well as patty cakes, an apricot pie Kieran's mum had made. She said Kieran helped, which made us giggle, but I heard her telling Mum he really was pretty good in the kitchen.

Our dads started letting off fireworks for real, lighting a bunch of wolf rockets and Roman candles all at once and something called a hurricane. Josh's dad had pulled the red beanie Mum had knitted him over his freshly shaven head, which made him look kind of like a rocket, too. The boys and I worked a line of fountains and showers until the sky was all colours and our ears were ringing. Megan and our mums cheered and clapped from their striped deckchairs.

Last, they let off the parachutes. They whistled and exploded with the biggest bang, and the little parasols came floating down, uplit by the fire. We ran around gathering them up, their plastic action men still attached. Ian's mum – who was captain of the open netball team – ran and leapt to rescue one from the flames.

'I've got five,' Kieran said.

'Six,' I said.

Josh had five, too, but one had lost its soldier so it didn't count. I think Ian had more, including the one his mother caught, but he didn't say anything. One soldier was still missing in action at the end of the night, snagged in a tree or out in the lucerne paddock. We would mount a rescue mission at first light.

The boys were sleeping over, and I helped settle them in the spare room bunks, bringing extra pillows, blankets and hot water bottles. They teased Ian about his *Star Wars* pyjamas, too short, and too kiddy. Kieran winked when I said goodnight and I thought he might follow me out, but Josh was between him and the door, and paying a little too much attention.

I stopped in the kitchen for a glass of water. Our parents were still going, in an orange circle around the dying fire. I could hear them laughing, and the clink of beer bottles landing in the crate, when I settled into bed.

JAYNE REACHED FOR the drop bars and pumped her legs to maintain speed uphill, imagining she was leading the first stage of the Tour. Flashing through pines, with glimpses of the lake, it wasn't such a stretch. She rose out of the saddle to pass a middle-aged man churning away on a mountain bike, seat set far too low. Fantasy over; you wouldn't see that on the Tour. The real thing started on the weekend. Armstrong had failed in his attempt to suppress the doping book. Hopefully it would put him off his game. The Australians, O'Grady and McEwen, were in good form, and she had a soft spot for the German, Jan Ullrich. He would have won the previous year, but had been too much of a gentleman, waiting for Armstrong while he recovered from a fall.

Getting out for a long ride helped allay the anxious feeling in her gut. It was the only thing that did. Everything had gone quiet at work. She had thought the gossip trying but the silence was worse.

She paused at Scrivener Dam, leaned her bike on the rail and drank from her water bottle. The aluminium was cold on her fingers, the Canberra water without tang. The lake's surface loomed above her. Five fish-belly flap gates held back the Molonglo, with the help of a whole lot of concrete.

Fog swaddled the valley to the south but couldn't obscure the raw hills that had been forest, before the fires. All those plantation pines, full of oil, had gone up like matches. It was hard not to stare, like seeing someone naked for the first time.

She and Sarah had been out of town when it happened. On a winery tour in the Adelaide Hills. By the time a local mentioned the fires, towards the end of a long degustation lunch, a state of emergency had been declared, and it was too late to get an earlier flight back. It had felt worse, somehow, watching it all unfold on the hotel television, fielding calls from family, and waiting to hear from Dana and Hopes, whose suburb had been evacuated.

Those volcanic skies, hillsides alight, fires closing in on the city from three directions, cinders and ash raining down – it was something no one would ever forget. It hadn't been a firestorm but a fire tornado. Dana and Hopes had been among the five hundred who lost their homes, and four people had died. They said it gave Canberra a heart. The city had always had a heart, of course, but it took a disaster for the rest of the nation to realise that humans lived there, not just politicians. Canberrans had learned that living in the bush capital meant that they were part of nature – more vulnerable, not less.

She shivered, sweat cooling under her jacket, and tucked her hands under her arms. It was still below zero. She needed to keep moving before she stiffened up, and her body was calling for coffee.

Sarah would be getting up now. Suiting up, too. The city was starting to crawl, going about its business. Cars swelled its arteries and pumped into the town centres. She was part of its rhythm, but outside it, too.

Currawongs warbled from the plane trees in the car park. The windows of the one car, an old brown Datsun, were fogged, as if it had stayed overnight, with heavy-breathing teenagers inside. She pushed off the railing and circled back down to the bike path.

She no longer missed having a car – but she remembered. Being able to drive meant more than just getting around. It was a space of your own. In her day, there had been plenty of 'parking' going on down back lanes and stock routes. The old Valiants were the best, with their wide bench seats. That's what Josh used to say, anyway. For the bachelor and spinster balls, the farm boys planned ahead, rigging up a mattress in the back of their utes under a tarp. All except Kieran.

She hadn't bought her Torana until she left home, with the money she had earned that summer. It had seen her through until the last month of uni, when a garbage truck had sideswiped it out the back of the Italian restaurant where she worked Wednesday and Saturday nights. She had come out around midnight and found it all concertinaed on one side, like an accordion. In a surreal touch, seagulls circled above, white in the light of the street lamp, although they were hours from the sea. She had taken it as a sign, and bought a ticket to Europe with the insurance payout.

She plunged back down into fog. The pine needles were damp, sharp in her nostrils. Fallen cones nestled in the grass like spiky creatures. From the next rise, she watched for a glimpse of

Government House, across the lake. The path was winding; she had to concentrate on the corners, shift her weight with precision.

Before she had understood that turning was all weight, rather than anything to do with the handlebars, she had come off her motorbike in spectacular style. Her father had explained how to stop and she had been zooming about without any problems. But when she had to take the corner and slip through the half-open gate all at once, she had panicked and shifted her hands, as if she were driving the ute, and used the front brake instead of changing down gears. She had sailed right over the handlebars and into the barbed wire fence. Her father had stopped, helped her pick up the bike, and explained again – but she had already learned for herself.

Her mother had been upset about the ripped sleeve of her jumper and the blood, shooting her father a scowl that suggested she had not been completely in favour of the bike, but patched her up all the same. Jayne could still see the white lines up the inside of her wrist when she rode, short and long, like morse code.

She hunched down low through the olive grove, picking up speed. After the darker pines, the olive trees were like puffs of smoke on a French slope, and she allowed herself another Tour moment.

What must it feel like to win, after all that training, after all those years? She would be happy with one stage, to wear the yellow jersey just one time.

SECURING PERMISSION TO camp had taken almost the whole holidays. We had more than enough gear between us, and the spring rain meant fire danger was low. The week before, we had all been on the phone, plotting a coup. 'They don't trust us,' Kieran said. 'It's fine to drive the header or work all day herding sheep, but not to have any fun.'

It sure looked that way. I had stopped speaking at home in protest. I shook my head and dragged my feet when asked to help clean out the garage. I even tried a hunger strike but Mum turned that around by making my favourite dessert: steamed chocolate pudding. The smell of it cooking had been too much; I ate three helpings.

Kieran refused to look after Matty, because he 'wasn't responsible enough', and even Josh stopped getting the mail or collecting the eggs and refused to wash the car.

Finally, on the Thursday, permission was granted. Matty was to stay home, deemed too young, which gave us even more reason to cheer.

Four silent households were transformed into nerve centres. We ran around writing lists and checking gear and making calls to decide who would bring what. Dad said he would drive us, which was lucky because our mothers cooked so much food we would need to stay away for a week to eat it.

———

The fire had died down, and the carved trees were shadows behind us. We toasted marshmallows, pink and white, until they were black. Josh popped one into his mouth while it was still on fire – that was his trick. Flame-Swallower, we called him. 'Guys, can I talk to you about something?' he said.

The fire popped, and an owl hooted deep inside a hollow tree on the other side of the river. I didn't know where to look. We all knew, and Josh knew we knew, but we still hadn't discussed his dad, who was now skinny as a stick and without any hair at all, not even eyebrows.

'What do you think of Kara Greyson?'

I laughed.

Kieran did, too. The kind of snort that is almost a sob because you are just so relieved.

'What?' Josh said.

'She's quiet,' Ian said.

Kieran shrugged. 'Pretty, though.'

'She's nice,' I said. She didn't gang up like some of the other girls. And she read books. Nancy Drew mainly, but still.

'I like her,' Josh said. 'I thought maybe I'd ask her out.'

'Just do it,' Kieran said.

We stared into the fire, the boys' faces reflecting its glow. It was a side to them no one else saw.

Kieran disappeared into the shadows for more fuel. He staggered back, a forked log in his outstretched arms. His shirt was too small, the sleeves creeping towards his elbows. 'Time for truth or dare, I reckon,' he said, as he dropped the log in the middle of the coals, sending sparks flying and us covering our faces. He brushed down his jumper and grinned. His teeth were bright in the dark.

I groaned. The game was one of our traditions when overnighting, as it was to feign reluctance, but lately Kieran's questions had developed an edge to them.

Ian gathered up four sticks and we each drew one from his fist. I was up last, which was a worry. Especially after Josh produced a half-bottle of rum from his jacket pocket. From his mother's kitchen cupboard, he said. Her rum balls were famous all around town. We had only discovered them when they were left on the kitchen bench too long last Christmas, almost eating the lot between us.

I filled the billy with water and set it on the grille over the reddest coals.

Kieran started. 'Josh. Truth or dare?'

'Dare,' Josh said.

We laughed. He always chose dare. The outcome was always horrible, too, but he never said truth. As if there was something he was hiding.

'I dare you to . . . run from your tent, around the trees, and back. Naked.'

'Geez, guys.'

It was about me being there.

Josh stripped off behind the tent and ran, holding his clothes in front of him, the length of the campsite, to our whistles. I didn't look until he had gone past, so as not to see anything, but I caught a glimpse of his bum, which had gotten hairy since Ian dacked him at the video night over the summer. He placed his palm on one of the smaller, leaning trees and headed back.

Ian and I made the hot chocolates by torchlight, poured in a splash of rum, and passed them around.

'Truth or dare?' I said.

'Truth,' Kieran said.

It was my big moment to ask him something awkward, to pay him back for last time, when he had asked me if I had my period yet, but the rum was only starting to warm my stomach and everyone was waiting. We were like pirates at sea. Or shipwrecked on a desert island. 'Did you hold hands with Alicia Landy on the bus on the way back from regionals?'

He dropped his head. 'True.'

I was glad of the dark then, and my hot chocolate. Alicia was from the year above us but really pretty and great at tennis. Even I could see she had great legs. Neither Ian nor Josh gave him a hard time, which meant they must have known already, which made me even madder.

Kieran poured another slug of rum into his enamel mug and passed the bottle without looking at me. I snatched it and handed it straight to Josh, although I was tempted to pour it on the fire. Or over Kieran. Something hit the ground behind me from a height and scurried.

'Righto, Ian,' Josh said. 'Truth or dare?'

Ian crossed his arms, as if there was nothing anyone could ask that would bother him in any way. 'Truth.'

Josh put his hand round his chin, as if he were thinking. But his eyes were smiling; he already had something in mind and was just trying to build the tension. 'What's the worst thing you've ever done to Kylie?'

Ian blinked and sipped his hot chocolate. 'One time, when she broke my Nintendo on purpose, I locked her in the shed. Mum and Dad were both up at the service station,' he said. 'Anyway, she banged on the door and yelled for a while but I ignored her. I made lunch and watched something on television. Lost track of time. When I saw Dad walking home, hours later, I remembered and ran to let Kylie out. She was blubbering and carrying on, all red in the face. It was real hot in there. There'd been a snake, she reckoned, and there was no calming her down. She starts punching my chest and yelling. Then I heard the front door, and Dad called out.'

'Then what?' Kieran said.

'Dad made me help him clean out the shed, in the heat, and sure enough, we found a brown snake, curled up under the old washing machine.' Ian stretched his legs out closer to the fire. 'He was so mad. I was grounded for two weeks and Kylie had to apologise for breaking my Nintendo,' Ian said. 'They didn't leave me alone with her after that.'

We watched the flames flicker on his face. It wasn't only a good story, it was the most Ian had ever said all at once.

'You weren't to know there was a snake in there,' Josh said.

Kieran poked at the fire. 'I've done far worse to Matty.'

I nodded – we all had. Ian shrugged, taking his time before he turned to me, but not in a mean way. He always went for soft questions, so I wasn't too worried. The stars were brighter than I had ever seen them and I could pick out particular rocks and trees and a shimmering on the water. The carved trees were beginning to feel like a friendly presence behind us, as if they were drawn to the fire. I had seen Ian with them at dusk, sitting a ways off, watching the light go.

'Truth or dare?' Ian said.

'Dare.'

The silence told me that threw them. Scared them, maybe. All of the things that were changing between us could work in my favour, too. Josh would have dared me to kiss Kieran for sure – but Ian wouldn't. The coals clinked like glass.

Ian grinned. 'I dare you to . . . drink a mouthful of rum straight from the bottle.'

Josh handed it over. I unscrewed the lid, tipped the liquid to my lips.

'That was just a sip!' Kieran said.

I shrugged and handed the bottle back to Josh. 'Truth or dare?'

'Truth.'

Not dare? I had it all planned. I had been going to dare him to sleep outside the tent. I had started doing that in the yard at home. It was scary at first, but then so peaceful, just staring up at the night sky. The cheering gave me a few seconds to think but thinking was getting hard. I tried to remember some of Ian's lame questions. 'What's your biggest fear?' I said.

Kieran elbowed me, hard in the ribs, but it was too late.

'Dad dying,' Josh said.

I focused on the fire, felt the strength of the carved trees behind me. My skin was prickling, like when Mum and Dad talked about chemotherapy and percentages after I'd gone to bed.

The branch sighed and collapsed into coals.

'Shit, man,' Ian said.

'He's not going to die.' Kieran touched his mug to Josh's. 'And we're all here for you, mate.'

We sat in our stone circle, beneath the star-shot dark.

THEY PERCHED ON cold metal seats at the cafe up the road from Sarah's apartment, a frequent breakfast spot on a Friday. In jackets, cuddled up close, with their backs to the sun, it was bearable under the outdoor heaters.

'Remind me why we live here again?' Sarah said.

'Your work.'

Sarah smiled. 'Yours, too.'

'Should we go inside?'

'Probably – but we're stuck inside all day,' Sarah said. 'I'm having French toast. I deserve it. I've been to the gym every day this week. Are you going to have the Florentine?'

Jayne had been going to order her usual but it wasn't good to be too predictable. That's how things got boring. That's what her ex, Suzie, said anyway – and she'd had plenty of experience. 'The corn fritters, I think.'

The waitress took their order, fingers pink, and hurried back inside. Come happy hour, the place was a dyke bar, with a long history as a women's only music venue. It was a Canberra institution. They were getting too old for happy hour now, often stuck at work until after it was over. And Suzie usually went, with the new flame, holding court with all the old crew. The fog thickened around them, obscuring the oak-lined street and the playing field beyond. A cluster of cyclists, lycra-bright, appeared on the roundabout – discussing the Tour in loud voices – then disappeared back into the mist.

'Did you end up putting in for the package?'

'I did,' Jayne said.

Sarah let out a noisy breath. Not quite disapproving, but not impressed. 'When do you find out?'

'A few weeks. A month tops.' The paperwork had been awful. In a perverse reversal of years of application rounds, she now had to demonstrate her lack of value to the organisation. It would be a race between the redundancy and the outcome of the investigation – torture by convoluted administrative process. Jayne filled their glasses from the bottle of water and sat on her hands to warm them again.

The waitress returned with their coffees, and cutlery stowed in her black apron. A tattoo crept out from under her sleeve, a plant tendril, perhaps. Or a dragon's tail. They exchanged that particular half-smile, recognition.

Sarah cradled her cup against her chest. 'Cute,' she said, once the girl was out of earshot.

Jayne shrugged. She wasn't even in the same league as Sarah. 'Thank God it's Friday, hey?'

'Oh.' Sarah slumped.

'What?'

'I have to go in this weekend.'

'Really?'

'Sorry,' Sarah said. 'I know we were supposed to go out to the wineries.' Sarah's Subaru had barely had a proper run since she'd bought it, and there was a vertical tasting – a decade of pinots – at Sarah's favourite vineyard. The tasting shed had views off into the hills, and the owners were a great couple.

'Both days?'

'Sunday morning, but it's early. Five. I thought you could come over tonight and have dinner instead?' she said. 'Maybe we can pick up some Indian? And we could go to the markets on Saturday morning?'

'What's going on?'

'Just a situation we're monitoring.'

'Around the clock?'

Sarah sipped her coffee, kept her face blank. She was getting good at that.

'Indian sounds great, but I don't think I can do the markets Saturday,' Jayne said. 'I have a kitchen guy coming around.'

'Another one?'

'A friend of someone from work. They use sustainable timbers. Solid, not laminate.'

Their food arrived, steam rising from each plate. 'I'm not going to see much of you this week, then,' Sarah said.

Jayne cut into a fritter, smeared it with avocado and relish. 'Is it Iraq again?'

Sarah closed her mouth and shook her head.

'Surely no one's around to get your reports on a Sunday?'

'Stop.'

'All right, all right,' she said. There was plenty to do at home, and the Tour preview to watch. 'I don't need to know.'

———

Dan opened the micrographs, Jayne and Marnie leaning in behind him.

'Whoa.' She had expected the images to show a flaky surface, typical of aged brass leaf. Dutch metal, as it was called, was often used as a cheaper substitute for gold. Because brass couldn't be beaten as thin, it couldn't be laid as flat either, so larger areas tended to wrinkle.

'It's gold!' Marnie said.

Jayne smiled. 'What makes you so sure?'

'The uniform craquelure, with hardly any loss of paper support,' Marnie said.

Dan touched the next image with his pen. 'And there's no tarnishing, like you get with brass or silver,' he said.

Jayne put an arm around Marnie and a hand on Dan's back. 'You guys are brilliant,' she said. The metal leaf had been applied precisely to the highlighted areas, with several shades of watercolour on top, to produce subtle gradated effects – the shimmering scales that had caught her eye. It was gold all right, and a skilled artist had applied it.

'Wow,' Dan said. 'But would they have had access to those materials at that time?'

Marnie frowned. 'Maybe they weren't done here?'

'Those are exactly the right questions,' Jayne said. 'Let's see if we can answer them.'

MUM AND DAD watched *Four Corners* every Monday night, like a religion. Sometimes I watched it with them while I finished my homework. The night Dad got stirred up I was colouring in a title page for Asian studies. We were studying Japan and I had drawn a samurai warrior. His armour had to be metallic but my gold pen was splotching. I blotted it on a piece of scrap paper to get it running and wiped paint off my finger with a tissue. When I threw the tissue in the fire it went *whoof* and burned blue.

Dad brought in the mini Mars bars he had put in the freezer after dinner. It had become a winter tradition, to eat them in front of the fire. Why they needed to be as hard as a caramel, I didn't know, but since my parents otherwise frowned on sweets and lollies, frozen was fine with me. They lasted longer that way. I had finally figured out that if Dad liked something, it was allowed. Like ice-cream and Turkish delight. All I had to do was get him to try something good and next thing he would be writing it on the shopping list, or bringing it home himself.

On the long weekend we were going to the liquorice factory, because he was interested in the old building, and I was hopeful of bringing home some chocolate-coated samples. Kieran was going to come with us. He liked machines and engines and how they worked and Dad liked him liking that stuff because he did too. I just wanted to eat liquorice.

When my samurai was finished, and the paint dry, I packed up and looked through Mum's pile of library books for something new to read, settling on one with a bear on the cover.

'That might be a bit old for you, love.'

I shrugged. She was already reading the next one in the series so I figured it must be good.

This was winter: Mum on the couch, me in the chair, and Dad sprawled in front of the fire, exhausted. He'd read his book for a while, but then put his head down and sleep. I nibbled on the corner of my chocolate and watched the fire, my feet up on the hearth. Different wood burned different ways and the flames were always changing. This wood was from old ironbark fence posts, and really throwing out some heat. Kieran, Josh and Ian said their parents didn't sit around reading, but then they didn't have an open fire either.

My Mars bar was soft enough to bite into and I opened my book. It was easy enough – no big words – but pretty soon I could tell why Mum didn't really want me reading about cavemen and women.

She stood up to turn on the television and the music for *Four Corners* was already starting. It was something about land rights and a court case and protests and I knew Dad was really interested because he wasn't even trying to read his book at the same time. I listened because Mum said I should study law at university and I didn't really know what it was yet. I liked history, and the idea that you could still make discoveries and have adventures, but Mum was right about most things.

I licked chocolate from my hand while Mum was concentrating on the screen. They were interviewing a lot of different people and I had lost track of the story.

Then Dad said something about our property having been in his family for bloody generations and Mum tried to shoosh him for swearing.

'This is a watershed,' he said. 'That's what he's saying.'

'We'll see,' Mum said.

'I'm telling you, this is a problem for all of us.'

She tapped her palm on the arm of the lounge. 'Can we listen?'

When they started talking about traditional owners and establishing a connection to the land, I understood. Dad was rolling one of the stone tools from the bottom paddock around in his hands. We had a whole collection of them on the hearth, turned up by the plough, or found on walks. He liked to test me on their possible uses, and trick me with the occasional river stone, but now they were a worry.

'That bloody Hawke.'

'I liked what he said.' Mum switched off the television. 'Anyway, Gough started this. And you voted for him.'

'I thought you did, too. We wanted out of Vietnam.'

Mum nodded. 'And free education. And land rights.'

'In the Territory. Not here.' Dad put down the rock. 'You can't undo everything for landowners four generations later.'

'I don't think we need to panic. I have a feeling it will take a long time to sort out.' Mum sat back down on the couch and opened her book.

I tried to keep reading but couldn't concentrate. A good daughter, a farmer's daughter – and certainly a farmer's son – would have chosen that moment to say something about the grove. To protect the farm. It wasn't so much a decision not to, as a feeling. Those trees were part of things: past, present, future – they held it all together. And we had sworn an oath. I could only hope the others would keep it.

JAYNE CHANGED THE paper on the sander, finer this time, and worked over the back deck. Sarah had made her promise to wear a mask, but it made her face itch worse than wood dust, so it hung around her neck. She moved lengthways, with the grain. The boards looked like ironbark and were tough enough. For whatever reason, the previous owners had never finished them properly, and they had roughed and weathered. Now that she had put a roof over the deck she wanted to bring out their colour and protect them.

A crimson rosella hung upside down in one of the apple trees, despite the noise and dust billowing out into the yard, feasting in a world of its own. The neighbour's cat was patrolling the top of the fence again, tightroping her way towards the rosella, who would only take off as soon as she was close enough to pounce.

It was going to be a long weekend, without any news on the investigation. One night at a time, during the week, was bearable, with the chance of new information each day, but two nights seemed much harder.

Jayne rubbed at a board, wet it with her finger. They had come up well; one more fine sand should do it. It wasn't ironbark, though – the grain wasn't right. Sydney blue gum, perhaps.

The sun was on her back now, as she worked. She turned off the sander, unbuttoned her flannel shirt. It was one step away from a red rag but all the more comfortable for its wear. She started on the final section, near the wall of the house.

Word was that two conservationists had put in for a redundancy. She couldn't be sure who the other person was, and although their case for superfluity was unlikely to be any stronger than her own, they wouldn't both get one. She couldn't count on anything.

The waiting was wearing her down. Meanwhile, the application, and all the meetings about the cuts, were getting in the way of finding her fish artist. Geoff was charged up about outputs and outcomes, none of which took account of the quality of the work or the value of collection items. All the time spent trying to measure and document the worth of the section was *reducing* their productivity but no one else seemed to see it that way.

She flicked the cord out of the way and pushed down on the sander. Her wrists were sore, from all the vibration, and the corner was awkward, requiring shorter movements, like trying to cycle in a tight pack. She gave it one more going over and switched off the machine.

She brushed down her jeans and wiped her feet on the towel in the doorway. Still her socks left dusty prints all the way to the fridge. She made herself a rough sandwich with leftover haloumi and salad and took it back outside to eat in the sun. With practical tasks, at least, the outcomes were quick and visible. If there was an upside to Sarah's hours, it was getting more jobs done. That, and eating her dinner in front of the Tour.

Fabian Cancellara, the Swiss cyclist they called Spartacus, had won the opening time trial and would wear the yellow jersey when the race proper started late tonight. As the voice of cycling, Phil Liggett, always said, when you put on the yellow jersey, you ride like two men.

The salty cheese and the sun made her think about a beer, but she had to finish the job first. That was the deal. It was like mowing the lawn – the beer tasted much better when you could wash the dust out of your throat and survey the results of your labour.

She had first learned to appreciate beer – and hard work – the summer they had finished school. She and Ian had carted wheat to the silo for old man Baker. There was nothing quite like the tickle of wheat dust in your throat or the itch on the back of your sweating legs in the hot cab. It had been a hard summer, too, hitting forty for almost a week straight. Nothing cleared that itch and tickle better than a beer at the end of the day.

Ian always ordered tap beer; he said it was the only way to go. Cheaper, too. Not that they were short of money. It was more than they had ever seen in their lives, paid in cash. They drank up at the front bar of the Criterion that summer, with the men. The others were down at the Railway or the Exchange. Or gone already.

That harvest was theirs; they were part of it, almost part of the land itself. Working a long week and partying hard when it ended. The weeks between their final exam in November and the arrival of their results in January was a suspension of time, seeing off the last of their childhood, and all that had happened, before the rest of their lives began.

More than one night out had ended with them tumbling down the quiet streets to Ian's after the pub had closed and sneaking in the screen door to fall asleep watching *Rage* beneath the air conditioner.

She would need the central heating as well as the fire tonight, rather than air conditioning, and drink red wine not beer, but she might well fall asleep in front of the Tour. Perhaps things hadn't changed so much after all.

DAD WORKED HIS way along the fallen tree with the chainsaw. I carried those pieces I could lift to the ute and threw them on the back. It was lucky the tree had come down right there, during the last rain by the look of it, or we would have continued on to the river and cut up dropped limbs instead. Dad hadn't said where we were going and I'd had to sit on my hands, wondering how to keep him away from the grove. Instead we were in the little valley between wooded hills, by the willow on the creek.

Normally there were lots of smaller birds, but not today – not with all the noise. There was always green grass in the valley, and the kangaroos and wallabies liked to come down to feed. I kept an eye out for them while I dragged any branches too big to break up myself to Dad for sawing.

Dad said the valley had always been like this, that his grandfather's diaries described it exactly as it looked now. Though the creek had run all year round then and was full of yabbies and even fish. I would have liked to read Grandfather's diaries, to see if they mentioned the trees, but they were locked in the safe with all of the other important papers.

I bent to take hold of a larger piece of wood, lifting with my legs the way Dad had taught me, but felt something moving up my jeans. A huntsman. As big as Dad's hand but hairy. I dropped the wood and grabbed a stick to flick it off. 'Yuk!' I watched the spider scuttle back to the woodpile even though it made me feel sick. They had too many legs.

Dad was still sawing, back to me. He hadn't heard me squeal. The machine spluttered and failed, out of fuel. 'That'll do, I reckon,' he said.

I gathered up small pieces, inspecting them first for spiders, and banging them on the ground just in case

'Josh's dad is pretty crook,' he said.

'Yeah.'

Dad had stopped loading and placed his hands on the tray. 'Jay, you know, he might not get better.'

'I thought they were treating him.'

'With cancer, sometimes . . .' He dug into his pocket for a tissue and blew his nose. 'Whatever happens, Josh is going to need you to be a good friend.'

I leaned into him. 'Okay, Dad.'

———

Josh was my responsibility in electives and our shared responsibility in core classes. If you didn't know him you wouldn't have guessed anything was wrong. Sometimes he tried a bit too hard to be funny; other times he was too quiet. He had asked Kara out and they had gone together for a while but then she dumped him when she found out about his dad. She wasn't so nice after all.

I even indulged his matchmaking tendencies to cheer him up, especially in needlework, which I hated. We both did. We sat up the back plotting and scheming instead of hemming and seaming. I made an octopus out of my pin container, attaching eight purple fabric legs to match its purple pins for eyes. I slid him around on the lino floor whenever Mrs Finsler was writing instructions on the board. Everyone was in on it, scooting Occy back under the desk when they could. Josh and I started to use Occy to signal who liked who, or who we thought would look good together, just to stir up trouble. Mrs Finsler would turn around and glare at me, as if she knew I was responsible, but say nothing. Until Liam kicked Occy the wrong way and he hit the back of her heel. That was the only time we were all dead quiet – waiting for her to blow her stack.

Mrs Finsler confiscated Occy for the rest of term and I was sent outside 'to think about my behaviour'. From the look on her face I thought she was going to hit me for sure, and I backed out the door just in case.

Josh told the others about it as soon as we got out for lunch and they threw themselves around laughing and holding their stomachs. Kieran gave me a thumbs up and I knew I was doing my job. From then on, I stopped caring if it wasn't cool to hang out with the boys; we needed to stick together.

Without pins I couldn't sew, even if I wanted to. I never completed my skirt, which I wasn't ever going to wear anyway, and when Josh finally finished his shorts, they were too tight. That's how fast he was growing.

When our reports came out I got my first D. Mum was not happy, especially since I'd managed an A for metalwork the term before. Dad said I needed to 'lift my game' – but winked when Mum wasn't looking. He understood. Josh got a C for needlework. He got nearly *all* Cs but no one said anything about his marks.

JAYNE STARTED BY following the trail from the donor, the estate of the last childless woman descendant of an early settler family. Her grandfather had purchased part of the Norris collection when the former chief surveyor's family home and its contents were sold off in the thirties. Natural history was an expensive obsession. More than one collection had been broken up to clear debts rather than acquired whole by libraries and museums. Now conservators like her were putting them back together, piece by piece.

The Norris collection had been copied by other artists, the source material for numerous works. These were the deepest notches on her time line. Family records and recollections were far less reliable, and every time items were moved, the trail divided and blurred. The contents of these particular boxes had the look of things thrown together from a high shelf and forgotten.

A number of the Norris drawings had been attributed to the naval surgeon Thomas Gatton. Unlike many natural history artists, he had signed his later work. Quite a colourful character, apparently, and quite an ego. Having that one name had opened up a wealth of information, but it was now recognised that Gatton had at least one other artist working under him – and that he had signed their works, too.

She compared her fish with Gatton pieces in the New South Wales State Library database, especially those using metallic media. The artist had used similar techniques to heighten the plumage of pigeons and cuckoos. Her fish was a fit with the Gatton pictures but it was hard to be certain, especially when relying on online photographs. And the museum wasn't about to send her up to Sydney in the current climate. She needed to examine the rest of these drawings, everything in the boxes, before drawing any conclusions. It was too easy to miss other possibilities if you focused on a particular suspect too soon.

Before logging off, she took the opportunity to check on another entry, an arborglyph from near home. She frowned and re-entered its record number, and then its name and location. Gone. One of the arborglyphs had disappeared from the record. She knew the piece by heart – another Wiradjuri tree, from near home. How could it just vanish?

As if the thought had summoned him, she heard the lift, and Max's voice. She shut down the database, her file, and ducked across the hall, into the stores room. *Pathetic*. She was avoiding the inevitable, like trying to drag out the last day of the school holidays.

She covered a yawn, loud in the close space. Overnight the Australian, McEwen, had won the second stage, and tonight they would be leaving Belgium, racing between Waterloo and Wasquehal, crossing back into France. She had woken up late with ABBA's

'Waterloo' stuck in her head and now it was back. Max had stopped right outside the door and she couldn't escape if she wanted to.

Her phone buzzed in her pocket. *Fuck.* She covered her mouth, whispered. 'Hey.'

'Where are you? It's echoey,' Sarah said.

Max moved off down the corridor with one of the maintenance men, something about the air conditioning. False alarm. 'I'm on an important mission. Surveilling staplers, folders and notepads.' Jayne stood on an elephant stool to reach the recycled manila folders.

'I keep forgetting you can take your mobile into work with you. I was just going to leave a message.'

'What's up?'

'I'll be late home,' Sarah said. 'I don't think I can catch up tonight after all.'

'I could cook?'

Jayne heard a car in the background. Male voices.

'I'm not sure when I'll get away,' Sarah said.

'Oh.' She climbed down and gathered up blue fine-point pens, a notepad and another pack of post-its. Her greatest paper consumption.

'I'll call when I can.'

'Everything okay?'

'Just work. Can't really talk right now,' Sarah said.

'Love you.'

She was gone. Jayne sighed – she was an intelligence widow. She sorted pens and highlighters by colour and straightened boxes. Sometimes she missed the stationery shelves. Those had been the moments of peace in her early jobs, the physical work: putting away stock, delivering mail, dropping cars off for servicing, doing the stationery run. The days had rushed by.

The job she had taken at the Queensland Art Gallery had given her a false sense of what the real work would be like. She and the other intern had unpacked great wooden crates from Spain and installed each of the pieces with the ground crew. Their retiring supervisor had spent more time at functions than with them. They had done the labels, invites and mail-outs and manned the door at the launch, giving them more ownership of the project than she had ever had since.

The experience hadn't won her over to the sunshine state. Too far from home, from civilisation, good coffee. The humidity, in combination with the steep hills, made cycling unpleasant. The staff had been friendly enough but she was a southerner, and she always would be.

It had been good to miss a winter, though, and work by the river. She had taken the CityCat to work and eaten her packed lunch on the riverbank. In those days, locals still turned their backs on the water, like Canberrans with their lake – there was hardly a cafe facing it.

The gallery didn't have any arborglyphs – she had checked during her first week – but the university did. She had ridden out to their Anthropology Museum, on the pretence of a masters project. Doors were always opened for a student of art. It was a Kamilaroi tree, carved with scattered stars and suns, boomerangs and lizards, and symbols she didn't recognise. The letters and other documents relating to that one tree had led her to many others, detailing where they had been taken from during the 1930s – and by whom.

She had left Brisbane at the end of the summer, offered another temporary position back at the museum, in conservation this time – when it was still a separate section. It was a sideways move, hardly a fast track to curating, but by then she was no longer sure she wanted that anyway. The trees were leading her down a path of her own. Once she won permanency, eleven and a half months later, getting the arborglyph out was only a matter of time.

WE WERE STUCK inside for the first weekend of the holidays. Wind was bending the trees and rain biting at the house. Everyone was glad of the storm but it wasn't what we had planned. We settled for a day playing board games in the sleep-out. Josh had brought Poleconomy. Dad said it was Monopoly on steroids but I liked it because all the companies were familiar and everything went faster than Monopoly – and for much more money. Kieran was winning, but Matty was treasurer and that led to trouble.

When I went in to fetch some old towels to stop water blowing under the door, Mum said we could watch a video in the lounge room instead. Ian had brought *The Lost Boys* and I thought Mum would veto it for sure but she shrugged and let it go.

Dad had taken Josh's dad to Orange for his treatment. He did that sometimes to give Josh's mum a break from all the driving. They used to stop at the pub on the way back, 'for a shandy', but they didn't do that anymore. Beer no longer tasted any good to

Josh's dad. When Dad told Mum that, he was sitting at the kitchen table with his face in his hands. Mum didn't say anything, just bent down and put her arms around him. Sometimes she was as strong as him but in a different way.

Mum had homemade pizzas in the oven, and the smell was driving us crazy even though vampires were being impaled with stakes and dissolved in garlic bathwater. When Mum finally brought in the pizzas, she sat with us for a while, nibbling on a single piece of ham and pineapple while we wolfed down the rest. Ian said it was the best pizza he'd ever had. Even Matty complimented Mum, making her smile.

It was a good feeling to have everyone together at our place again, even if it was inside. I started to think that high school was pretty good after all, because we were able to do more things and watch better movies and have sleepovers with a whole lot less babying.

Mum stood up when the credits started, and I helped her carry out the plates. 'Lucky we don't have any vampires around here,' I said.

Mum smiled. 'Only in California.'

I took the bottle of lemonade from the fridge and poured myself another glass. It wasn't often there was soft drink in our house; I had to make the most of it.

'Josh seems to be doing okay,' she said.

I nodded.

'Does he talk about it?'

'No,' I said. 'We just try and keep everything the same.'

'That's good, Jay.' But she didn't look at me.

———

Matty brought his new bug catcher to the river. Kieran gave him a hard time, calling it 'juvenile', but it was fun. When we grew tired of swinging, we caught dragonflies and skimmers and a big old horsefly. We let everything go again – it just meant we had a good look up close and Matty recorded each creature in his notebook.

Ian had something new, too: a Polaroid camera. We took a picture of two dragonflies stuck together and a grasshopper the same colour as the leaf he was eating and it printed them out right on the spot.

'Let's go up to the trees,' I said.

It was sunny there, and out of the breeze. We set about catching beetles and ants, and the highlight – a swallowtail butterfly.

Kieran was grumpy, perhaps because Matty's bug catcher was getting all the attention, or because he and I hadn't had much time together, just us, since that day in the hay shed. There had been so much going on, and I was still cranky about Alicia.

When Matty caught a spider I lost interest. I didn't need to see all of its hairy legs magnified or have the boys try to scare me with it. I started to set up our lunch and took the best spot – with my back against the biggest tree.

We ate and gossiped, and gave Matty a hard time about a girl from the Catholic school who had been passing him notes on the bus before we had finished for the year.

'You should take a picture of us,' Kieran said. 'With the trees.'

Ian reached for the camera behind him.

'Get Matty to take it,' Josh said.

'That's not fair!' Matty said.

'It has a timer,' Ian said. 'We can all be in it.' He set the camera up on the esky while we arranged ourselves. Kieran and I were in the middle, Josh on the right, and Matty in front. Ian pressed something and ran in to take his place on the left, next to me. The camera flashed and for a moment we stood, arms still around each other, blinking. And then we ran, pushing and shoving, to see how it had turned out.

We were all grinning and everyone had their eyes open for once. Ian must have been moving – his hand was blurred. It was exactly how I imagined us, right down to Kieran's arm around me and the peace sign he was making above Matty's head. The big carving was behind us, and the other trees leaned into the picture, like giant people.

Then a cloud went over the sun and Ian said he had better get going. I wished we had taken five pictures so that we could all have a copy. When I looked at the image again, the colours had already started to fade, as if it was a moment we could never have back.

THERE WAS SOMETHING in the artist's brushstrokes, and the wash they had used. Jayne had found a clutch of wildflowers in the middle of the second box. She set up a banksia and a grevillea on the bench for closer examination and opened her file of images on her desktop for comparison. She could pick this artist now: the skill level, the style, the connection to their subject. She was like a connoisseur, a collector – a curator, even. She was sure that the wildflowers were by the same artist as the fish, and that they belonged to the Gatton school. Watermark comparisons, and the gold leaf analysis, supported her conclusion.

Much more difficult to prove was her suspicion that this particular artist was a woman. The handwriting had been the starting point, soft and looping. The acknowledgement of the Aboriginal names was a point of difference, too, reminding her of the early women nature writers, whose accounts tended to be sympathetic to Aboriginal peoples, including their stories, rather than writing them out of the scene.

The wildflower pieces had also reminded her of another drawing in their collection, of a flowering matt rush, unsigned and unattributed. Identifying the artist had been one of the impossible training tasks she had given Marnie when she started. The piece had been donated by a women's mental hospital when it was cleaned out and demolished in 1979. They had hoped the picture had been a gift to a patient by a family member but the names had turned up only dead ends. When Jayne had pulled the picture out again this week, the similarities were overwhelming, and it was on the same paper stock.

If she could identify an individual artist, particularly a woman, from the Gatton school, it would not only make her career, but earn the museum some much-needed funding. If she was smart, like their former director, she would have the museum fund her research, publish an indulgent series of books, and then leave for a flash university position somewhere off the back of it all. But the publications section was history now. Her, too, probably.

Meanwhile, another arborglyph had gone missing – from the Melbourne Museum. It was still listed, but marked unavailable. She had started working through her list, checking each tree against its respective database and catalogue. But it was hard to sneak the time, with Dan or Marnie always popping in and out, and she had already taken more than a fortnight to get through half of the Norris boxes. With a growing backlog and the cuts coming, Geoff would soon be asking what was so interesting. It was his job he was worrying about, not that they ever got rid of dud managers – just promoted them. But perhaps he didn't realise he was a dud. Her searches were logged, too, of course. Since the cuts to IT, no one checked those things, but perhaps, given the investigation, now they would.

The phone rang. Internal call.

She wheeled her chair over to answer. 'Jayne Lawson.'

'Dalma here. Can you pop up? Noni would like a chat.'

'Now?'

'If you have a minute.'

'On my way.'

Jayne locked her screen, took her resignation letter from her top drawer, gathered up her diary and a pen, and took the stairwell.

Her first real mentor – at the gallery – had advised her to always carry a folder and pen when walking around the office, and to appear to be in a hurry. The executives stored these busy images of you, she said, and matched it to 'management material'. Jayne hadn't bothered with that charade since failing the last promotion round, and the world hadn't ended. Until now.

She stopped at the foyer windows and breathed from her stomach. There was a heavy dump of snow on the Brindabellas; there was bad weather coming.

Dalma looked up. 'Saw you cycling in this morning. Impressive! Left our bus for dead.'

'You should join me.'

'As if,' she said. 'The world is a *much* better place without my rear appearing in lycra. Go on through.'

Jayne tapped on the doorframe.

Noni didn't look up from her two-fingered typing. 'Come in. Come in.'

Jayne stood back from the desk.

'Sit. Sit.'

She did. On a freshly upholstered guest chair. It was funny how there was always room for certain upstairs frills in the budget – no matter the cuts going on below. Jayne's personnel file was open on the desk.

Jayne wiped her palms on her suit pants. There was a worn patch on one knee, where it rubbed against the light box under the lab bench. Had rubbed.

'I've just been reviewing your redundancy application.'

'Ah.'

'What would you do?'

Jayne shifted in the chair, which was uncomfortable despite its plush waratah-print fabric. 'Finish fixing up my place. Do some more study, perhaps.'

'Another qualification would certainly help you. In terms of career advancement. If you want that. Increasingly, we need people who can cover multiple areas.'

Jayne nodded.

'To be honest, I'd been hoping we'd keep you. I wouldn't lose you to endless rounds of maternity leave, at least – like the other girls.'

Jayne opened her mouth and closed it again.

Noni's ample cheeks turned pink. 'Though that's a bit of an assumption.'

'It is,' Jayne said.

'But accounting are happy with the figures. You're young. Twelve months and you can apply for jobs again. I'd write you a fine reference. Things won't stay like this. When the new government comes in . . .' She gestured out the window, towards Parliament House.

The new government, if they got in, were unlikely to boost funding to arts institutions. Like balloons, once the numbers went down, they rarely came back up.

'Okay,' Jayne said.

Noni breathed out her nose. 'Have you spoken to Sarah?'

'I have.'

'And you're sure? You haven't rushed your decision?'

Jayne tucked the letter in the back of her diary. 'I'm sure.'

GOING BACK TO school the next year wasn't as hard. I knew what to expect and looked forward to seeing everyone. We weren't the youngest anymore, and could laugh at the year sevens trying to find their room and looking as lost as we must have.

I had managed the contact on my books myself and although there were a few bubbles they turned out pretty well. We were in the same elective groups but now we had geography and ancient history and music. The music room was all new, with brand-new equipment, but I wished I didn't have to do it. I couldn't sing a note or imagine what instrument I would be able to play. The triangle, perhaps. I was brave enough to join in the handball games, and got up to king a few times but never ace.

Ian waited for a quiet moment at lunch on the second day to tell us. 'You know the picture of us with the trees?'

I had been watching two year twelve boys put a year seven upside down in a garbage bin but turned back at the tone of Ian's voice.

'Mum saw it.'

Josh slapped his hand to his forehead. 'You were supposed to keep it secret.'

Ian shrugged. 'I had it hidden,' he said. 'But she cleaned out my room in the holidays.'

We groaned; we had all been there.

He tossed a ball of foil up in the air and caught it. We gathered in closer. I had only been thinking recently that we had been lucky Matty had kept his mouth shut so long, even when we left him out or were mean.

'She says it's a burial place for my people,' he said. 'We shouldn't have played there.'

I felt my face flush.

Kieran frowned. 'But she's not going to tell anyone?'

Ian shook his head. 'She won't say anything.'

———

Ian's mum had taken the day off to drive me and Ian to cross-country regionals. It meant his dad had to work all day in the service station on his own, so Mum was going to drop him off some lunch after pottery. Mum had just started, but she was really good. Dad had even made her a wheel, setting it up in the garage, and picked up some special clay from Forbes.

I had only won the school race by accident, because I was always running back and forth from the river on foot. Once I knew I was going to regionals, I started to take it seriously, going for a long run three times a week. Mostly I went to the grove, but sometimes I ran to Kieran's or Josh's along the stock route.

Now that the day was here, I was so nervous I had hardly slept, which was not ideal preparation. It wasn't just the race – it was seeing Ian's mum for the first time since she found out about the trees.

She smiled as I climbed in the back, but also gave me one of those looks adults have that go right through you, to the list of all the things you shouldn't have done. The trees were at the top of that list.

'Thanks very much for driving me,' I said.

'It's a nice day out,' she said. 'I want to see you two do well, eh?'

Ian grinned at me from the front seat. It was all going to be okay.

─────

The junior girls were up first. It was a six-kilometre track, longer than I had done before in one go. Ian pushed to the front of the crowd and gave me a goofy thumbs up for the start, which stopped me being too nervous.

I got away well, keeping clear of all those legs. Then I sat just behind the lead group, like Ian said, and settled in along the flat part of the track, past ironbarks and Cootamundra wattles starting to flower. They were itching my nose and it was warming up. The ground was so dry our feet sent up little puffs of dust and I felt thirsty just looking around. A few of the leaders fell off the pace, and one girl dropped out. Soon it was only me, a thin girl with red hair I recognised from Little Athletics, and the four Aboriginal girls up front. They were all from the local school, with long dark hair and the sort of legs that could run for ages. One even ran barefoot. They were intimidating, and probably knew the track, but I thought the shorter one was starting to lose her rhythm, and I focused on my breathing to stay steady.

Then we started to climb a steep slope that went on forever.

Our school track was almost dead flat and I hadn't included any real hills in my training. It was costing me now. Halfway up, the red stick-girl passed me. I was in trouble. Flies kept crawling in my mouth and my lungs burned. I had to really push to stay with her and my breathing was all over the place. I wanted to stop but then we passed the shorter girl, limping now, and were still in touch with the lead girls.

From the top, I could see the bright green oval where we would finish. It was the only thing that kept me going. I let the hill take me down and held up my arm to breathe through the stitch grabbing at my left side. As soon as we reached the edge of the oval, I accelerated. I still had power in my legs, from the shorter distances I raced at Little Athletics. Four hundred and eight hundred metres were my best, and I knew how to judge the final turn. I passed stick-girl at the two hundred mark; she had nothing left.

The three remaining girls had spread out, their strides long and even. They were running their own races now – for the medals, and for the chance to compete at the state titles. I ran the last hundred pumping my arms as if it were the relay – as if my team and everything in the world depended on it. I still had a shot at third. The crowd was making a lot of noise for their local girls, and I knew Ian was there cheering for me. I was close, right on the heels of the girl in front. I could see she was sweating, her face tight. There was no point leaving anything behind. But to get off her heels, I had to move around her, and when we lunged for the line, she was a whisker in front. The locals took first, second and third.

I collapsed on the ground, face throbbing and thighs burning. All I could do was suck in air. Ian appeared above me offering a hand up. 'Not bad, girl.'

I stood, but with my hands on my knees. Ian's mum was talking to the winning girls. The one who ran barefoot had come in second. She had a nice smile. Ian's mum looked over, pointing out Ian with her chin.

Ian turned his back on them and put his arm around my shoulders. 'Thought you had her there for a minute.'

'I really tried,' I said.

'I know.'

Then they announced Ian's race, and everyone started clearing off the track.

———

I ate the chicken, lettuce and mayonnaise sandwiches Mum had packed for me under a currajong tree with Ian's mum. Ian's race was longer, eight kilometres, so we had some waiting to do before the boys would reappear. I hoped Ian would do better with the slope than I had, and take all the momentum from the downhill run onto the track. I should have told him about that.

I jogged to the toilets and back, trying to keep my muscles warm, drank from my water bottle, and did a few half-hearted stretches. A breeze had picked up, swirling around the oval. At least it wouldn't be so hot for Ian. I shivered.

Ian's mum poured me a cup of sweet, milky tea and gave me a chocolate cupcake with pink icing. 'You need to replace some energy,' she said.

The warmth and sweetness were exactly what I needed. I took my time with the cupcake, pulling it apart and spreading the icing right to the edges. At least with cross-country there was only the one race; I didn't have to regroup for any other events. I took a deep breath and faced Ian's mum. 'I'm really sorry about the trees,' I said. 'We didn't know.'

She watched me over the lip of her thermos lid and sipped her tea. 'It's one of Ian's ancestors buried there,' she said. 'Those trees keep him safe.'

I dropped my head.

'The carvings say who he was, and show the way to the Dreamtime.'

It wasn't a grove, it was a graveyard. A cupcake crumb stuck in my throat and I gulped at my tea so I wouldn't cough. My cheeks were burning, and it wasn't just not being able to breathe.

'I should have taught Ian more, I suppose,' she said. 'And you kids have the right idea – to protect them. It's Ian's responsibility, to look after that place. And there's not so many left, anymore.' She half-smiled.

Breathing was easier, and I smiled, too.

'Do Deidre and David know about them?'

'I'm not sure,' I said. 'Maybe.'

'Well, you make sure you tell them it's an important place, eh?'

'Okay.' I wasn't sure that was such a good idea, the way Dad was talking.

'Look.' Ian's mum was on her feet and tipping out her tea before I could even turn around. 'He's coming second!'

It wasn't like our race – there were big gaps between the first three and no others in sight. Ian cut to the inside of the track and was gaining on the first boy, whose face was strained. Ian's stride was longer and he was smiling.

His mother jumped up and down. 'C'mon!'

Ian waited until the home straight to push in front and cross the line with both arms in the air. His mum screamed. 'That's *my* boy!'

Everyone was clapping and cheering while the others came in, the locals in second and third this time. Then they announced that Ian had set a district record. The girls from my race were watching from the hill, and the one who had come second whistled with her fingers in her mouth.

I ran down to the track, where Ian was shaking people's hands, puffed but still smiling. When I hugged him, he lifted me into the air. 'I saved something for the end,' he said. 'Like you.'

'HEY, STRANGER,' JAYNE said. 'You must be tired?'

'Wrecked,' Sarah said. 'I've been writing briefs on the fly for days. I dream briefs. Only in the dream something always prevents me from finishing, or I make a mistake that causes a major international incident, and I get the sack. But no such luck in real life.'

Sarah was smaller in her arms, more frail. 'Beer?'

'Please.' Sarah slipped out of her shoes and left them in the doorway, heels against the wall. 'And I have six missed calls from my mother.'

'She rang here, too.' Jayne twisted the tops from two James Boags and threw them in the bin.

'Oh, no. Sorry.'

'She misses you.'

'I know, but six calls? And she shouldn't ring you.' Sarah peered out the French doors at the gleaming deck. 'You've been busy, I see.' She took the bottle Jayne offered. 'Thanks.'

'Cheers.'

'It looks great. Just needs a big pot plant, maybe.' Sarah released her breath, as if she had been holding it for a week.

'You okay?'

'I'm not sure I'm cut out for all of this. Some of them seem to thrive on it.'

'Adrenaline?'

'Bad coffee and biscuits, I think. Self-importance.' She gulped at her beer. 'I was the only woman there most days,' she said. 'What did the kitchen man say? Are these his samples?'

'He was really good. Pick one?'

'Oh, honey,' Sarah said. 'I don't think I can make another decision. Ever.'

'I'm stuck between the myrtle and the blackwood.'

'Blackwood's more modern.'

'I'm not sure I want that.'

'Then the myrtle.'

Jayne smiled. 'Decision made.'

'What else has been happening? How's your mystery woman?'

'I'm sure it's her,' Jayne said. 'But I still need evidence.' There was half a box left to go through. She couldn't see any more pictures, and none of the documents seemed to relate to the fish or the wildflowers, but she had resisted the urge to rush ahead and flick through the remaining items. Like making your Easter eggs last through to the end of the holidays.

'You'll find it,' Sarah said. 'If she wants to be found.'

Jayne poured the laksa into deep bowls and carried them to the coffee table, where she had set out spoons, chopsticks and serviettes.

Sarah poked at the fire, added a few small pieces. 'It's not putting out much heat,' she said.

'Wood's not very good. Still green,' Jayne said. 'I should get a load from home.'

Sarah sat next to her on the couch. 'We could go one weekend.'

'You'd like to?'

Sarah plucked a piece of fried tofu from the top of her soup with her chopsticks. 'Of course. I'd like to meet your folks, see where you grew up. They must be wondering if I really exist.'

Jayne's tofu kept slipping from her grasp. She gave up on chopsticks and spooned hot liquid into her mouth. Its chilli pinched at her throat.

'Perhaps after I go away?' Sarah said.

'Away?'

'To Indo,' she said. 'End of next week.'

'For how long?'

'Ten days.'

'Right.' It was beginning to feel like a long-distance relationship, with her stuck at home like some wife. Chances were she would find out about the package and the investigation while Sarah was gone. But maybe that was for the best.

'What about the long weekend?' Sarah sipped her beer.

'That's when the wedding is.'

'Was I invited?'

'*Yes.*'

Sarah smiled. 'I'll check my diary.'

'What did your mum say?'

'It wasn't anything urgent. She wants to know when she can come visit,' Sarah said. 'She's keen on Floriade.'

'She mentioned that to me, too,' Jayne said. 'We should make it happen.'

'I know, it's just so hard for me to plan ahead.'

Jayne glanced at the clock. 'Do you want to watch something?' She had hoped to sneak in the week's Tour highlights. The other Australian, O'Grady, had won a stage, the last half of which she had slept through on the TV room couch.

Sarah stretched her legs out in front of the fire. 'Let's stay here. I feel like I haven't seen you properly for weeks,' she said. 'Is there wine? My mother was talking about her funeral. So exhausting.'

'Is she unwell?'

'Fit as a fiddle. But a friend of hers died recently. She's feeling morbid.'

Jayne pulled a local pinot down from the rack. 'You can just bury me in a cardboard box beneath a tree.'

'Don't you start,' Sarah said. 'Is that even legal?'

'They have green burials in Japan. There's not enough space left for cemeteries. It's ecological, too – no chemicals, no expensive lacquered box, all those nutrients released back into the ground.' She filled their glasses and sat the bottle on the coffee table. 'Whole woodlands are being regenerated, with little winding paths where people can visit their relatives.'

Sarah sipped, nodded. 'You're right into this.'

Jayne shrugged.

'Any particular reason?'

'Tree burials are traditional in a lot of cultures. Interring a body inside the trunk, beneath the roots, or even up in the branches.'

'And you like your trees.'

'Better than graveyards.'

Sarah smiled. 'Too many ghosts?'

'All those rows of marble and cement, mowed lawn. Dark suits despite the hot sun. Give me a tree for my tombstone any day.'

'Noted – not that you're allowed to die on me,' Sarah said. 'I think I saw one of those burial woods, in South Korea.'

Jayne sipped her wine, a little too sweet for a pinot, but not bad after dinner. 'Korea? Is there a country you haven't been to?'

'A lot of it has been for work.'

'Still.' It started to rain, loud on the iron roof.

'You've been to Europe.'

'London, for the internship. The rest was weekend trips to all the galleries. The Uffizi, the Louvre, the Prado, the Munch.'

'In Norway, right?'

'Yeah. I love him.'

'His paintings, you mean.'

Jayne grinned. 'Yes.'

'So where would you go? If we could go anywhere in the world for a real holiday tomorrow.'

'Tomorrow?' Leaving the country wasn't a bad idea. Maybe when the package came through. If the package came through. 'Italy maybe,' she said.

'More galleries?' Sarah placed her glass on the coffee table next to Jayne's and curled in beside her.

'I think I need a break from cultural institutions. Italy is *sexy*. The food, the wine, the landscapes, the climate. All that history.'

'Is that right?' Sarah bit her neck where it met her shoulder, goosebumping her skin. Jayne tried to turn, to kiss her, but Sarah was pushing her onto her belly, and her arm was already under her, unbuttoning her jeans. She pressed into Sarah's fingers, shut her eyes beneath her weight. The room was warm, too warm.

'I've missed you,' Sarah said, into her hair.

Her own words were gone, lost in skin and heat.

THAT WINTER WAS the driest on record since Mum and Dad were young, and followed on from a tough summer. We were already feeding the cattle. It wasn't about fattening them up but keeping them alive. Dad said that the market was so bad, it wasn't worth selling them even if they had been fat.

The cattle had the run of the valley and the river paddock, where the grass was still good. I didn't like that much – they made a mess in the grove and rubbed up against the carved trees. I had seen the way they burnished fence posts smooth with their necks and didn't want them rubbing out the carvings. They messed up our beach when they went down to drink, too, leaving stinking manure pats and holes in the sand. The river was already low and muddy and the cattle stirred it all up. But they had to drink. If you sat by the water for a few hours you would see nearly every animal and bird, even ones you didn't often see, like cranes and egrets and robin redbreasts. The river kept them all alive.

My job that winter, every second morning before school, was to push hay bales off the tray of the truck or to control the flow of grain from the contraption Dad had rigged up, while he drove.

That day, it was grain. The chain was dragging behind the truck in the dust, the big metal hook catching on clods and tussocks. We were only carrying a small herd, under two hundred, and I had begun to recognise the pushiest of them as they milled around at the gate and followed us down the paddock. Food was how you tamed animals. Even the most rebellious steers and heifers now followed us around more like sheep.

My breath made fog in front of my face. Sun caught the dew on spider webs along the fence. A pair of crows had flown in, as miserable as the drought itself, their beady eyes on the grain the cattle would miss and trample into the dirt.

Big Angus bull was first in line as usual, muscling his way to the front. Dad joked that he needed to keep his energy up. I knew exactly what he meant, and it was too gross to be funny. The truck was crawling forward, in low gear, and as we passed the stand of river oaks that provided shade – and extra feed in hard times – I pulled the lever that opened the flow of grain. Bull was waiting, nosing right into the trail we left behind.

Dad braked, obstructed by cattle circling around the front of the truck, and then crept forward. Somehow the hook must have ended up under the grain. When I looked back, it was caught in Bull's nose – through the strip of coarse pink flesh between his nostrils.

'Dad. Stop!'

But the truck rolled on, and Bull was hooked. He dug in his heels, pulling, fighting the chain, with an awful bawling.

'DAD!'

The truck finally stopped. By the time Dad jumped out, Bull had torn free, torn through his own nose, leaving a great bloody gash, like when Melinda Davis caught her finger in Elaine Star's earring during a netball final and ripped it right out, tearing her earlobe into two ragged pieces.

This was worse. There was blood everywhere. All the cattle were bellowing. I turned away, sure I was going to throw up.

'Oh, shit,' Dad said. 'Sorry, Bull.'

When I turned back, Dad was still standing there, hand over his mouth. Blood streamed from the bull's nose.

'*Do* something.'

'Not much we can do now,' he said. He bent to pick up the chain and hooked it onto the rail running beneath the back of the tray where it should have been. 'It will heal. He'll be all right.'

I cut the flow of grain, which had formed a great pyramid, as yet untouched.

Dad blew out long and hard, making his lips and cheeks wobble. 'You okay?'

'Yeah.'

'Sorry, kiddo,' he said. 'We'd better get this finished. I'll drive you to school if you miss the bus.'

SHE HAD TO wipe down the deck table after all the rain, but in partial sun, out of the wind, and with the extra heat of the barbecue, it was pleasant enough – for midwinter. There must have been a frost; there were still patches of white on the brick path in the shade. There were plenty of things wrong with Canberra, but she had always appreciated the air – clean and clear.

'Hon, your burial tree is in the *Canberra Times*.'

'What?'

Sarah held up the front page. STOLEN.

So, someone had blabbed. 'Who wrote the article?'

'Mary Gleason.'

An interesting choice – she was thorough but far from penetrating. 'I'll have a look after you.' Jayne loaded up her fork with French toast, banana and yoghurt, and dipped it in maple syrup.

'This is what's been going on?'

Jayne chewed, nodded. It was usually her figuring out what was happening at Sarah's work from the papers. Like the *Australian*'s latest headlines about the Middle East.

'It says there are only a handful left now – in their original locations?'

'Well, they're wood. They don't last forever. Conserving them is hard out in the elements. But yes, a lot were cleared by settlers, and some were removed and put in public institutions during the early twentieth century. The rest have been destroyed since – whether accidentally or deliberately.'

'And now this one has been stolen. That's awful.'

Jayne shrugged. 'Some pieces are better off lost than found.'

'How can you say that?'

'Their monetary value goes up, for one,' she said. 'No one gave a fuck about that tree when it was parked in storage.'

'They didn't know about it.'

'Exactly.' She flipped over to the sports pages. *But they do now.* McEwen had won another stage and Armstrong was yet to feature, but he always finished better than he started. Perhaps it took a while for the drugs to kick in. Jayne pushed her plate out of the way. 'Another coffee?'

'Sure.'

She carried their mugs to the kitchen, rinsed the jug and refilled it. The whine of milk heating filled the kitchen. Outside, a king parrot edged his way along a thin branch towards a pomegranate. Jayne tamped down the grounds and pushed the handle into place. She watched Sarah reading and tried to think over the noise of the machine while the mugs filled. This part she had no plan for.

She poured the milk, turned the machine off and carried their coffees out to the table. 'There you go, love.' She touched Sarah's shoulder.

'Thanks.'

Jayne leafed through the television guide with as much flapping as possible. 'I've been following the Tour de France and the Australians are doing pretty well. There are highlights tonight – might be some good scenery.'

'You watch it. I have some reading to catch up on.'

Jayne sighed. 'It goes through some really beautiful areas. Little stone villages perched on the hillsides.'

'Your DG says no one has claimed responsibility. No ransom request.'

Noni had done an interview? Jayne snorted. 'As if anyone would pay it.'

'Sorry?'

She shook her head.

'I hate it when you do that.'

'I don't like repeating myself.'

'You mumble.'

Jayne shrugged. 'It wasn't important.'

'I think that perhaps it was.'

Jayne closed the *Herald*, and tried to shuffle it back into shape. Sarah was still looking at her, coffee going cold. 'What?'

'Is there something you're not telling me?'

Jayne frowned and fiddled with the cup's handle.

'This tree was one of the first things you told me about when we met. You should be more upset about this.'

'Should I?' Jayne reached for the *Australian*. They hadn't even read Mystic Medusa yet and Saturday morning was blown. 'It was stolen decades ago. That's the real crime.'

Sarah lifted her mug, set it down again. Nodded. 'Honey, did you have something to do with this?'

The neighbour's ginger cat jumped down from the fence and slinked across her backyard. Why couldn't it hunt on its own turf?

'Jay?'

She stared at the map of France, imagining herself on the Tour. Hurtling down the mountain pass.

'*Jay!* I asked you a question.'

She watched the cat conceal itself in the unmown grass. 'Yes and no.'

'What is that supposed to mean?'

'It means I facilitated its return to its rightful owners.'

'*Facilitated?*'

The cat crouched, eyes on the parrot in the pomegranate. The cat didn't have a chance but it was going to have a shot anyway.

Sarah shook her head. 'Far out, Jay. What the hell were you thinking?'

The cat pounced, and the parrot fled, leaving the bare branch trembling.

Jayne closed her mouth.

'What about your job?' Sarah said. 'What about *my* job? Did you even think about that?'

'Oh, I'm a security threat now?'

'I could lose my clearance. You know that.'

'That's crap. Do they even know about me? It's not like we live together.'

'That's *your* choice. Not mine.'

'Oh, here we go.' Jayne shivered. The sun had risen above the roof, leaving them in shadow.

'You must have planned all of this. You've been sitting on it. And I had no idea,' Sarah said. 'Who are you?'

'For fuck's sake. We live with your secrets every day. All those silences while the news runs.'

'That's *work*,' she said. 'Meeting the conditions of my employment. Being professional. Stealing an Aboriginal artefact from your own fucking museum! That's personal.'

'Yes. It is.'

'Just tell me *why*?'

'I don't feel like you're interested in anything I have to say right now.'

Sarah let out her breath and tucked her hair behind her ears. 'I'm sorry. It's a shock.'

The breeze had swung around, fluttering the papers.

Sarah pushed her chair back. 'I'm going to get a glass of water. Would you like one?'

'No thanks.'

'Will you explain, at least?'

'You wouldn't understand.'

Sarah stood in the doorway, hands on hips. 'Try me.'

THERE WAS A good climbing tree between the grove and the river, a big old river red gum with plenty of low branches and lumps and hollows all the way up the trunk.

Now that we couldn't play in the grove, we had talked about building a tree house, or a platform at least, so as to watch over the trees and to see anyone coming. But we hadn't figured out how to get the materials down there without Mum and Dad knowing, and there weren't many people likely to show up anyway. If they did, it was by the river, which is what happened that day.

There were three older teenagers in the water, using our swing. There was a public access point a little way upstream, and sometimes people came down exploring or looking for privacy.

It was early for swimming, but it was a warm day. We didn't know the boys; they weren't from our school. There was a girl, too, in a bikini, and Kieran wanted to tell them to get off the swing, but when we saw her kiss one of the boys, we decided not to let on that we were there.

Matty was with us, which is why what we did was so stupid. I hoisted him up so that he could reach the lowest branch and then left him to it. We had started doing that more and more; he was bigger now and going into high school the year after next.

We manoeuvred up the tree and out onto riverside branches, each on a different spoke of the wheel. When I found a spot where I could see, the teenagers had stripped off; they were swimming naked. The girl had proper breasts and they were as brown as the rest of her, so I figured she went topless a lot. I was brooding about how this conflicted with my mother making me stop going topless because I was getting older, when Matty let out one of his sooky half-cries.

He was behind me. I had to turn around, and I did so reluctantly. Somehow his foot had gone through a rotten part of the branch he was on, and it was stuck. We were up pretty high, and he was looking down and trying to pull his foot out and making a lot of noise, which was going to wreck everything.

Kieran was closest, on the branch above him. 'Shh. Hang on,' he said, 'I'm coming,' and swung down.

When I turned back to the river, the girl and the boy were close together and it was embarrassing but I couldn't look away. She had her legs around his middle, underwater. The water was murky, so I couldn't see, but from some of the books I had read, I could kind of imagine. They were really kissing hard now, and I was feeling silly because of what had happened with Kieran and was glad he wasn't watching.

Then there was a crack behind me, and Kieran made his impatient noise, that *bah*, but whooshier, and I turned in time to see him, and the branch, hit the ground.

'Kieran!' I don't remember climbing down, but Matty must have managed to free himself, because he was there, next to Kieran with the rest of us. In the dirt.

'He's breathing,' Josh said.

It was bad, though. His eyes were shut, his face white, and his legs at an odd angle. 'Shit.'

'I'll go for help,' Ian said. 'I'm quickest.'

'Dad should still be in the front paddock,' I said.

Ian was hunting around for his other shoe.

'But we can't bring everyone here,' I said. 'The trees.'

Ian stopped, looked over my head, at the grove.

Josh waved his arms. 'We could move him down to the top of the beach track. That's as far as a vehicle is going to get anyway.'

'I'll meet you there,' Ian said, and set off at a sprint that even he couldn't maintain.

I laid the picnic blanket out beside Kieran and put my hand on his shoulder. His freckles stood out. I'd never really noticed them before.

Josh ran down to the river for help, but the teenagers were gone. As if they had never been there and we needn't have climbed the bloody tree in the first place.

'Are you sure we should be moving him?' Matty said.

I wasn't sure of anything, but together we rolled him onto the blanket and half-carried, half-dragged him downhill. We stopped in the shade, right by the track, where I knew Dad would back in. Kieran hadn't moved or woken, but I thought I could feel his breath on my cheek when I leaned in close. It was too hard not doing anything but stand there, so I wet the tea towel that had been around my drink bottle and put it to Kieran's forehead.

We heard the ambulance coming out from town at the same time as we saw the dust behind Dad's ute. He was going so fast I knew Ian wasn't on the back. They left the gates open behind them.

He pulled up short, on the other side of the track, to leave room for the ambulance. I hadn't seen him move that fast for years, out the door and to Kieran.

'Oh, no,' Dad said. 'No. C'mon, little mate.' He checked Kieran's pulse, ran his hands over his head, his limbs.

Ian wasn't with him. He must have stayed behind to direct the ambulance.

Josh was blinking back tears and Matty was full on sobbing.

Dad patted Kieran's clothes and looked around. 'Ian said he fell. I thought you must have been on the swing?'

I shook my head.

He looked towards the grove and then at me, his face asking a question.

I made a noise in my throat trying to stop the sick coming up.

'Okay, kiddo?'

I nodded, and managed to swallow and then breathe again.

The ambulance turned off its siren. It was flying across our paddocks, through the open gates. Josh and I stood close, Matty between us.

'How high was he, do you think?'

'Maybe twenty-five feet,' I said.

The ambulance backed up in a cloud of dust. The doors opened and the trolley came clunking out. Ian came behind, the top of his shorts wet with sweat.

We knew one of the ambulance officers from first aid but the other was new. They looked Kieran over, too, and put a brace around his neck before strapping him to a board, then lifting him onto the trolley. I started to panic then, about moving him, about everything – but Dad had his arm around me, holding me tight.

They jacked up the trolley, wheeled Kieran to the back of the ambulance and loaded him in. Their faces were serious, even in front of us. There was talk of Matty going in the ambulance but in the end he came with us.

'Your mum and dad will meet him at the hospital,' Dad said, lifting Matty into the passenger seat of the ute. I wished he would lift me in beside him, too, but I climbed on the back with Ian and Josh.

It was a slow trip after all that rushing. I thought Dad would drop Josh and Ian home but he took us all back to our place. We looked at each other without speaking; we knew we were in for it. Then Mum was there, with hot chocolates for all of us in the lounge, which was odd on a hot day and with us so filthy, but it did feel better to sit there together.

It was only when we realised that there would be no shouting, no lecture, that we understood how bad it was. And then we couldn't look at each other anymore.

THEY CROSSED THE park opposite the shops, following the deep
furrow worn in the grass, and hurried through the stile. Last time,
they had dawdled through and a branch had fallen from the big
blue gum overhead, landing only a few centimetres from Sarah's
sneakers. They didn't call gums widow makers for nothing.

They took the track around the base of the mountain. 'So where's
the arborglyph now?'

'I don't know.' The track overlooked the houses lucky enough to
back onto the reserve. Some owners had put in decks and glass
to catch the morning sun. All of the original cottages had been
built to face the road rather than north, with poky windows and
small rooms. Eighty years later, Canberrans were finally adapting
to the environment.

'Is this why you wanted the package?'

Jayne nodded. 'Now I'm just sweating on the investigation . . .'

'Investigation?'

'It's only internal.'

'Christ.' Sarah pulled her beanie lower, half-covering her eyes.

A woman walking her Staffy from the other direction detoured around them. They weren't putting out a good vibe.

Sarah walked faster. 'They can take the money back, you know. If you're convicted. And I'd have to tell my employer.'

'*If* I'm convicted. And, I think, only if I benefited from the crime somehow. Which I didn't.'

'Well, you've planned everything, haven't you?'

'Don't.' Jayne hunched into her jacket, hands in pockets.

'Did you think through what would happen?'

A gaggle of mountain bike riders whirred past. The track had never been so busy. 'I guess I knew I'd either get away with it or I wouldn't.'

'And if you didn't?'

'I was prepared to accept the consequences.'

'To me? To us?' Sarah stared at the water tank ahead, bright with fresh graffiti tags.

'We weren't together when I started.'

'We are now.'

Present tense. *Don't panic.* 'I guess I see it as being bigger than us.'

'More important?'

'In some ways,' Jayne said. They stopped to look out over the city, its trees without leaves, parks browned off by winter. Spring couldn't come soon enough.

'Right.'

'Hundreds of those trees were bulldozed into piles and burnt. Or sold off to museums and galleries – like they were ours to sell!

It's not just the individual trees – they were part of a burial site, a place for the initiation of young men. It was bad enough taking the land, but we're talking about deliberately destroying a people's cultural heritage.'

They turned onto the path heading up the slope. 'I agree,' Sarah said. 'But—'

'But what?'

'You aren't responsible for the past.'

'But I am,' she said. 'Sometimes, someone has to do something.'

'What about your professional responsibilities? It's separate to our personal views. That's what being a grown-up is.'

'Oh, I'm a child, now?' She kicked a stone off the path. 'I can't separate those things. Anyway, we serve the taxpayers, not the government of the day. What I did was in the public interest.'

Sarah shook her head.

'Please understand.'

'I don't know, Jay. I have so much going on already, I can hardly think straight. I need some time.' She let Jayne take her hand. 'I didn't know about any of this. You've kept so much from me,' she said. 'We see things so differently.'

A young goanna scuttled up an ironbark. Parrots chattered and called overhead.

'Can we talk about it more when I get back?'

'Back?'

'From Indo,' Sarah said. 'I fly out Monday morning now, remember.'

Jayne had forgotten again, with everything. 'I can drive you to the airport.'

'Thanks, but work has organised a car.'

Jayne tightened her grip on Sarah's hand. What sort of job was it, where you couldn't even say goodbye at the airport?

THE MORNING AFTER, I slept late. Mum was already washing up our picnic stuff, which I had planned to sneak out and get. Dad must have been down to the river already, which was not good. Our secret was probably out. But that was the least of our worries.

'Morning, love.'

I cuddled into her from the side, and she leaned over but didn't stop washing.

'Want something to eat?'

I shook my head. 'Have you heard anything?'

'He was stable overnight, but it's too early to tell, they're saying.'

I groaned.

'Fingers crossed, love.'

I watched her tip potato salad in the bin and then push the container under the sudsy water.

'The police were out early, to take some pictures and so on,' she said. 'They want to talk to you later.'

I pulled away to open the fridge and took the juice from the door. Kieran said I was lucky to be an only child. In his house he had to fight for everything. There wasn't much juice left, so I only poured half a glass, pretending I had to share. How would Kieran fight for anything now?

'What were you doing up that tree?'

'Just climbing,' I said.

'It's very high.'

I shrugged.

She was wiping up Tupperware and sorting it into piles by family. 'Why don't I make you some eggs?'

'Okay,' I said.

She cracked eggs and whisked and I put on a piece of toast and fetched the parsley from the back step. When Mum put the plate down it smelled so good, I found that I was hungry after all.

Mum washed up the whisk and bowl and wooden spoon while I ate. With her back to me she said, 'When the police come back, just tell the truth. Okay, love?'

My mouth was full but I managed to make an affirmative sound.

———

Mum and Dad let me stay home from school when term started. The others were home, too, but it didn't feel like holidays. We didn't call or see each other. I lay on my bed in my room and listened to music and read every library book in the house. Mum tried to coax me out to play Monopoly, which was a rare offer, but I was too tired and too much had happened. Dad brought in a book one night about a girl and a giant manta ray. He sat on my bed for a while and said that the girl reminded him of me.

I read the book twice even though it was sad. The girl dives on the reef and makes friends with the manta ray. After her father dies, she has to protect the manta, keeping it a secret from the fishermen and her own brother. She was much braver than I could ever be.

I wondered if Dad was trying to tell me he knew about the trees, and that it was okay, but he didn't say anything else. The police hadn't said anything either, just asked questions until I couldn't remember what I had said and put my head down on the table and Mum told them that was enough.

On Sunday night there must have been some sort of parent conference, because over dinner mum said we were all going back to school the next day. Except Kieran.

I said I wasn't ready, but Mum said I was going all the same. When she offered to drive me in, I said I'd rather take the bus.

———

Josh was the next stop along. He dropped his bag and sat in the seat behind me. 'Hey.'

'Hey.'

Every kid between Josh's place and town looked up at us as they got on and then looked away. Everyone knew what had happened but not what to say. I stared out the grimy window at all the paddocks fading from green. Josh speed-read *Day of the Triffids* for English.

When the driver – old Gary Newlands – pulled up out the front of school with a lurch, the red-brick building looked different. Smaller somehow. Josh and I were last off, lingering in our seats, along the aisle and at the door, as if stepping outside would make it more real. Ian was waiting by the gate, hands in pockets. Everyone else swarmed around talking and laughing too loud.

We walked down the steps together. There was nothing that needed saying.

THE PRESS HAD staked out the front steps of the museum. Jayne wheeled her bike into the car park, locked it, and left her helmet and glasses on until she was inside the lift. The head of publicity, Tamsin, would have her work cut out for her today. It wasn't often that the Canberra cultural institutions made the news. Except when asbestos turned up in the air conditioning, or they paid too much for an American modernist painting.

The lift doors opened at the foyer. Max had employed extra security staff and the cafe had put on an extra barista. The line for coffee was out the door. What a circus.

'Morning.' Marnie held the lift for Dan with one hand, her coffee with the other. He ran to catch up, carrying two takeaway cups.

He handed one to Jayne. 'Thought you might need this.'

'Oh, thanks.'

'Some guy from the ABC tried to talk to me in the queue,' he said. 'I'm not going out there again.'

Jayne smiled. He was a sweetie. At least she wouldn't be around to watch that ground out of him.

They had reached their floor. 'Lunch today?' Marnie said over her shoulder. 'Get off site somewhere?'

'Sure,' Jayne said. 'Grab me on your way out.'

She dropped her pannier and coat and switched her computer on. She sipped her coffee while her emails came in. Tamsin's was marked urgent, and sent at five in the morning – instructing them not to comment to the press. Noni would make a statement at noon. Tamsin had probably had to come in early to draft the media release, but the woman was a climber, that was clear. She never let her efforts go unnoticed.

The next email, sent several hours later, let Jayne know her redundancy application had been approved. It was done; she was surplus to the organisation's requirements.

For a long time, she hadn't known what to do about the arborglyph – how to get it out. The most successful schemes for stealing paintings involved finding a skilled artist to produce a fake and creating an opportunity to swap it for the original. It was sad, but only a few people could tell the difference. Her position on the inside gave her the opportunity and she had plenty of artist friends – but you couldn't fake a four-hundred-year-old carved tree.

As the years went by, and the tree wasn't exhibited, she began to realise that like those forgeries, few people would notice it was gone, despite its size. There was an audit every four or five years, and items were routinely written off or decommissioned. Taking it from Mitchell, though, was a problem. The perimeter was fenced, shut down and secured at night and she rarely had a reason to visit the site after hours. It would be difficult to remove the tree from the room it was in, at the back of the facility, and the loading dock was visible from an adult shop across the street, which was open all night. She would need help. A lot of help.

She had been down at the loading dock when she figured out she needed to bring it in from the cold, back to the museum first – but how? If she requested it for treatment it would be linked to her on the system. She needed it to be loaned out to an exhibition – and returned. There would be too much attention if it failed to show up at the other end.

When she was sure she could pull it off, she approached Ian. It had been a strange conversation, both of them sidling up to and stepping around the idea. She had thought he would be a little more surprised, reluctant perhaps. But in the end he just listened and asked her to leave it with him. It was his idea to use a gallery outside Wiradjuri country. A red herring. He had a contact who did occasional consultancy work for the Tweed Gallery, authenticating Indigenous items. She would plant the idea for an exhibition, offering to facilitate the permissions process with the various communities. Ian said he thought he could talk the council round. She didn't ask too many questions. The less they knew about each other's part in it the better.

It took over a year to set up. The exhibition was a broad one, so as not to trigger any suspicion later: carved timber objects from across New South Wales. There were canoes, woomeras, spears and message sticks. And the tree. The whole thing almost fell over so many times. She nearly told Sarah in bed one night when, after all that planning, it had looked like the tree wasn't going to be released.

When it turned up in the loading area, and she prepared it for its journey to the gallery, it was quite an anticlimax. The exhibition was for five months: a long wait. But the time frame and the patience required were, in many ways, appropriate for a tree.

It had taken seven years – like a sentence for stealing a loaf of bread – but now the arborglyph was free.

It was the greatest success of her career. Yet she couldn't tell anyone, or list it on her résumé.

The redundancy package was a gift, a get out of jail free card. But it wasn't exactly how she had imagined her career panning out. Sarah was on the up and up, planning each move, doing important work – and Jayne was on the way out.

THE DAY THEY flew Kieran to Sydney, Dad came home with a new motorbike. After years of saying no. It wasn't just a Honda 90, like the boys had, but a Yamaha 125 – yellow, with a matching helmet. A real trail bike. I spent the weekend riding around all of the tracks and dams and learning how to do burnouts. I wasn't allowed to go on the main road except to cross over, and the stock route was out of bounds.

There had been no punishment for what happened. Dad told Mum we had been 'punished enough'. If anything, our parents fussed over us, listening to what we said and doing things we wanted. I didn't even have to ask to stay over at Ian's for his birthday, and there was cake and Coke and videos till midnight.

We got special treatment in school, too. When I punched Stacey Harwood in the arm during maths, I was sent outside and told to apologise – that was it. And when Ian and Josh water-bombed the year twelves waiting to go into their trial exams, they weren't even called up to the principal's office.

I high-fived them at lunch, and we grinned for a bit, but everything was flat without Kieran. As a group, we only really worked with him there, and it was hard to enjoy anything knowing he might never play sport or even walk again.

———

The motorbike had a catch. I had to help round up cattle, bringing them back from the river to the yards. It took most of the morning, and the first time I stacked it on a rock because I was watching the cattle, not the ground. It was good being outside, though, and I saw three rabbits and an eagle – which was after one of the rabbits.

A few cattle hung wide, among the trees. I was worried Dad would go after them, into the grove, so I took the river side as we approached, which meant dodging all of the logs and roots. The cattle didn't go near the carved trees, but rushed down to drink as if they had been driven across the state, not just our property. They eyed the other bank, and for a moment I thought the steers would make a run for it. I didn't blame them; it was better than where they were going.

When I beeped the bike's horn and revved from the side, they turned and ran back up the track. I had to accelerate to make it up the bank and launched into the air. My first jump. Dad grinned and gave me a thumbs up.

While we waited for the cattle to push through each of the gates, Dad told me stories about when he was a boy. He said everything was a lot wetter then, that the river was higher on its banks and the creek almost always flowed. 'Once, when it rained heavily upstream, all the fish came up,' he said.

'What do you mean?'

'The water was really muddy, and all the fish came up to the surface. All we could see was fish. We went down to the edge with nets, and scooped them up by the dozen.'

'Wow,' I said. 'That wouldn't happen anymore.'

'Probably not.'

———

The cattle were less cooperative going into the yards. It was as if the fear off all of those who had gone before was stored in the timber rails, and they could sense it. Sometimes we yarded them for drenching or marking calves, but today the truck was backing up to the ramp – to take the best steers to the market in Forbes. I tried not to think about it.

I didn't go inside the yards, not since I saw one of the Hereford steers charge Dad and gore him, leaving a big slash on his back that had to be sewn up at the hospital. Mum sewed up his shirt in the same place. In the race, when he was trying to move them on or force the drench gun in their mouths, cattle would often kick or squash him into the rail and he would have bruises for weeks.

I stayed on the fence and whacked a long piece of poly pipe, yelling my special 'heyup' to help separate the fat steers into the holding yard. After a while the whole place stunk of manure and so did we. When I opened the gate to release the cows, calves, and steers too skinny for market, they ran off into the paddock without looking back.

———

One Monday morning the bus stopped at Kieran's gate. Matty was there waiting by the mailbox. We had never been so glad to see him. His hair was cut short and his face didn't look as babyish. Josh moved over to share his seat and we didn't give him a hard time, the way we used to. He didn't say anything about Kieran, though he looked out the back window, towards home, as the bus pulled away.

In the end we didn't ask him any questions. He probably felt as bad as I did, having been the one Kieran was trying to rescue. Instead, I told Matty about my motorbike and Josh told him bits and pieces of gossip he had missed out on, like a girl from Matty's school going out with a boy from ours. Josh didn't mention his dad either, and we didn't ask. Mostly we heard updates through our parents, if we hung around enough and kept our ears open. There were so many things that we couldn't talk about now, even though they were the most important.

SHE RODE ON, around the end of the lake, past the public toilets and car park. It was a well-known beat, incongruous in its setting between lake and forest. There was always a car or two parked beneath the trees, waiting for another to arrive. It was lonely if you thought about it.

She flushed a bevy of quail from the grass, the last of the young skittling out from under her front tyre just in time. She didn't stop at the dam, but continued on, out towards Sutton Forest. She could get more speed up on the road, but the quiet, and the gentle curves and slopes of the bike path, allowed for Tour de France fantasy moments. Armstrong had won his first stage. They were into the mountains now, which tended to sort out the Australians.

The sensation of speeding downhill through trees was the pinnacle of riding – the sound of cogs, gears, spokes and wheels all working together and bouncing off trunks, the smell of pine sap, the light all shafts and shadows. There was something primal about it, a return to the forest. Followed closely by the exhilaration of re-emerging into the open, into the light.

The sky was without cloud, the air crisp. In a trick of the altitude, eyes closed, she could imagine she was in the northern hemisphere, sitting just inside the lead pack, locked onto that wheel. She made her move, through the gap, sprinting to the finishing line beneath plane trees, the motorbikes leading her in, the crowds three deep at the side of the road. She raised her arms in the air and did a double fist pump. 'Queen of the mountain!'

A mob of grey kangaroos grazing beside the path took flight, bounding away towards a gully. She cruised the easy downhill stretch to Uriarra Crossing. What had been Sutton Forest was now bare slope – but green grass had grown through the black.

A temporary wire fence encircled the ruins of the once-white Mount Stromlo Observatory, where some of the world's best astronomers had gazed at galaxies far away. All but one of the telescopes, and the library, had been consumed, while only metres away, the visitors' centre and cafe were left untouched. Fire was outside logic.

A surviving straggle of trees were covered in fuzzy new growth, and the site office, an orange crane and blue portaloo were bright on the hillside. But this was a site of deconstruction rather than construction. The observatory was not going to be rebuilt. And she was a long way from France.

———

Mount Ainslie was gold in the late afternoon light. She could see every detail of every treetop, like an oil painting. The air was so dry it crackled, and the back of her head, behind her ears, ached with cold. But the air was so clear, she could see everything as it really was. An afternoon on the bike had been what she needed.

She ducked into the supermarket to avoid one of the gallery preservationists – an occupational hazard, living in the same town and the same inner north suburb as so many other public servants her age.

She chose a bottle of cabernet on special, picked up a round loaf of Italian bread and some parmesan, and carried it to the check-out. Her bike shoes clacked on the lino.

Couples and friends were drinking around lit braziers outside the pub on the corner as she made her way back to her bike. She was feeling Sarah's absence more than she'd thought she would. More than she would like. It was hard to settle to anything.

It was her old uni friend, Gemma, who had introduced them. She and Jayne had done honours together, under the same useless supervisor: bonded for life. Gemma was an academic now, a senior lecturer already. To keep herself sane, she always had her next overseas trip planned. And her next painting.

Gemma admitted later that it had been no accident. Sarah had been miserable longer than Gemma could stand, still pining after a year for a drama queen she was better off without. The ex worked for AusAid, and had postings and breakdowns in equal proportions. It was good work – you had to respect it. But what was the point helping others if your own life was a mess?

Gemma was probably sick of Jayne whingeing, too, about the statistical improbability of meeting a suitable mate in a public service town of three hundred thousand. She had seen something in her and Sarah that they might have missed themselves.

———

She forced open the door of the shed behind the carport, bringing down a shower of dust. The notebooks were in a box on a high shelf. On tiptoes, she lifted the lid and felt around for her first sketchbook, marked and scuffed from numerous camping trips. She had even dropped it in the fire once, requiring quick rescue.

It was on the last page: the first shading she had done – of the tree. She could almost smell the grove: grass, yellow box, red gums, the river. In all of the catalogues, books, photos and visits, she had never seen another quite like 'her' tree, the chevrons, diamonds and scrolls snug around the river lines. She didn't know who this man had been or his story, but she knew the tree, the place. The patterns left behind.

She carried the book inside with more reverence than her drawing skills warranted and placed it on the kitchen bench. The white corner of a photograph nosed out. It was faded now, but there they were, their child selves standing in front of the trees. It was evidence of another place in time, not just the past, but when the world was different. Where the trees once were, and their childhood – before Kieran fell.

She stuck the photo on the fridge door with a silver magnet, switched on the lights, and the kettle, for tea. While she waited for it to boil, she played around with the design, just black felt pen on the shopping docket. She conflated the river and the chevrons, and repeated the pattern, then compressed it into the shape of a shield.

AT THE END of that year it seemed that all of Kieran's dad's talking had paid off. We went into sheep. Prices were at record lows and we still had feed. Dad bought a big mob of wethers from the other side of town, from a family selling up.

Mum drove us over there in the ute, our motorbikes tied on the back, early one morning, and we walked the sheep back along the stock routes. You couldn't hurry them too much because they had to go so far; it was just a matter of keeping them moving. There wasn't much grass left, between the gravel and the fences, but sheep didn't need much. Dad said it was good for them to eat as they went, less stressful, and that way they wouldn't lose condition. We could have trucked them home but that cost more and stressed out the sheep.

Sheep were easier to manage than cattle – but so stupid. They circled around and around like a single creature; they all had to go the same way. If one got stuck on its own it panicked and went crazy. You didn't see them sneaking off, figuring out ways to escape or getting cranky and fighting back like cattle. Their manure didn't stink as much either. If you ran over the little pellets it wasn't a big deal, not like hitting a cow pat that splashed up all over your legs.

Sometimes Dad stood up high on the foot pedals, only his fingers touching the handlebars, to see ahead over the mob. By the end of that first day I could do it, too, although I couldn't see as far.

When a ute or truck came along they had to drive through the sheep. Mostly we knew the driver, but even if we didn't, they would always lift one finger from the steering wheel and nod their heads. We had to travel along the main road for a mile or so to get to our own stock route, and there was more traffic then. You could tell those who weren't locals; they hung back, afraid to push into the sheep or beep their horns, and the animals just milled around the front of the car. Dad would exclaim at their stupidity and ride alongside the vehicle, telling them to rev their engine and move forward.

When we had to cross the bridge the sheep baulked. They could see daylight between the boards and when a car crossed it rattled. Even when we both revved our bikes and rode at them, they turned back in circles and baaed like nobody's business. In the end, Dad got off his bike, grabbed a sheep and dragged it over. It was freaking out, kicking and making a lot of noise, but once it was on the other side, and Dad let it go, it just stood there looking back. The rest of them streamed across the bridge without any more fuss. Dad said they were just like people.

The sheep were happier once we were back on the stock route, fanning out to chomp on grass in the shade. More trees meant

more birds, too. Galahs especially. Dad said there was another type
of galah that was white with pink under its wings, although you
only saw them out west nowadays.

We would stop under the shade of a tree, turn off the bikes and
let the sheep wander. As long as it was in a steady forward motion,
we were making progress. One dead gum was full of hollows, and
I saw a rosella poke its head out of two different holes. Or perhaps
it was two different rosellas. I looked for any trees with carvings on
them, like ours, but the only marks were on those that had been
ringbarked with an axe.

'So, Kieran is coming home next week,' Dad said.

I wiped dust off my petrol cap, loosened it and tightened it again.

'He's not going to be the same as before.'

I frowned. Dad didn't know Kieran like I did.

'He's probably going to be in a wheelchair the rest of his life, kiddo.'

I looked out over the brown paddocks, at an eddy of dust travelling fast, and shut down tears.

'It's going to be pretty tough for him,' he said. 'For all of them.'

I tried to imagine Kieran not running, not climbing, not
laughing. 'When can we go over?'

'Once they get settled again. When he's ready.'

———

Mum had packed us lunch, which I had been carrying in the little
esky strapped to the back of my bike. We ate it beneath a yellow
box, though its narrow leaves didn't cast much shade with the sun
right overhead. Dad and I lay flat on our backs once we had finished
our sandwiches. Sitting down all day was harder than it sounded.
Going slow was the worst. The slower you went, the harder it was

to balance, and stopping all the time meant putting your leg down, taking more of the bike's weight.

We left the sheep overnight in the Grangers' paddock and rode home. We had been up at five and didn't get home until six. Lamb chops and mashed potato had never tasted so good, although I had a moment of doubt, having stared at the wethers' backsides all day.

'So, what did you make of your first day of droving?' Mum said.

'Good,' I said.

'How's your bum?' Dad said.

'Sore!'

Mum and Dad laughed more than they needed to and then talked about some of the tech classes being shut down, including pottery.

'There's a petition we can sign,' Mum said. 'I can't believe they'll go through with it.'

Dad had started going along to the evening class, and in the holidays they sometimes took me along. I had done pottery at school and for a while I knew more about it than them, but that didn't last long. The raku firings were the best. They built a new kiln out in the courtyard every time, with special white bricks, and stacked all of their pots and vases and cups and bowls inside. Then they lit the fire and sealed it up. It went all afternoon and into the night. The kiln glowed red and everyone sat around with drinks, and there was a barbecue later.

The next day, everyone came back to see what had happened inside. When the teacher opened it up, you didn't know what you would find. How each piece turned out was determined by the heat, and where the ash fell. The glazes reacted in different ways depending where they were in the kiln. One side of a pot could be blue and the other side more green.

Dad liked his pieces to be matching but Mum chose glazes that reacted the most. There was one that turned grey and crazed all over, with red running down like lava. That was best on a vase, something with high sides. There were mugs that were one colour inside, dark and smooth, and another colour outside. It was all a mystery until the pots cooled and we started unloading the kiln. A few pots always cracked, or didn't work out, but the rest were gold.

There were always other kids there, and we ran around the grounds, climbing over everything and hiding in the shadows, but if there was no one my age, once the firing had started, I preferred to listen to the adults talking.

The first pottery teacher was Japanese. Hiroki knew about raku from home. He said that people had been doing it for thousands of years and explained the different effects created by burning cedar or pine. He had been experimenting with eucalypts, but his favourite Australian wood was brush box. 'It burns so hot!' He had gone back to Japan, but they had kept going with the raku firing once a year. Until now.

'They're trying to make everything more vocational, I suppose,' Mum said.

Dad shook his head. 'It's the crafts and hobbies that get people there. What else have we got?'

I yawned.

'Night, kiddo,' Mum said. 'Early start again tomorrow.'

I brushed my teeth leaning on the sink, and climbed into bed. When I closed my eyes, I could still see sheep.

SHE HAD BOOKED in twice before and cancelled so it was little wonder Cas looked surprised to see her open the door. It was more like a dentist's surgery than a tattoo parlour: white, sterile, with an adjustable brown leather chair under bright lights, as if for torture.

Cas had had an exhibition when Jayne was still at the gallery – all feathers and landscapes, celebrating her capacity for detail. She had set herself up out in the burbs. No sign. She was trying to fly under the bikies' radar. Rumour had it that she had taken a circular saw to someone's Harley, but she was just a big old softy.

'So, let's see it,' Cas said.

Jayne handed over the docket. 'It's only rough.'

'Nice,' she said. 'Original.'

It wasn't, but she hoped that somewhere between her childhood representation, adult interpretation and Cas's re-creation, there would be something of her own, of what it meant to her. And it was too late to back out now.

'Where?'

Jayne touched her left shoulder.

'Good. The shape, though. It's a bit nothing. We could go longer, like a traditional shield, down onto your bicep, or wider, more like a superman symbol, filling out to fit this shoulder of yours,' Cas said.

Jayne blinked. 'Broader, I think. Not cartoonish, though.'

'But strong, for protection.'

'Yes.'

Cas redrew it on tracing paper and gave it a more muscular look, with cleaner lines – the difference between the artist and the arts administrator. 'What do you think?'

'Perfect,' Jayne said.

'Okay. You haven't been drinking?'

'No.'

'No blood issues?'

'No.'

'Let's get that jacket out of the way then. Get yourself comfortable.'

She had only worn a singlet underneath, which left her a little cold. Cas prepped the area, the alcohol raising goosebumps on Jayne's skin. 'Tell me when you need a break, okay?'

Jayne nodded. She had thought about asking Hopes or Dana to sit with her, but it had been a while since she had been in touch, and they were probably busy with the new house. They were rebuilding in one of the new suburbs, a forest of new houses where pines had been. But it had good views and was to be powered by its own solar grid.

The outline hurt, like a thousand small cuts – which was probably less than she deserved – but if she breathed deep and steady it was bearable, and she settled into a kind of meditative trance.

The fog still hadn't burned off outside. It was one of those days that got colder as it went on.

'You work out?'

'Cycle,' Jayne said. 'Some yoga.' And her twenty push-ups and fifty sit-ups most days.

Cas wiped down Jayne's shoulder and changed the attachment on her machine. 'Okay?'

Jayne nodded.

It was the filling in that got to her. The pain was duller but seemed to intensify over time, until it was maddening. She started to worry that she hadn't heard anything from Sarah, and what that might mean. And to dwell on all of the things she could and should have said before she left. Yogic breathing no longer helped.

'You look kind of pale,' Cas said. 'How about a rest?'

'Thanks.' She shook out her left hand, unused to being so still.

'Tea?'

Jayne laughed. 'Sure.'

'Expecting bourbon?'

'Maybe.'

'Alcohol thins your blood. Makes you bleed more,' Cas said. 'Heavy drinking will blur the clarity of the tattoo over the years. That and sun. Just look at all those navy guys. Terrible. Mind you, they were backyard jobs to start with.'

Top deck jobs, more like it. Or down below. The tea was good. Sweet and warm.

'Better?'

Jayne nodded. 'Thanks.'

'There's no hurry. Can't have any of my girls passing out in the chair,' Cas said.

Jayne smiled.

'So is there a story behind this one? I like a piece with a story.'

THE FIRST MORNING back at school I was glad to be away from sheep and cattle and dust – and adults. We had been waiting for Kieran to ask us over, but he never did, and the best Josh and I had managed was one night at Ian's and a day at the pool. None of us had wanted to go to the river, and it was low and stinking anyway. School had never looked better. Only the library was air-conditioned, and that was for the books, not us, but there were fans and water fights and a lot more distractions.

Matty wasn't at their stop and we worried, until Josh said that maybe Kieran was coming back and their mum was driving them. I hadn't figured out that he wouldn't be able to go on the bus with the chair – ever again. Now it was all too real.

'They were building those ramps at school over the holidays,' he said.

'For Kieran?'

'Must be. So he can get up to the second floor – and down from the entrance.'

I hadn't thought of that either, although I thought about Kieran all the time. Legs were something you took for granted when you had them. 'Ian will be happy,' I said.

'Yeah.'

Ian had been stuck in electives on his own the last term, including needlework. He had our sympathy there. Josh said some of older boys – farmers' sons – were giving Ian a hard time, calling him names. The cool girls had started to gang up on me, too, locking me out of handball. We had all relied on Kieran's legs.

A caravan all the way from South Australia was holding up the cars ahead of us, dragging out our trip to town. My stomach churned at the idea of seeing Kieran, even though I wanted to.

———

In the end you couldn't have predicted how it would be, but it all made sense afterwards. We grinned at each other and Josh made bad jokes. Kieran asked him what the gossip was, because Josh always knew. The hardest part was standing up while he was sitting down and not being sure when to help or how.

At recess, Ian thought to offer to go to the tuckshop – the counter was too high and the covered area crowded. Then the door into maths was only just wide enough so I lined his chair up straight and pushed while he tucked in his arms. I felt better after that, knowing what to do.

At first the class went quiet whenever he rolled in. It took a while to get used to him pushing the chair away from the desk and kind of parking there, unpacking his bags sitting down. He was good at it, and I realised he must have been practising lots of things at home.

The first time we were alone was at lunch, waiting for Josh and Ian. 'So, what have I missed, Jay-girl?' he said and put his hand on my arm. And I laughed and cried all at the same time because I didn't know where to start.

———

Dad had been waiting for a fine weekend to take Josh's dad gliding, and after a lot of nagging he let me go along to watch. There was an airstrip between us and the next town, where they had both learned to fly before Dad met Mum. Whenever we drove past, Dad checked the yellow windsock and told one story or another about the place. He said he had taken Mum up once, but she wasn't that keen on flying.

They were quiet in the car, no stories, and Josh's dad dozed off in the winter sun.

The hangar was nothing like the movies; it was just a shed with an office in one corner and an old couch out the front. There were two pilots, Brian and Graham, one to fly the glider and one to fly the plane. It was too long since Dad had learned to fly on his own, and there was only one passenger seat, so they had to go up one at a time. Josh's dad went in the glider first, but Dad kidded Brian to take him in the plane as a passenger. I watched the plane tow the glider down the runway and off the ground, climbing until it was nothing but a glint in the blue sky.

It wasn't long until the plane buzzed back and touched down, the glider left out there on its own. Dad did a training session while we waited – in a special cockpit they had rigged up that seemed real when you were inside it. You could even crash – but I didn't want to think about that. Dad was set on flying himself. He wasn't like that about many things, but when he was, he was over the top. They were humouring him, maybe because he was trying to do something for Josh's dad. He wanted to go up together, just them, like when they were young.

I searched the sky for the glider but couldn't see anything. Only a hawk on the fence line, patrolling for mice. Mum had suggested I bring a book, but I hadn't listened. There was a lot of waiting around with flying. I stretched out on the couch, the local radio station blaring from a speaker right above me. They were counting down the top forty. The same soppy song had been number one for ten weeks and if it didn't get voted off soon I was done with radio.

When the glider landed, like a great white bird, they had to help Josh's dad out of the cockpit, partly because he was laughing so hard. 'It was so good to be up there again.'

———

Dad was laughing after his go, too. He had taken the controls, from the back seat – but they still wouldn't let him fly on his own. Josh's dad said he was too tired to go again, anyway, and gave me his turn instead.

I was that excited I could hardly sit still long enough for them to strap me in. The moment we left the ground, when we were first flying, took my breath away, but the best part was when the plane let us go. The glider itself was silent; it had no engine. We rode the thermals like an eagle, watching the ground below. Graham wasn't a talker. We were each in our own bubble in the sky, away in our own thoughts. We flew over our farms, all fenced into squares.

I picked out the grove by the pattern of the treetops and the curve of the river. We followed its course for a while, then the road into town, past the ovals, then the school and the showground. The houses were small and all the same from above.

Then we dipped a wing and circled upwards, inside a funnel of warm air rising from near the showground. The horizon was angled, and my stomach tippy, until we levelled and set our course back to the hangar.

It was so peaceful up there, with the clouds, that I didn't ever want to come down. It was as if all of the things that had happened were smaller, paused somehow, while I was in the air. As if the glider were a time machine that might set me down at a moment and place of my choosing. With the whole world to choose from.

Paddocks, fences and scrubby hills floated by, and more, all the same, curving out either side to the horizon. The glider's shadow flickered over the ground. The sick feeling came back, and with it the understanding that this was what being grown-up would be like, looking back on things from far away. We were flying because Josh's dad was dying, and one day my own parents would die, too. I wouldn't always have Kieran and Josh and Ian – it would all change. It had already started.

We landed with a bump, and pulled up in front of the hangar. Dad was there to help me out. I grabbed on to his arm and hid my face in his jumper.

'Were you scared, kiddo?'

I shook my head. But I was glad to have both feet back on the ground.

Kieran lobbed a scrunched-up ball of paper onto my desk while Mr White's back was turned. It landed millimetres from the Bunsen burner. I was tempted to leave it to catch fire and upset Mr White's deadpan explanation of evaporation – which anyone with a dam already knew all about – but when the edge of the paper began to singe brown, I chickened out and flicked it into the sink.

There was a knock on the door and the principal stuck his head in. For a moment I celebrated a close call, but when he gestured Mr White over and whispered, I felt sick instead. The whole room had stopped.

'Josh, could Mr Krieger speak with you outside, please?'

Josh walked to the front of the classroom, back straight, all our eyes on him. The door closed.

Mr White said something but we weren't listening. Mr Krieger's voice was low and gentle, which was shock enough, and then we heard Josh's voice break in an awful kind of sob.

Kieran hid his face in his hands. Ian packed up Josh's things and put them in his bag. The zipper closing was too loud, took too long. Mr White carried the bag to the door, handed it out. Mr Krieger walked Josh past the open windows up the steps to the office.

All I could hear was the hiss of Bunsen burners and boiling water in beakers. I hated science.

'All right,' Mr White said. 'Let's pack up for today.'

———

Mum was waiting for me at the school gate when I went for the bus. She had that worried look, as if she wasn't sure she could pick me out of the crowd of other kids, but I saw her first.

She took my bag, like that lightened the load, and we walked to the ute. 'Your dad has the car,' she said.

I climbed into the passenger seat, which was cleaner than usual. Our mail was sitting on the dash, as if everything was normal. I strapped myself in, feeling Mum's eyes on me. 'I already know,' I said. 'They came and told him in class.'

'Really?'

'Mr Krieger took him outside. But everyone knew. He cried.'

Mum made a noise in her throat. She started the ute and pulled out with a bunny hop. She still wasn't that good in a manual.

I looked out the window, at the gardens passing and the houses behind them. Every single one had people inside and things that went wrong. 'What will happen now?'

'There'll be a funeral. Friday, I think. And we'll all help out as much as we can. Your dad and Kieran's will get the crops in. You can help me do some cooking. Fran's sister is coming down from Wollongong.'

None of that seemed enough, somehow.

———

Dad's whole class was at the funeral. Josh's father had been the first of them to go. The biggest and strongest of them, too. He had played rugby for country versus city and been offered a contract with a big Sydney team. He took over the farm instead. He had been one of those invincibles, a superman, and not only to Josh and my dad. He worked the hardest, didn't take a day off, not even Sunday. And he was first to help anyone out, if they needed to get their crop in before the rain, or an extra driver to cart grain.

The priest didn't talk about him working Sundays, but said that he was the one always coming up with new ideas, and building new machines that they could share. Like the auger that shifted grain from truck to silo faster.

I had never seen a man cry, until then. I didn't think they did. Especially not *my* dad. But there he was with tears streaming down his stubbled cheeks, and Josh and his mother and Megan in a complete mess, and Kieran parked at the back of the church because the chair would be in the way in the aisle. It was the worst day of my life. Of all our lives.

HER ARM ACHED, but it was a euphoric ride home, as if she were flying just above the ground. She left her helmet off, stuffed into a pannier, to feel everything better: the wind in her ears, the cold nipping at her face. The detail of every changing leaf. The cars, buses, people, were nothing. There was only her breathing. She slowed for the intersection and assumed starting position, balanced on the line, anticipating the green light. Armstrong had won the second mountain stage and looked to be gaining momentum. McEwen was holding on. It was a three-week endurance test and still anyone's to take.

There was a power in choosing your own path. Taking action. She didn't know where any of it was going to end – but for the moment, she was free.

Suzie always used to say that it was the journey that was important, rather than the destination. She had said that a lot, although they didn't go the journey themselves in the end. The years she had on Jayne meant that when it all died down, they were at different points in their lives. Maybe that's all it ever was when people parted ways.

She had hoped to have heard from Sarah by now, but perhaps she was having trouble accessing her email – it wasn't necessarily about their fight. About the tree.

Jayne had been caught off guard when they met. Sarah had twigged to the set-up straight away, arriving last. Her blush, more around her neck than her cheeks, had been endearing. They had stayed on after Gemma left, ordering wine and then pasta and more wine, talking politics and the changing nature of the northern suburbs and art and travel and life. It had been easy at the start.

That was before the promotion and the new job and high-level security clearance. Jayne liked to imagine that the Sarah she first met, the Sarah of that first year, would have supported her actions, cheered her on. It was sad to think that a job could change you, and your relationship.

IT WAS LATE when I finished my history assignment. I changed into my pyjamas and went out to say goodnight, but stopped in the kitchen. Mum and Dad were having the closest thing I had ever heard to an argument. Land rights again.

'This is serious, love. The kids have seen them. We have to think about our livelihood. Our future. Colin Tythe has already ploughed in the old ovens along their creek.'

'Ovens?'

'For cooking crays and fish, I suppose,' Dad said.

'Deliberately? That's terrible! We can trust Jay. We should be teaching her about these things, not covering them up.'

'It's not Jay I'm worried about.'

I backed into the stove, knocking over a block of wood. He meant Ian.

There was a pause in the lounge room.

'Don't you even think about it, David.'

I pulled my tent and sleeping-bag from the cupboard in the garage and started gathering together a list of gear. I was sneaking sausages from the freezer when Mum found me.

'What are you doing, kiddo?' She stepped over my knapsack and a smaller bag packed with potatoes, flour, sugar and oats.

'Camping – down at the river.'

'On your own?'

I shrugged.

She frowned. 'Just for one night?'

'Maybe two,' I said.

'Did you ask your father?'

'No.'

'You won't be scared?'

'No.' I checked off items on my list.

Mum looked over my shoulder. 'What about tomato sauce?'

'Oh, yeah.'

She put some in a smaller container, from the picnic basket.

'You'll ride the bike down?'

'Yep.'

'I guess we're only ten minutes away.'

I hugged her around the waist.

I packed everything in my knapsack, tightened it. Mum was fussing around in the kitchen, putting Mint Slice biscuits into a Tupperware container and apples in a string bag.

'Are you sure you don't want one of us to come with you?'

'I'll be fine, Mum.' What I really wanted was to think about things without anyone watching over me, or having to worry about what not to say in front of Kieran or Josh or Dad or Matty or anyone.

'What about water?'

'I have my drink bottle,' I said.

'Will that be enough?'

'I'll be right by the river, Mum.'

'You can't drink the river water!'

'We do all the time and no one's died,' I said.

We stopped then, in the middle of the kitchen, because someone had died. Josh's dad. And Kieran had come close. Sometimes he said he might as well be dead, and we could only hope he didn't mean it and try harder.

Mum put her hand on my shoulder.

'I'll boil it,' I said. I pulled the straps tight and tied my billy to the outside of my pack.

'Are you sure you don't need me to drive you?'

'Mum!' The whole point was to load up the bike and head out on my own. Like the boy in *My Side of the Mountain* who ran away and lived in a tree.

'Just trying to help.'

Feeling bad, more like it.

The hardest decision had been choosing what book to pack. I could only take one. In the end I had taken Dad's copy of *Robinson Crusoe*. It was leather bound, and unsuitable for camping trips, but I didn't care. Though I did put it in a plastic bag before I hid it in the bottom of my bag.

I applied sunscreen there and then, to save Mum nagging, and slipped the tube in the outside pocket of my bag. 'Right,' I said. 'I'm off.'

'That's just what your father would say.'

I pulled a face but let her hug me. 'See you Sunday night for dinner.'

'Okay, love,' she said. 'But if you want to come home earlier . . .'

I rolled my eyes. 'See ya.'

I slipped my arms into the pack, grabbed my gear from the bench and staggered to the laundry. Mum held the back door open and followed me out to help attach the tent and bed-roll to the bike's rack, behind the seat, with ockie straps.

I kickstarted the bike and took off with more care than usual. All of the extra weight was difficult to balance. Mum stood on the verandah, arms folded, as I wobbled away.

———

I stood at the edge of the grove, looking in. Rain had washed away our miniature land. There was no point rebuilding. It belonged to a time that had passed. Like stupid games and climbing trees and playing where we shouldn't. But I sat for a while, on the log beneath the pine, like Ian, watching and listening.

The river was flowing well again and I watched it, too, trying to imagine it crowded with fish and creatures washed down from upstream. I gathered up stones to skim, but ended up making a circle on the beach instead. Inside, I set out the only constellations I knew by heart – the Southern Cross, the Big Dipper and Taurus, my star sign – with gumnuts for stars.

They knew about the trees. And they knew we knew. The only possible explanation for Dad's comment was that he was worried Ian would tell his parents. His mum. The only thing left between us and disaster was that Mum didn't agree with Dad.

I took an apple and my book back up to the log near the grove and tried to read. The words kept blurring, so I watched the treetops against the sky, the birds busy in their branches, and all of the flowers and insects that you only noticed when you were still, the sounds and smells that made a place and were the whole world. Eventually, I felt still again, too.

I was scared, that first night, although I wouldn't have admitted it to Mum. Or the boys. When I looked towards the grove, but not directly, I thought I saw shadows sneaking out of those trees, heading for my fire.

After I went to bed, there were footsteps, and I couldn't help thinking about the shadows, even though I knew it was probably only a possum. My heart pounded and I thought about going home and what a stupid idea camping had been. Everything sounded louder at night, especially from inside the tent. I turned my radio up and fell asleep.

In the morning the battery was flat.

After that night, the grove had my back, keeping watch. Sometimes the river made gurgling sounds or something splashed: fish, river rat, platypus or cray, I couldn't tell; it was all a mystery under there.

There was a quietness in the grove, as if the trees were listening, motionless despite the breeze. The next night, I edged closer in the moonlight, but the shadows made me uneasy, and the carvings were so much darker, like scars.

They were scars.

THE MEDIA HAD gone from the front of the building but the stories were still running. A former gallery director – now in the hunt for a parliamentary seat – had waded in, calling for an overhaul of collection practices.

Jayne had taken the lift up from the basement to avoid facing Frank, who was looking older and thinner every day. She wasn't the only one sweating on the outcome of the investigation.

She was almost through the last box. She reached for the next item, removed it from its plastic sleeve and laid it out on her desk. Another grevillea. Watercolour. The usual Gatton signature. The same gentle handwriting listing its local name. She chewed on the end of her pencil. What had Sarah said about this woman wanting to be found? Today, Jayne could almost feel the artist's presence, her frustration.

At uni, a guest lecturer from the Louvre had told them that a forger always left a tell. Although the aim was to copy the piece exactly and pass undetected, the artist couldn't resist expressing themselves with a tiny flourish, a hidden sign, as if challenging the world to find him out. Or her. As if being caught was better than anonymity.

Jayne leaned back in her chair, staring at the flowers. Some of these early artists *had* been forgers, but these pieces were not forgeries – they were original artworks, although they were not considered so at the time. The artists had been kept anonymous because of their rank and status. She leaned over the grevillea, examining the image again, through her magnifying glass. There, tucked into the flower's scrolls, was a set of initials: E.C. She leapt up and pumped her fists in the air. 'Gotcha!' Her stool clattered into the pillar behind her.

She took the printout of all her cross-referenced catalogue numbers with her to the compactus. Her shoes squeaked on the concrete as she pushed open one section, then another, skidding between the shelves and pulling out each item.

She spread all of the pictures out on the bench in rough chronological order: half guesswork, half science. With the help of the magnifying glass – the simplest of all her tools – she found the initials even on the hospital piece, tiny, faint, but there, in the rear leaf of the matt rush. How she had missed them on the leaf of the banksia, she didn't know. Once you knew what to look for they were obvious.

The initials gave her a surer grouping and chronology, and a picture of an artist gaining confidence over time. This was someone who didn't want her work accredited to someone else, a lesser artist. Someone who didn't want to be invisible. Or forgotten.

She unlocked the stores cabinet and signed out the camera. With its high-powered lens, she captured the initials on each image. She uploaded them to the computer but hesitated before adding them to the system, storing them on her personal drive instead.

E.C. fitted one of her suspects. Emily Calwell had been sentenced for theft, arriving in New South Wales in 1791, and assigned to Norris as a housemaid. What she had stolen wasn't clear, but women tended not to be the hardened criminals that the male convicts were. At that time, all women offenders had been sent out – to help balance the sexes in the colony.

Calwell had disappeared from view once Norris died, possibly into marriage. Into the desert for all Jayne knew. Once convicts were free, they wanted to blend in, forget their past. And who could blame them. Perhaps she had ended up in that women's hospital. There was no proof of that – but for now, at least Jayne had a name for one of the Gatton school painters.

———

Duty officer for the weekend just meant being on call, carrying a pager wherever she went – and extra money in her next pay. It wasn't like Sarah's job, where the chances of having to check in at least, were high. In five years, Jayne had been called in once – and the one night she *should* have been called, she wasn't.

Something had happened to another one of the arborglyphs. When helping Dan search the Australian museum database – outdated before it was launched – she had run a search of her own while he fixed yet another printer jam. She didn't feel good about it, but she couldn't risk using her own login details. There was something bigger going on. All of the missing trees were from Wiradjuri country.

The duty officer could also take home a work car. She didn't normally bother, but she needed to pick up paint and other supplies from the hardware store, out at Tuggeranong. It was impossible on her bike, and took too long on the bus. She could have organised to borrow Sarah's car while she was away, but she hadn't.

She filled in the book at the registry office and took the keys for the van. It had plenty of room for her bike in the back, and she could use loading zones, which came in handy.

It was a trick she had learned from the plumber she had dated for a while. That relationship was never going to last, but Erica had been fun, and looked cute in her overalls. She always took her work van when they went out, because she could park it anywhere. Jayne would ride up front, dance music blaring, and they would pull up in the loading zone intended for delivery vans right behind the club. Erica would slide open the door to the back, and her friends, in leather, satin and denim, would tumble out, laughing, from around her tools, pumps and pipes, like Canberra's own Village People.

JOSH DIDN'T COME back to school the rest of that term. It was only me on the bus. I sat in the same seat, the blue vinyl hot on the back of my legs with summer coming. Unless I was studying for a test, I read from the moment I sat down until we pulled up in front of school, and I tried to keep the story with me right through the day, until I was back on the bus and could open the book again. The year twelves teased me but I pretended not to hear. I carried my own world with me.

It was harder in class, when the teacher might ask a question at any moment. Miss Hanaman had already separated me from Ian and Kieran. She was new and didn't seem to know about cutting us a break. I had to sit right up front, next to her desk. When she asked if I thought there was any hope at the end of *Z for Zachariah*, I couldn't answer. She seemed sure it was because I hadn't read it, or because I was daydreaming, which I wasn't. It was clear there wasn't much hope, I just didn't know how to say that, or if I should. She was very black and white for an English teacher. Either she didn't really like reading or she had read all the wrong books.

I missed Josh in woodwork. He had made me laugh and helped me set up the machines, and showed me how to hold some of the tools. We were turning the legs for a stool on the lathe, in our groups. Without Josh, our stool was going to be missing some pieces. I didn't mind – it was about right for the year we'd had.

I finished year eight with more Bs than As or Cs, which fit well, too. Miss Hanaman gave me a C for English. I could only hope I didn't have her again. Ever. I didn't see Kieran and Josh's reports, but they can't have been good. They had missed so much school. Ian didn't say anything about his marks, and I didn't ask.

The biggest news was that Matty, in year six now, had been elected school captain. We couldn't believe it at first. He wasn't as good as Kieran at anything, but he was a lot more sensible – I just hadn't realised it till now. That was one problem I didn't have, being in someone else's shadow.

———

After harvest, we drove up to Coffs Harbour and stayed at a caravan park right on the beach for two weeks. It was Mum's idea. We hadn't been since I was small. You could hear the sea all night and soon everything was damp and salty. Dad went fishing early each morning, off the rocks. Some days he caught a fish, and we barbecued it for lunch or dinner. Most days he didn't catch anything, but Mum said to leave him in peace. I guess when he was standing there looking out to sea he was thinking about Josh's dad.

One evening he fished off the beach instead and asked me to go with him. We caught four yellowfin bream and Dad grinned for the first time in months. I had a go at scaling a fish, and gutting it, on the special wooden table between the beach and the caravan park. Dried fish scales crunched under my thongs, and I rinsed the inside of the fish under the tap.

Dad bought us boogie boards and we were in the surf every morning. Through the middle of the day we slept or read or played a game. I would go back to the beach in the late afternoon to ride the waves with some of the teenagers from the caravan park. I wished Ian and Josh and Kieran were there with me instead, but one of the boys loaned me a flipper so that I could go out deeper and catch bigger waves.

The day it rained we drove up into the mountains and looked at shops and had burgers and milkshakes by a river much bigger than ours. Mum said that sometimes it flooded and cut off part of the town.

I thought about the trees then, and our river, and what had happened to Josh and Kieran. Home seemed a long way away.

I nearly told Mum all about the burial trees that night. The first sentence was out of my mouth before I thought it through. Mum didn't hear me properly because of a mower outside. When she asked me to repeat myself, I muttered something about a lookout I had walked to. I wasn't sure if what Ian's mum had told me would help or make things worse. Perhaps there would be a better time once we were home.

SHE WAS ALREADY tired, and coverage of the Tour was starting, but she had to get another coat of paint on if she was going to finish everything before Sarah got back. Armstrong had won three stages in a row. If he won another, she might have to drink paint.

When she and her mother had been painting the windows at the front of the house one year – white as usual – they had left the lid off the tin while they went inside to have lunch. When they came back, the poddy calf they had been keeping in the yard had drunk from the tin, thinking it was milk. It was too late when they found her. They always kept the lid on after that, even when there were no calves.

She changed into army pants and a singlet, put on an old Eagles CD and poured paint in the tray. She attached a new woolly pad to the roller and screwed in the extender.

A fine spray of paint splattered the back of her hands and forearms with each upward movement of the roller. She adjusted the drop sheet and reattached it to the skirting board.

The tattoo was starting to settle and feel a part of her. Her skin. It moved when she did, when she flexed or gripped. Not that anyone would see it until summer.

Cas had shown her some real tribal work, hammered into her legs with bone by a Maori man. A repeating pattern. When Jayne had asked if it hurt, Cas had laughed. 'I won't ever forget it, that's for sure. Had to stay overnight.'

But you did forget, everyone said that. Even when the pain was what you needed to remember.

There was something about the smell of fresh paint, a flawless wall. Something hopeful. With the paperwork signed off, she should be feeling free. But the investigation was still hanging over her head. Like an axe. It was to be another weekend of waiting.

The rumour was that Max's report had already gone up to Noni. Jayne had caught another glimpse of Frank at the security desk when she left work, looking grim. She hadn't banked on him just turning off the alarm, not following protocol. If he lost his job, it was his own doing.

She stood back, checking for any spots she had missed. It was going to come up well, the colour deepening with each coat.

The email she'd had from Sarah was encouraging. It was hard, though, to forget the look on her face when Jayne had told her about the tree. Her words. At least she was missing the shit storm in the media. The parts of history people didn't like talking about were in the public arena, and collection practices on the political agenda. A Wiradjuri spokeswoman had compared the theft, destruction and incarceration of their arborglyphs to Hitler's theft of Jewish artworks during World War II. It was an old story: destroy a people's culture, destroy the people. And it made good headlines.

When interviewed on the *7.30 Report*, Noni had tried to focus on
the pressures brought about by the constant decline in government
funding for the arts, but crumbled under attack. Kerry O'Brien had
likened acquiring Indigenous artefacts to receiving stolen goods.
He was right, but she felt bad for Noni. The museum was far from
alone in that, and it wasn't as if it had been her decision. At least
they hadn't found out about the human remains.

Jayne washed out the tray and roller in the laundry tub and
scrubbed her hands, but couldn't quite get them free of paint.

IN YEAR NINE we finally got to choose our own subjects. I did art, history and Asian studies. I had wanted to do Japanese but Mr Nixon had left over the summer and it was French or nothing. I did try it for a few weeks, but the teacher was a pain and the grammar too hard. Josh and Kieran did agriculture, industrial arts and commerce. Ian did commerce and industrial arts, too, but with music. None of us did home economics, which was probably a relief for Mrs Finsler.

Geography was the one elective we took together. Josh wasn't quite as keen but we talked him round. The teacher, Mr Vaas, was straight out of college. They sent the new ones to towns like ours. Mostly they went back to the city after a few years but sometimes they stayed, like Mrs Keys, and married farmers or another teacher. Mr Vaas was from Sri Lanka and was crazy about cricket. He started every Monday's class by throwing us a cricket ball. We had to speak for one minute and then throw the ball to someone else. We could talk about anything or anyone as long as we didn't stop.

I don't know what it was about Mr Vaas – the talking ball, his cricket stories or learning about the world – but he knew how to get the best out of Kieran. Mr Vaas treated him just like the rest of us. He would ask him to write on the board or hand out books or go and pick things up from the library. Kieran was happy to speed around in his chair – he had gotten so good at manoeuvring it that he was quicker than he would have been without it.

When Kieran came to class late one morning, which he had been getting away with since the accident, Mr Vaas yelled and made him stay back the exact same number of minutes at recess every day for a week. After that, Kieran never mucked up in geography and was on time for every class. He got the highest mark for our first assignment, on the rivers of the world, and Mr Vaas gave him a special cricket ball, signed by Dennis Lillee. One of Kieran's Monday talks had been about how hard Lillee had trained after his back injury to play for Australia again. Kieran nearly cried, holding that ball. I was sitting next to him.

———

The bus dropped me off early, on the way home from a sporting exchange with the neighbouring town. We had been thrashed overall, as usual – they were a much bigger school – but the junior girls won hockey and I scored a goal in our second game. They put me on the wing because I was fast, but I didn't really like it out there. When someone made a big pass, it was hard stopping it, let alone clearing it or driving forwards. Ian had the same problem playing footy. 'Too much pressure,' he said. Inner was better, you could just attack, but those girls had better stick skills and were heavier. It was only because Alison rolled an ankle that I got a half up front at all.

It was strange going away for sport without Kieran but we were getting used to it. We didn't win as many things and it wasn't as much fun on the way home. It was quieter, though, and there was less trouble.

Ian gave me the last of his lollies and I ran down the bus steps while the driver pulled my bag out from underneath. Mum must have seen the bus because she walked out to meet me. Our driveway wasn't long, and the breeze rustled the poplars either side.

I didn't pay much attention to the other sound at first. It wasn't unusual for Dad to cut wood and it was a relief to hear that he was out of the shed. Life was almost back to normal since the holidays. Mum did a good job of asking about all my events, exclaiming about the goal, and getting me into the kitchen. I was part of the four-hundred-metre relay team that won, too, which meant I might go to the state titles.

When I smelled smoke, I just knew. The breeze had been coming up from the river when I got off the bus – that's why the sound carried so well. The rain had made things safer for fires, but only just. It wasn't the right season.

I ran outside, still in my pleated blue sports skirt and long socks. 'Jayne, wait!'

Mum was out the door after me but I had already started my motorbike and roared off down the drive.

I wished I could jump all the gates, like Dale Buggins, but I had to stop and open each one. When I pulled up in front of the last, I could see exactly where the smoke was coming from. The breeze had dropped but it was still furling my way. I tore along the sandy track and up the rise.

I was too late.

They had cut down every single one of the trees and dragged them into a pile three times the size of our stupid Queen's Birthday bonfire. Dad, Kieran's father and Bill, who sometimes did odd jobs for Josh's family, were standing back watching, hands in pockets. The trunks were well alight. I could only see the markings on the largest one, disappearing fast.

I rode at the men flat out, skidding to a stop at the back of their boots and revving the bike's engine.

Dad turned. 'Jay? Shit.'

'I *hate* you,' I said. 'I hate all of you!'

The other men looked away, back to the fire. Dad's face twitched – perhaps it was the heat and smoke. Ash floated on the air. He held up both palms. 'Jay, please.'

I shook my head and pushed off with my socked foot, giving the bike too much throttle for the loose ground. The back wheel slid out and I overcorrected, fishtailing, nearly losing it, but somehow I kept myself steady.

I flew back through the open gates and onto the main road. I tore all the way into town, without shoes, without a helmet, to Ian's house – and no one stopped me.

'YOU GOT A TATTOO?'

'I did.' She had taken off her shirt to help bring in the furniture and forgotten to put it back on. It was meant to be a surprise – for later. If they got that far.

'It looks nice.' Sarah's skirt was crushed, her eyes puffy.

'Nice?'

Sarah shrugged. 'It does. I like the design.'

'It will look better when it's not all scabby.'

'That makes it sound less nice.'

'Good.'

'Ah, you were aiming for tough?'

Jayne laughed and leaned on the kitchen bench. Her guts were swirling. 'How was your trip?'

'Everything was through translators, which was kind of exhausting. Harder to read all the subtext.' Sarah touched Jayne's shoulder with her little finger. 'Is it still sore?'

'Not really.' She'd had her first normal shower not ten minutes ago. Without the plastic patch. She had shaved her legs, scrubbed off all the paint and glue and washed her hair, hoping for the best. Looking her best, at least.

'I missed you.'

'Missed you, too.'

'Why are you grinning like that?'

'Just glad to see you.'

Sarah turned around. 'Oh, my god. Is that wallpaper? Do they even make it still?'

'I guess they do.'

'It reminds me of that painting you like.'

She meant the Mondrian. 'I tried to get something Australian, but—'

'I love it. The green on the other walls, too. You did all this?'

'I did.' Her aching arms proved it.

'It will be like dining in a forest.'

'Thanks.' Afternoon sun lifted the room even better than she had hoped.

Sarah ran her hands over the fabric of the dining chairs, a simple botanical print, in honour of her found artist. 'I love this material.'

'I saw it in a magazine. That store in Kingston ordered it in.'

'You know, when I met you,' Sarah said, 'I had no idea you spent so much time looking at home magazines.'

Jayne smiled.

'And the table?'

'I ordered it ages ago. A two-man operation in Fyshwick. Art school graduates. I did a drawing and they turned that into a proper design. And they had an upholsterer finish the chairs.' She was talking too much, trying too hard.

Sarah fingered the table's glossy surface. 'Is it maple? Like your cupboards.'

'And the contrast on the dovetails is blackwood.'

'It's gorgeous, Jay.'

Still she hung back. No hug. No kiss. 'Are you hungry?'

'If we can eat at this table. The whole room is perfect. Even the table runner.'

'I made that from the leftover fabric.' She'd had to sew it by hand, while watching bloody Armstrong win the last time trial.

Sarah shook her head. 'You are the one thing in my life that still surprises me, woman,' she said. 'But it must be my turn. I brought back some gin, of course, and Dutch liquorice. And a present.' Sarah held out a parcel, wrapped in pink and orange.

Jayne slipped off the string, unfolded the paper.

'It's a burial mask.'

'It's beautiful.' She touched the cheek, a hint of red on fine-grained timber, and turned it over.

'It's just a replica. But hand carved. I saw him do it,' Sarah said. 'I only had an hour between meetings, but found a little market near the hotel.'

'Thank you.'

'You like it?'

'I love it.' Jayne sat the mask on the table runner, the gin on the sideboard, and turned over two of the good tumblers.

'I see your tree has been in the papers.'

'In Indonesia?' She poured three fingers of gin in each glass.

'It was in one of our intel reports. The British prime minister has made some comments about the Aboriginal artefacts in their institutions.'

She meant human remains. 'That's an old conversation.' Jayne walked away, to the kitchen, and took the ice from the freezer, a cucumber from the crisper. She glanced, again, at the photo on the fridge. The only evidence that the grove, those five carved trees, had ever existed.

Sarah followed her. 'It's a new conversation now. The UK is going to pass fresh legislation around human remains. All those items will have to come home. I think it will impact on your trees.'

Jayne twisted out ice cubes on the side of the sink with a clatter. 'We'll see.'

'Can you stop?' Sarah leaned over the bench and placed her hand on Jayne's arm. 'I don't agree with your methods, but I understand your reasons,' she said. 'I'm trying to say I'm on your side. I just wish you could have talked to me about it.'

Jayne looked up. Sarah's eyes were soft. Things were shifting. 'Thank you,' she said. 'And I'm sorry. I didn't want to involve you. Like you said, your job . . .'

Sarah smiled a sad smile. 'You're my partner. I'm already involved.'

THE NEXT TIME I went camping Mum fussed a whole lot less. She was probably glad to get me out of the house and I was glad to go. I took a whole lot less stuff, too. No books, no radio. Just Mum's camera tucked in the front pocket of my new pack.

I parked my bike and carried my gear the rest of the way, dumping it on the ground. The breeze worked the treetops, the river moved along. Everything went out of me and I could breathe.

I laid the tent out facing the river, its back to where the grove had been.

Mum and Dad were having friends from pottery over while I was away. Once I would have been sorry to miss out on their conversation, which was always full of gossip and big ideas. Angela and Gareth had lived in Sydney, running a bookstore and going to art school. They always had great stories. Mum and Dad loved them, too. The life they might have had, perhaps. They would have a better time without having to make sure their talk after dinner was child-friendly.

For weeks now, I had managed to avoid the dinner table, citing homework, and ate breakfast after my parents had started work for the day. The holidays were harder.

I had spent the first weekend at Ian's, mostly hanging out at the public pool. We would swim a few laps, jump from the diving board and then lie around up the back on the grass under the trees eating lollies or chips Ian had brought from the service station. Since our end of year party, it had become our class's spot. Others turned up throughout the day all weekend, still talking about all of the things that had happened. The pool owners had put in a ramp at the entrance for Kieran, and he had come even though he didn't swim.

He and Josh came back into town on the Sunday night and stayed at Ian's. It was a bit of a rigmarole with Kieran's chair but we were getting used to it and he didn't mind us helping him anymore. But one night at a time was all he could manage, and Josh had to get back to the harvest.

When I went home, Mum put her foot down. I not only had to eat with them but help her cook the slaughtered animal that was to be our dinner. I did as I was asked but nothing could make me speak. I didn't even look at Dad, despite his attempts at conversation. When he stood in the doorway of my room after dinner, to ask if I would like to watch a movie with them, I rolled over and put my headphones on.

Now I set up my tent in record time. I'd been practising in the backyard, timing myself. Not that there was any real hurry – it was hours off dark. I rigged the fly the way Dad had shown me, with the spacers he had made to keep it clear of the roof of the tent. The pegs pushed in easy after the rain we'd had; I only had to finish off one of the corners with the mallet, where it was rocky.

I laid out my bed-roll and sleeping-bag, dark green on the outside, blue flannelette check inside. It smelled of camp fire, eucalyptus and freedom, no matter how much you aired it on the clothes line.

The lorikeets were raucous in the gums along the river, feeding on blossom. I gathered an armload of kindling and piled it high in my fireplace. The cattle had kicked a few stones out of place and I pushed them back. Finding wood was getting harder. I had to walk further, and smash up smaller branches with my boots.

I wouldn't be seeing the others the rest of the summer break. Kieran was going to Sydney. He said it was for a holiday, but Mum said it was for another operation. I had given up asking about him walking, and didn't get the feeling that was on the cards – but I still thought about it. We all did. Josh was visiting his sick grandmother in Canberra, and Ian was off to Melbourne, staying with cousins. We had joked that it was deliberate, splitting us up, part of some grand plan. We knew it wasn't true, but it was easier to blame our parents than talk about how much things had changed.

I carried three loads of wood and built up a store by the fireplace. Enough to last the night and breakfast. In the dying light, ants piled out of one log, all rotten inside. I pulled the matches from the top pocket of my shirt and lit the leaves at the base of the pile. It crackled and caught, the flames warm on my face. I sat back on my heels while it took hold. I fed in larger sticks, then a small branch, and left it to settle.

From the corner of my eye I saw a possum make a run for it, behind the tent. 'I see you,' I said. She lived in the old hollow yellow box near where I parked the bike. I fished out my potatoes, already wrapped in foil, and a serve of sausages, from my food bag. No greens. Broccoli, beans, peas – none of them were much good for camping.

I stacked everything on my enamel camping plate, felt around in the bag for my splade, rezipped the tent, and headed fireside.

I tried not to look where the grove had been, where there was now only the mound. There was still something there, despite the emptiness. Someone.

Ian's ancestor had probably made his journey to the Dreamtime long ago, but still. What if some portal had been closed and he was wandering, lost? The trees had protected his earthly remains, too. What would happen to them now?

While I waited for the flames to die down, the sky turned pink, then a deep red. I nestled the potatoes into the coals, only their silver tops showing. The first star winked down from above and I made a wish. The same wish I always made.

———

I blew air into my lilo, pushing out all the crinkles and folds. It was much harder blowing it up from scratch. We used to leave them in the ute or the garage, and they only lost a little air between times, but camping meant packing light, being compact – and doing some things the hard way.

An egret fished upstream, between the reeds. A breeze wrinkled the river. When the lilo was tight, I pushed it out into the water and climbed on. I was more careful paddling than usual: arms in, arms out, with a precision our house swimming coach would have been proud of. The quieter I was, the more likely the platypus would come.

I let the current take me away from the camp site. Away from where the trees had been. It was another tree I was after. The leaves rustled and the river whispered and whistled. When on the water alone, it was a conversation I was still part of.

The old apple tree was heavy with fruit. If Kieran had been here we'd have been throwing high fives and carrying on. There were years it had borne none, and many with miserable, gnarly lumps. Nothing like this.

I beached on soft sand and scrambled up the bank with my string bag. The tree had low, horizontal branches, as if it had once been tended. I plucked the largest fruit, placing them in the bottom of my bag. There were other harvesters at work: rosellas, moths, and – in the rotting fallen fruit below – ants and flies. The best thing about camping was noticing the hum of everything, the way it worked together.

When my bag was full, I ducked out from under the branches. There was enough fruit left for the owners, if they came. And plenty for the birds if they did not. I slid down the bank, the bag against my belly. I made my escape by water, like a poacher fleeing the scene. A cockatoo sounded the alarm and I imagined gunshots flying over my head. I crossed the river pressed flat on the lilo.

———

I peeled an apple with my knife, cut out its core, and filled it with sultanas, sugar and oats. Once I had wrapped it in two layers of foil, I set it in red coals. The night was clear, revealing a roof of stars.

The Southern Cross hung upside down, its pointers bright. Ian said it was really a warrior spearing a giant emu, but I couldn't see it.

An owl called and another answered. I wasn't scared anymore, even though I was alone. If I needed to, I could live by the river, catching fish and eating blackberries and apples.

I poked the apple with a fork. It was soft already and I dragged it out with the tongs to cool. I set it on my plate and ate it with a spoon. Ice-cream would have been nice, to melt into the crumble part, but the apple was flavourful as it was, sweet and sharp all at once – like being outside. Better than whatever my parents were having at home.

I had been staying in my room so much that even Mum was cranky. I didn't care. Dad had destroyed those trees, the grove, all of those beautiful carvings, and she hadn't stopped him.

By the time Ian and I rang Kieran that day, he and Matty had already heard. They had been on the way home from school and said they hadn't known what was going to happen. Kieran said it was 'fucking unbelievable' and that he was never speaking to his father again. 'I wish I could drive in and get you,' he said. 'We could run away together.' But Kieran couldn't run anywhere, and we weren't going to be together. Too much had changed.

I hung up on Josh when he said that it was probably for the best. 'We can't lose our farms,' he said. He was thinking like a landowner now, not one of us. Later I felt bad that Kieran and I weren't speaking to our dads and Josh didn't even have one. He was just trying to fill the space his father had left. Be a man. When Josh rang back to apologise, I said sorry, too.

Ian's mum said that what my dad had done was terrible, and now bad things would happen. I thought enough bad things had happened already, but I'd thought that after Kieran fell, too, and things got worse. I don't know if Ian's mum spoke to mine but they let me stay over that night and Ian and I walked around town until there was no one left on the streets.

We didn't go to school in the morning. We were tired, and I didn't have my uniform, but that wasn't the problem. We should never have sworn a pact on those trees. We had meant to keep the outside world away. Instead, we had tracked it in. I had known how important they were, and how Dad was thinking, and still said nothing.

———

It was just light when I woke, the sky soft pink with cloud wisps. The kookaburras had called it up. I crawled out of the tent, stoked the fire and threw on the last small branches. I took my towel from the fly line and walked barefoot down to the river. I left my pyjamas and towel on a rock and ran into the breath-stealing water. Mum wouldn't have done it, or approved. 'What if someone turned up?' she'd say. But I thought Dad might understand how it was too cold but also felt good – like you were more alive afterwards. He said he sometimes cooled off in the river in summer and I couldn't imagine he left his work clothes on.

My body felt better in the water. Lighter. My hips had started to get heavy, and it was no longer possible to ignore the bumps on my chest, the puffy nipples. In the cold, at least they shrank and puckered hard. I burst out of the water, ran to my towel, and shivered on the shore.

I dressed by the fire, some bits of me too hot and some too cold and some not sure if they were burning or freezing. When the water came to the boil, I dropped in the eggs and browned my toast.

The second cup of tea was too strong, but I nursed it by the fire while it went out, and watched the river. I'd seen the platypus again, on the first morning. But only from a distance. She didn't like to show herself anymore, even to me. As if she could sense I was getting older. She didn't trust adults – and I didn't blame her.

I tried taking a picture of the mist over the water but it was hard to fit everything in. I focused on lichens instead: the flat spreading one, pale green on rocks, and the hairy kind sprouting from bark.

I used the last of the film to photograph the black holes where the trees had once been, and the bare mound, left exposed to the world. Mum would have the film developed in town, and always looked through the results before I got home. It was why I had never taken a picture of the grove – to protect it. Now it was gone. There was only part of one stump left – and Mum was welcome to see what sort of picture that made.

I poured a billy full of water over the coals, kicked sand on top, and made sure it was out. A shadow passed over, a hawk hovering to see what I flushed out. I let down the lilo, squashed out all of the air as I rolled it, and packed it in with the rest of my gear – much more neatly than I needed to for the short trip home. The sun was high already, and I had promised Mum I'd be back for Sunday lunch. Aunt Margot was coming out, which didn't happen so often anymore. I loaded up my bike, checked the site over for any rubbish, anything forgotten.

Sometimes the longer I stayed, the harder it was to leave.

JAYNE CARRIED THE rug and pillows out to the apple trees and spread them in their shade. It was a wilderness – long grass, weeds through the beds, the brick path overgrown with lavender, and the passionfruit vine taking over the side fence – but it was outside, and the sun was shining.

The neighbours all had much nicer gardens. Even the common, which the house backed onto, was better kept. Children were playing football out there today, or she would have carried their picnic to the stand of blue gums instead.

Judging by the smell, the vegetables were almost done. Jayne prepared the rest of the salad. The last patch of cloud drifted off and the breeze stilled. Perfect. She turned off the oven, slipped on the mitt and removed the baking dish, placing it on the breadboard on the bench.

The tapping of keys from the dining room slowed, then stopped. Sarah padded into the kitchen in bare feet.

Jayne smiled. 'Hey.'

'Smells great. What's going on?'

'I thought if we can't get away on a picnic, I can bring the picnic to us.'

'Sweet.'

'How's the report?'

'Coming along.' Sarah glanced around. 'I didn't hear you sneak out to the bakery.'

'Took the bike.' Jayne pulled the champagne from the freezer, removed the foil, and released the cork with a gentle pop.

'What are we celebrating?'

'My package came through.'

'When did you find out?'

'While you were away.' She filled two of the fancy flutes she used for bubbles, a twenty-first gift from Kieran.

'I'm sorry I wasn't here,' Sarah said.

'It's okay.'

Sarah lifted her glass. 'Well, congratulations! Happy?'

Jayne tinked her glass against Sarah's. 'Relieved.'

'When do you finish up?'

'End of the month.'

'And the payout?'

'A few weeks after that, I guess.'

'Any plans?'

Jayne dipped a Turkish bread finger into the beetroot dip. 'Not really,' she said. 'Buy a new bike.'

'That's exciting. You have one in mind?'

'The most beautiful bike ever made is hanging in the window of that new store in Braddon at the moment.' It was a Bianchi EV3.

The same model Jan Ullrich had ridden to second place in last year's Tour. With aluminium frame and carbon forks, it weighed in at just seven and a half kilos. No wonder he had been floating on the pedals.

'What colour is it?'

'Celeste,' Jayne said. 'It's a kind of retro sky blue.' Ullrich's signature colour.

'You'll have to show me,' Sarah sipped her champagne. 'I've been thinking about your mystery woman. If you're right, and she stole materials to practise her art, it's such a great story. Maybe you could do a masters, get a scholarship. Gemma would help you, wouldn't she?'

'Maybe.' Gemma had already asked several times, though about the arborglyphs, not her convict artist.

'Just an idea.'

'It's a good idea,' Jayne said.

———

Sarah lay back on the pillows, leaf-patterned shade on her face. 'This is the life.'

'Dessert? Coffee?'

'Only because I know there are tarts,' she said. 'Can I help clear?'

'Relax,' Jayne said. 'I'm the unemployed one.'

'Not yet, you're not.'

When Jayne returned, Sarah was in the middle of what had once been a herb garden, pulling weeds. 'Pear or blood orange?'

'Pear.' Sarah wiped her hands on her jeans.

Jayne frowned at the mess of capeweed and thistles on the path. 'Gardening urge?' She set down the tarts, forks and coffees, and sat, cross-legged, opposite Sarah.

'It's easy after rain. They come out by the roots.'

'You had a big garden at home?'

'When I was a kid?'

'Yeah.' She sucked citrus jelly from her fork, sharp and sweet at the same time.

'The house we had in Launceston, before Mum and Dad split, had a wonderful garden: lawns and sculptures and hedges, a vegetable plot. It was where Mum preferred to be. I learned how to help out. It was the only time she really talked.'

'Perhaps you can teach me,' Jayne said. 'I've let this go too long.'

'Wouldn't take much to get it back.'

The phone was ringing inside. 'That'll be Mum,' Jayne said. 'I'd better get it.' She took her coffee and popped the last mouthful of custard and pastry in her mouth.

———

Sarah was on all fours, her back obscured by a great pile of weeds.

'I should be doing that, babe. You need to finish your report.' A breeze tickled the apples' leaves, as if the two trees were rubbing together.

'Fuck it,' Sarah said. 'I'll go in early tomorrow. This is far more satisfying.'

'You sure?'

'I just want to finish this bed, then I'll clean up.' She flicked a snail shell at Jayne's feet. 'We're going to reclaim your garden.'

'Mum says hi.'

'How is she?'

'Making lots of plans for our visit.'

'She knows the wedding will take up most of the weekend, right?'

'She's just excited. Angling for longer – guilt tripping. I've explained how busy you are.' As a hook, her mother had revealed that her old room had been repainted, made over as an adult room for the occasion, complete with a new queen-sized bed. It was much more appealing than her childhood single bunks.

BEFORE WE KNEW it, Matty was in year seven. When I saw him lined up at assembly with his class he was one of the tallest and kind of cute. Built, too, from swimming and the extra farm work. Kieran worried that Matty would be teased, but at the swimming carnival, Matty won all of his races, and the next day he was going out with the prettiest girl in his year, Maria Bardell. He didn't need Kieran – he was doing just fine.

Kieran didn't go out with anyone. I didn't go out with anyone either. It was a thing. The sort of thing everyone knows but doesn't mention and that you try not to think about. I told myself it wasn't about the chair – his legs – but probably it was. Part of it, anyway. I wanted everything to be the same but it wasn't. It meant that I wasn't a very nice person and that was hard to face.

––––

Liam Davis wrestled Mark Cunningham on the square of grass in the corner of the quadrangle. Showing off. Kieran and Ian were stuck in detention again, leaving Josh and me on our own – with Mark and Liam the only entertainment.

Josh wrapped a slice of white bread around his sausage roll and sauce. There was so much sauce it was more like sauce with sausage roll and bread. He not only managed to fit his mouth around it, but took almost half in one bite. 'Have you done that science assignment?'

Or that's what I guessed he said, cheeks fat like a chipmunk. I nodded. 'I just followed the example he gave us. Nothing fancy.'

'Right.'

'I'm serious. There's not much you can do with *aim*, *method*, *outcome*. It's a formula all right. For boredom.'

'No pictures?'

'Nope.'

'Headings?'

'Blue pen. Underlined.' I had given up on title pages and headings and lettering. I didn't have time with all of the assignments and essays and the exams coming up. And I couldn't be bothered anymore.

He laughed. 'No one is going to believe it,' he said. 'I don't mind doing the experiment. Following the steps. It's writing it up that sucks.'

I was the opposite. All that measuring and recording. Just to see water boil. Or smell stinking gases. It was a shame we couldn't team up. 'Apparently the experiments get more interesting in senior. In chemistry.'

'I doubt I'll find out,' he said.

'You're staying on, too, aren't you? You'll probably get better scores than me with your maths marks, and two sciences.'

He shrugged. 'It's not like I'm really going to need it.'

'I guess,' I said. 'There's no way I'm doing any science.'

'I thought you had to.'

'Hope not,' I said. 'Who'll keep Kieran in line if you leave?'

Josh looked up to the detention room. 'I'm not sure anyone can do that anymore.'

'True.' There was a lot to be angry about. Mr Vaas had left after only one year and Kieran was taking it personally. In geography, Ian had put Kool Mints on top of the fans. It was Kieran's idea but he couldn't reach. When Ms Walsh – Mr Vaas's replacement – turned them on, the white balls went flying and rattled all over the floor. She slipped over in her new heels trying to get out of the way and split her skirt. The whole class was in stitches, but she didn't see the funny side and sent them both outside. It wasn't her fault – she had never even met Mr Vaas and knew nothing about cricket or any of us.

Liam's nose was dripping blood, but he didn't wipe it or let up. He had Mark pinned down now, grass stains on the back of his pale blue shirt. The boys were all turning into animals. Except Josh. It was like he had skipped a step, through losing his father. The reason was sad, but he was better company than the others. He didn't bother with the matchmaking anymore, but he still picked up on everything that was going on.

'You know Kieran still likes you, right?'

'Yeah.'

'We always thought . . .'

'Me, too.' I crunched my carrot stick. 'But everything's so weird now, you know?'

Josh threw his iced-coffee carton at the bin and got it in first go. Slam dunk. 'You can say that again.'

———

The river was low, not much flow. We stuck to the beach area, where it was still deep and cool. Josh had taken to diving down to the bottom, bringing up odd items.

He was the biggest now, all muscled up from working the farm. My dad and Kieran's helped with the big jobs but a lot of the day-to-day, before and after school, was on Josh. His mum did what she could and had gone back to growing vegetables, to keep food on the table. We all helped. Whenever we butchered a steer dad took over two eskies full of meat.

There was more to Josh's growing; with Kieran gone from our river play, there was more space for Josh to fill. Now he was the strongest, in all sorts of ways. He was eight months older, too, which had never mattered, but now it meant that he had his licence already and could drive us down to the river.

Sometimes, on really hot days, we thought to pick up Matty. Kieran always wheeled himself out and said hello but wouldn't come with us. It was too hard, he said. At first I thought he meant loading up the chair, but he really meant seeing the river – and all of us in our swimmers with our bodies working as they should.

Ian was up where the trees had been. He still sat there sometimes, just looking and listening. I left him to it. He didn't get much time there anymore and I could come whenever I wanted.

Josh's head spun round. 'What was that?'

I scanned the surface of the river. 'What?'

'I saw something.'

Ian was back on the beach. I hadn't heard him come down. 'Bunyip?' he said.

Josh pointed. 'Look. Ripples.'

There was a hint of a sleek dark head, further upstream this time. And then it was gone.

'It's the platypus,' I said.

Josh shook his head. 'There aren't any platypus in this river.'

'There used to be,' I said.

'There used to be a lot of things,' Josh said.

The tone in his voice was how I felt sometimes. I splashed him. 'We all saw it.'

'It might have been a water rat,' Ian said. He dived in and backstroked downriver, away from us.

'Fine,' I said.

I wished we could go back to that day in the tree, and undo it. Wind everything back and stay on the ground, hold on tighter to what we had. But it was gone.

THE BIKE PATH curved through Commonwealth Park, past the flowerbeds being prepared for Floriade, beneath the elms and on into Kings Park. She sped past the chiming Carillon, ringed by poplars, an echo of distant church bells ringing out in the cities and towns of Europe. Lance Armstrong had won the Tour de France. Again. The French newcomer, Voeckler, had given him a run for his money, hanging on to the yellow jersey for ten stages before losing out to the veteran. Poor old McEwen won on individual points but that didn't get the glory. Next year, perhaps.

She passed the defence and intelligence agencies and, where the path ran parallel with the road, the entrance to Sarah's building. Once, when Jayne had dropped her off in the car, Sarah had asked her to keep going, to stop at the Lake House instead. There was some sort of signal, an alarm out front to warn staff when the media were about. It was more for the agency they shared the building with, Sarah said, not wanting the faces of their field staff all over the television, but she had taken a long walk all the same.

Traffic rushed by, reshuffling on the roundabout, cars on their way to the airport or south of the border. The lake narrowed back into river, green with willows. The path was bumpy and cracked with roots, jarring her ride. Like the cobblestone sections of the Tour. She pulled up in the park opposite the grounds of the military college, just short of all the nurseries she should be visiting to figure out what to do with her garden. It was the wrong route to get away from the city, but it was the river she needed right now.

She leaned her bike against a park bench and walked to the water's edge. Her cleats left deep holes in the muddy ground. She found a willow with a twisting trunk close to shore into whose arms she could climb. The breeze was quicker over the water, the current gentle. Weeping green leaves curtained her from the world.

The Executive had signed off on Max's report, recommending increased security staff and an upgrade in monitoring equipment. That and the media storm would help Noni with her budget bid. Frank would take his retirement early with no ill effects, his record clear, and his payout.

Jayne was officially off the hook. Breathing, and sleeping, should get easier from here. She couldn't have gone one more weekend waiting. Especially not at home with her parents, where it all began.

They were leaving after work tomorrow and she still hadn't picked out a wedding present for Matt and Catherine. She had only met Catherine once, at the engagement party, and it was hard to imagine the Matty she had known liking towels or sheets or crockery. Sarah had suggested an artwork, which Jayne should have thought of herself. Now there was only tomorrow left to buy something.

Waterbirds patrolled the muddy banks, their red webbed feet so sure. The air was cooling fast, and mountain bikes whizzed by at steady intervals. Sarah didn't seem nervous, but Jayne was worried enough for the both of them. A wedding and meeting the parents all at once. The tree in the news. Her career over.

With nothing left to lose, she had run a search on all of the remaining Wiradjuri arborglyphs and found another missing. It had to be more than a coincidence, but she couldn't figure it out, and the records alone told her nothing. She could poke around, call in a few favours, and find out more – but perhaps she should ask Ian first.

There was so much sky, turning from blue to pink as she watched. The city was low to the ground, tucked into the landscape, and not so far from home.

JOSH LEFT AT the end of year ten, to work the farm. It wasn't as if he had much choice. The rest of us pushed on, against the tide – or so it seemed. As seniors, everything was harder. I did three-unit modern history on my own, and ancient history by correspondence; I lived in the library.

For the rest of our classes, Ian and I took the ramp to the second floor, with Kieran, while everyone else raced up the stairs. I had to do biology, after all, and made sure the teacher, Ms Parnel, knew I hated every minute. I thought we would never get to the end of cells. The only time I raised my head all year was when we did genetics. Dominant and recessive genes and the way we all carried things from the generations before us was like a light being switched on – it explained how people worked. I was part Mum and part Dad and part their parents and grandparents and we should know everything they knew rather than starting from scratch every time. Maybe we did, deep down.

I couldn't help thinking about the trees. Despite doing every history unit available, despite all we were learning, there was nothing about the people who had been here before us, or those who were here still – Ian, right here in our own classroom. He was one of us, always had been. But for the first time, it occurred to me that he might not feel that way.

I sniffed back tears and rummaged in my bag for a tissue.

Ian frowned. 'What's up?'

Kieran chose that moment to elbow me in the ribs, except he hit my breast instead. It hurt so much, I punched him back. My fist on his shoulder made a slapping sound, and I managed to drop my bag and knock my textbook off the bench.

'Right,' Ms Parnel said. 'I've had quite enough of the three of you. Outside.'

———

Every school day, I was up at five, for a run, then homework, then school, then study, then bed. We saw less and less of each other, but I only had to look across the classroom, or the quadrangle, and catch Ian's eye, or Kieran's, and know we were still together. And yet, apart.

Kieran was changed, and not just his body. He was angry, and sometimes mean. He had gone through puberty in a chair. His shoulders, arms and chest were big and he was handsome. You could see who he would have been.

Our school had made the district rugby final, and along with half the town, the school filed down to the ground to watch. But Kieran sneaked rum in with his Coke and got messy. He yelled, 'Take that, motherfuckers,' at the opposition in the same wholehearted way he would have fed the ruck or pushed his way through to the tryline. When he was finally thrown out, Ian, Matty and me went with him.

While I phoned Mum from the office, Kieran somehow managed to pick a fight with Ian. I never found out what was said but when I went back outside, the three of them weren't talking and the Coke bottle was inside the home ec classroom, the other side of a broken window.

That cost us another hour, and a week's suspension. Mum didn't ask, when she arrived, for which I was thankful. I'd had a gutful of everyone.

———

We had to go to another funeral before that year was out. Brad Marsden drove his Falcon ute right into a tree on Pipers Lane one Saturday night. He'd been drinking, his blood alcohol way over the legal limit, but that was nothing new. We all drank down at the pub with our teachers – at the Railway Hotel – and until now, had driven home afterwards without major incident.

I had passed my licence exam first try. All of the girls did. I wore my school skirt, like everyone said. Most of the boys failed and had to resit the test. Kieran said the instructor was a perv but Dad said boys were overconfident and needed that knocked out of them as soon as possible – girls were better drivers. I drove the car to school most days and could take the ute when I went out on Friday or Saturday nights.

They never checked our ID at the hotels until we had turned eighteen; they didn't want to throw us out. I don't know where the cops were when we left the pub and headed out of town. Kieran said they drank – for free – at the Exchange. But they never pulled us over. Kieran couldn't drive, so Josh or I would pick him up and drop him home, or he would crash at Ian's.

At the funeral, Ian's mum and dad didn't sit with mine, or Kieran's, or Josh's mum. Ian hadn't said anything, but of course they were angry. I tried to catch Ian's mum's eye, but she didn't look my way. She was angry at me, too – and I didn't blame her.

For weeks afterwards, the boys were all talking about Brad and the lack of skid marks, the straight road, and nodding among themselves, like they knew something we didn't. It was far from the first time a young man had written himself off, but he was one of ours. Another one of us gone. In one of those moments you couldn't make up, the wreck was towed right by the school when we were milling about in the senior common room on Monday morning, allowing us a perfect view of the twisted white metal.

I'd read an American novel in year eight that was about surviving childhood. At the time I had thought it all a bit exaggerated, but now I wasn't so sure. It wasn't as if there was gang fighting and overdoses where we lived, like the kid in the book had gone through, but big things still happened in small towns. The year before, Harvey Nielson fell off his BMX while mucking around in a culvert. A skinned knee and a bump on the head. Nothing unusual. But he was groggy, so his brother took him home, and their mother drove him up to the hospital. It was Sunday afternoon, and there weren't any doctors on, so the nurses sent him home with a fresh bandage and smelling of Dettol.

When he wasn't up for breakfast, his brother burst into his bedroom and whacked him with a pillow. But Harvey couldn't get up. He was dead. A brain haemorrhage, they said. He should have had a scan, but they couldn't do that at our hospital anymore. You had to drive to the next town, an hour away.

It wasn't like we didn't already know about life and death. By then most of us had seen lambs or calves – and their mothers – die in childbirth, helped slaughter animals and eaten them, and shot roos or feral pigs.

It was what getting older was, realising that we weren't special after all. Our class was just one of many, and part of a world where anything could happen – even to us.

———

In a way, Kieran still led us. At the school dance at the end of year, he smuggled in booze. 'They're not going to search my chair,' he said. And he was right. So we sipped rum and Coke under the trees outside as the sun went down and the air cooled, with the Angels as our soundtrack. The warmth slid through our bellies and into our legs and for a while things were like they used to be, only better. We could have been ten and we could have been twenty, on the bank of the river, watching time flow by. But we were sixteen and the rum was going to our heads.

Ian and I watched Kieran open his second can and spike it, while Ms Johnston headed up to the girls toilets, prowling for smokers.

'What are you doing over the holidays?' Kieran said.

'Helping with harvest,' I said. 'And then a few weeks in a vineyard.'

'Which one?'

'Calare,' I said. Dad had asked around for me – they bought wine there sometimes.

'Mum found me some work with forestry,' Ian said. 'Clearing trails.'

We didn't want to go on too much. Kieran was working in the asparagus canning factory. We all hated asparagus. Factories, too.

Liam had already walked by twice, his shirt glittery in the quadrangle lights. Now he headed right for us. I knew what he wanted. Kieran did, too. 'Go on,' he said. But a mean look set on his face.

I stood. One dance was better than whatever might come out of Kieran's mouth if Liam walked past one more time, and what would happen after.

The song was an old one, a bit slow. We danced with my hands on his shoulders and his on my waist. He was kind of good-looking, in an interesting way.

The others still hadn't come inside. Liam's hands slipped down, his fingertips inside the top of my jeans. Whether it was the drink still warming my skin, or the music, I didn't mind.

'I love this song,' Liam said.

It was Tears for Fears – I liked it, too.

The music got better and time whirled by. Liam said he was going to go to uni, in Sydney. To study archaeology or architecture. His eyes were dark, and soft and made you want to look at them.

Ian spun past a few times, towering over Diane Hamley with a goofy smile. He must have finally found the nerve to ask her out. The next time I saw him he was up talking to the DJ. Requesting something, no doubt.

We were still dancing for the last song. I couldn't see Ian anymore. The lights were low, and the coloured ones they had put up were kind of beautiful. I almost backed out then, feeling something wash over me I wasn't sure I liked. But Liam pulled me closer. 'Please?'

When I was lost in the song and the lights and that tingle running over my skin, he kissed me. He was sure but not pushy.

I could breathe. Our tongues touched, and the feeling seemed to thread all the way to the warmth between my legs.

Then the music faded, and the fluorescent lights of the hall flickered on, row by row. We turned away from the stage, Liam still holding my hand.

Kieran was parked in the doorway, watching.

KIERAN'S PLACE WAS on the edge of town, in one of the newer estates. He was far from the only one never to have left the area. Or to have wandered back. The boys, in particular, had a way of returning, whether it was to take over the family farm or pursue business opportunities springing up between the old ways and the new.

He answered the door in a suit, tie half done up, and peered around behind her.

'Where's your woman?' he said.

'She's meeting us there.'

'Worried I'll sweep her off her feet?'

'Hilarious.'

He wheeled back into the house, all tiles and floorboards, no carpet. 'Our girls are ring bearer and flower girl, so Al took them in early.' He opened the fridge door and removed two beers. Crown.

'I thought you were never going to drink those again?' They'd had a thing for Crown after the end of year ten party, until Kieran got into a fight with some old-timer about drinking wanker beer. They were the only ones to have been thrown out of the pub before they were old enough to drink there, which was quite an achievement. Now the Railway was full of designer beers and ciders. It was hard to get a middy of New. And Kieran was a bit of an old-timer himself.

'I've said that a few times now. Keep coming back to them.' He flipped the tops and held one out for her.

'Thanks.' Their light fittings were almost chandeliers. Al's work, surely. And the heavy curtains.

'To the heister,' he said.

'Shut up.' But she clinked the base of her beer bottle, and then the neck, against his. 'Cheers.'

'Reckon you're going to get away with it?'

'Probably not,' she said. 'Did we ever get away with anything?'

'True.'

She set her beer on the granite bench, which was low enough for Kieran to work at, and bent her knees to tie his tie.

'I can do that myself, you know.'

'I know,' she said. 'I like doing it.' She could smell the alcohol on him. He was just topping up from last night.

'Do chicks wear ties?'

'Sometimes,' she said.

He grabbed her hand.

'Kieran, don't.'

'Promise me you'll stop now,' he said. 'Enough.'

She tried to pull away.

'I'm serious,' he said. 'It wasn't your fault. Not Matt's. Not anyone's.'

She reached for her beer, took a gulp, then another. *Beer* at eleven in the morning on the day of a wedding. Sarah would be unimpressed. 'We both know that's not true.'

'It was an accident. I fell. *I* made a mistake. The damage was most likely done when I hit the ground. And our parents knew about those damn trees before we were even born,' he said. 'There was nothing we could have done. We were just *kids*.'

The clock ticked, the room's air close. She tipped her head back and sculled. Just like the old days. Except now she sniffed back tears. 'How can I . . .' She gestured at his chair.

'Don't you dare pity me,' he said. 'I have a good life, Jay.' He wheeled back, opened the fridge. Two more beers. 'I'm happy. I have a beautiful wife, two great kids, a successful business, a great home. Top mates. I'm fit and healthy, swim a kilometre every day. It's *you* we worry about.'

She leaned on the bench. 'What?'

'C'mon, Jay.'

She registered a car pulling in. There was half a knock on the door and Matt was inside, sunglasses still on. He was tall and freshly scrubbed in a groom's suit.

'Hey, handsome.'

'Hey, Jay-girl.' He bent to hug her, kiss her cheek. 'You missed a good night last night.'

'So I hear,' Jayne said. It was a major break in tradition to invite a woman, and she probably would have gone if Sarah hadn't been along. 'But I reckon I'm feeling a whole lot better than the two of you this morning.'

'Soon fix that.'

She smiled. 'How's the farm?'

'Good,' he said. 'Went into canola this year. It's all contracted up front. Good return. Less risk. Pretty happy with that.'

'Dad's done that, too.'

Matt slid his sunglasses up onto his head. 'Did you hear about Josh?'

'What?' There was an old cricket ball mounted on a piece of wood in a glass box on the sideboard. She was pretty sure that if she went over and picked it up, it would be the one Mr Vaas had given Kieran.

'He bought up Barr's place – you remember it adjoins his, at the back.'

'Wow.'

'I think it was part favour. Old John has cancer.'

'Well, Josh would be sympathetic there.'

'Yeah.'

Kieran opened the fridge. 'Beer, bro?'

Matt checked his watch. His hands were trembling. 'We probably need to get going soon. Have to allow time to get the chair in and out.'

Kieran waved his arm. 'Drop the crip shit. You can take it with you. Settle your nerves.'

'I feel sick all right. I'm probably still over the limit from last night.'

'I'll drive,' Jayne said.

NOTHING REALLY HAPPENED with Liam. I didn't hear from him over the break and then we were back at school like it had never happened. Whether Kieran did or said something, I didn't know and I didn't care enough to find out. I didn't want any dramas, or to feel any more guilty than I already did. And I had my hands full with schoolwork. There had been enough distractions. All my marks from here on counted towards my final score, and it had finally dawned on me that I could do well if I tried.

There was a new girl at school, too, Donna Favenc. I was charged with showing her around, not that there was a whole lot to see. She had moved from Melbourne and talked about coffee shops and galleries and clothes and seeing big games at the Melbourne Cricket Ground – all of the things she was missing. She said her father worked for government and her mother had run an Italian restaurant and that they ate pasta every night.

We only had maths and English together, and art. We were doing printmaking when she arrived, which she had already done. Unlike my own smudgy attempts, hers were crisp and clean and bold. We teamed up to do a series, which I'm sure she didn't appreciate, but it turned out I wasn't so bad at the design and carving of the patterns – and Donna nailed the printing process. By the end of term, we were quite the team. For the first time, I topped the class – tied with Donna.

Her parents had bought the Maynard property, wanting to turn it into a llama farm. Alpacas were what Donna called them, but all the farmers around called them llamas. They started calling the Favencs that too: the llama people. It was a first for the district, and that always got people talking. Donna said alpacas protected sheep, and that every farmer should have a few. She brought in little fluffy alpacas made from real alpaca wool, which were cute and soft and that won most of us over. The girls, anyway.

In English we did *Julius Caesar*, the first Shakespeare most of us had read. More than a few rolled their eyes, but once we started taking parts to read the scenes, it came to life. It was like a new person at school – once you talked to them, you realised they were not so strange after all. Kieran was Caesar, chair and all, and Liam played Brutus. Mr Tait must have known something. I had to be Calpurnia. We were to perform for the whole school at the end of the term. On top of assignments and essays and studying, I had to learn my lines and the year started going by super fast.

———

Dad had dug the footings for the new shearing shed himself but needed me to help him lay out the weld mesh. The metal was rough on my hands. Mum had given me a pair of gloves but they were too big and made me clumsy.

She was working in the library for the week, while Mrs Anderson was on holiday in Paris, which was probably why Dad needed me to help and was prepared to pay me.

The day before, Ian's mum had come into the library. There had been some sort of conversation, and Mum had been crying when I walked into the kitchen, but she and Dad stopped talking.

'Grab that end and try and get it in snug at your corner,' Dad said.

Getting weld mesh to do anything you wanted was much harder than it looked.

'Seeing much of Kieran?' Dad said.

I shook my head. Kieran was too closed off and cranky to talk most of the time, but there was no point giving our parents more to worry about. Matty was becoming a handful, too. After his first detention, the principal called him up, warning him not to follow in Kieran's footsteps. That had made Kieran all the madder. 'I don't even make fucking footsteps,' he said. 'I leave tracks.'

Dad hammered in a stake. 'What about at school? Is he keeping out of trouble?'

I nodded, picturing Kieran as I had last seen him, parked outside the principal's office, his shirt wet and torn. We had been on the balcony waiting to go into maths when Owen Cartwright from the year eleven class threw a water bomb and called him Wheelie – and Ian and me the Chopper Bunch. Everyone knew Kieran had a short fuse, but they didn't realise how strong he was. Kieran grabbed hold of Owen's sleeve and punched him in the face, again and again, splitting his lip and breaking his nose. He had to go up to the hospital and there was talk of his parents laying charges.

Mum said hardships brought out the best in us but I couldn't see it. It was more like that one day had ruined our lives, and everything that had gone wrong since prevented us from being the best we could have been. But there was no point explaining all that. Kieran was the son Dad didn't have and now he was broken. There was only me. Spending time with Donna was like a holiday; she didn't know about any of it – and didn't care.

'Hello? Earth to kiddo?'

'Got it.'

'Maybe use a brick to weigh it down?'

'Okay.'

Mum said we should have converted the old machinery shed instead – it was full of wood and metal and parts, most of which should have been thrown out or sold for scrap. Or we could have kept borrowing Kieran's dad's. Dad said to do things properly he needed a purpose-built shed with a proper race and ramps and shoots and four shearing stations. Mum said it was ridiculous to build a shed you would only use for two weeks of the year. Mum and Dad had argued about it for a whole weekend. They argued about a lot of things now, but it was always about the trees.

'What about you?'

I looked over the edge of the trench.

'Are you doing okay?'

'Yeah, Dad.'

He bent to tie the mesh to the rods, and I thought maybe he let a lot of breath out. Once all I would have wanted was to talk to him, but he wasn't who I thought he was, and neither was I. Now it was like I'd gone out too far on my own. We all had. Like Kieran on that bloody branch.

THE BAND HAD started knocking back Jack Daniels and the volume was on the rise, shaking the walls out the back of the golf club. Jayne watched Sarah on the dance floor, twirling and grinning with the bride and bridesmaids. She was biased, no doubt, but Sarah's simple green dress left those frilly numbers for dead.

Kieran touched his beer bottle to her wineglass. 'She's great, Jay,' he said.

Jayne smiled. 'You like her?'

'Yep. Keep this one, eh?'

Jay pushed at the wheel of his chair with her boot.

'How long has it been?'

'About eighteen months,' she said.

'And you're just bringing her home now?'

'Yeah, yeah. I know.' She emptied her glass. 'Where have your girls gone?'

'Asleep in the back of the car.'

They were both very pretty but little terrors – like Kieran. Josh returned from the bar with his farmer's hands around a fresh round. Jay's mum had driven her dad and Kieran's parents home, and Josh's mum was helping clean up out in the kitchen. They were like teenagers again, up late drinking in the room where so many balls had been held in their day.

'What's this crap?' Kieran said. 'Play some rock'n'roll!'

'They can't hear you,' Josh said. 'Why don't you request something?'

Kieran sped off, around the table to the side of the stage.

'I hear you've bought up half the neighbourhood,' Jayne said.

'I've expanded a bit, yeah. Too much, probably.' His schooner, she noticed, was lemon squash. 'What's your dad going to do?'

'I don't know,' Jayne said. 'You want to buy them out?'

He laughed. 'Well, we all want that river access. Tell him to talk to me when he's ready.'

The band started in on a Bon Jovi riff. Kieran's work. The song called Ian in from the garden, smelling of cigarettes. He squatted beside her chair.

'Hey,' she said.

'Come for a drive?'

'What?'

'Something to show you,' he said. 'Meet me in the car park?'

She nodded. Sarah and Josh's wife were lip-synching now, complete with air guitar and thrashing hair. It seemed a shame to interrupt. 'Can you tell Sarah I'll meet her at home?'

'Sure, mate. We can drop her off,' Josh said.

She found Ian's white station wagon guzzling petrol by the entrance. 'What's going on?'

'Thought you might like to see where the tree is.'

She blinked. 'You right to drive?'

'We'll be okay. Keep to the back roads.'

They headed out into the night. She counted less than five kilometres before they left the sealed road, heading west. She had a rough idea where they might be going. The trail she had followed from that first tree she'd found in Brisbane had suggested that hers was one of half-a-dozen taken from a homestead near a neighbouring town. They had been removed from their original location on the property in 1933, topped and tailed, and displayed around the garden, like sculptures. When the property was sold, the trees were sold off, too – for twenty pounds each – and sent by rail to museums around the country. Cut up, split up, and kept in storage – a long way from country. It was more than a metaphor.

They took another turn, on loose gravel. The back of the station wagon slewed, and Ian grinned. She thought they were headed north-west but her directions were out with the booze and the dark.

'Been a while since you were out here, eh?'

'Yeah,' she said. Tree trunks flashed past, just shadows. She caught glimpses of the moon, higher now.

'Remember when we broke into the pool, to have a midnight swim?' His teeth were green in the dashboard lights.

'I remember how mad your dad was when we got home,' she said. They had woken up under the stringy barks, their T-shirts and jeans bleached white, when the swim squad arrived at five.

'I copped more of an earful after you left, I tell you,' Ian said. 'I tried to tell him how hot it was that night but he didn't care.'

She smiled. It had been after their last day carting wheat. Still forty-two degrees at four in the afternoon. She remembered someone dropping a shot of Drambuie in her fifth schooner and not much else.

When the time had come for her to go, the next morning, Ian had followed her out to the car. 'Might not see you for a while,' he said. 'You'll be at uni when I get back from Melbourne.' It was too soon to say goodbye and they were hung-over; a hug was all they managed. That's when he had given her the photo, of them and the trees. To take with her wherever she went. 'I keep a picture here,' he said, touching his forehead. She had cried all the way home; it had been the end of so many things.

'Okay?' Ian said.

'Yeah.' The initials of the next town were marked on the old cement guideposts. She knew where they were going. 'You don't see Kieran much these days?'

Ian shook his head and kept his eyes on the road.

'What did he say to you that day? When we got suspended?'

'Called me a black cunt, the bastard,' he said. 'It doesn't matter now.' He dropped the headlights for a car coming the other way. 'It mattered *then*. I didn't want to know who I was,' he said. 'Only time I punched anyone in my whole life, and he was in a fucking wheelchair.'

'He was so out of control then,' she said. 'I don't think he really meant it.'

'But he *said* it, you know?'

'Yeah.'

They turned onto bitumen and travelled on, with a gentle, winding motion that lulled Jayne almost to sleep. She sat up at the purr of gravel. Ian pulled up beneath an old ironbark.

'Okay.' He handed her a black and white bandana. 'I have to ask you to tie this over your eyes. Sorry.'

'It's all right.'

Eventually she felt the car turn left again, and then right. The road was rough but flat and straight. When they stopped, she heard running water and frogs. Ian's door opened and closed. He opened hers and helped her out. 'Okay?'

'All good.'

'Just a bit longer.' He led her downhill on what felt, to her city feet, like a rough track with deep furrows. She smelled damp earth. Moonlight crept in around the edges of the cloth. She hadn't done much of a job of the tying.

'Is it okay for me to be here?'

'Got special permission from the elders,' he said.

She squeezed his hand.

'Righto. Open sesame.'

She slipped off the bandana and blinked. If she had known how the evening would end up, she might have had a few less wines and worn more sensible shoes. She breathed, listened. There was a stillness she recognised, from the grove.

'We can't go any further,' he said. 'But you can see them from here. Look.'

Them? Seven bare trunks huddled inside a protective circle of younger living trees, pillars in the forest. She picked out the tree she had last seen bubble-wrapped on the tray of the truck from its height and girth, though its chevrons and spirals were out of view. Silhouetted there in the dark with the others, it was proud, powerful once more.

'How?'

Ian grinned. 'We have some of our mob inside those places, too, you know.'

They were standing between the trees and the creek, which flowed slow and steady, as it always had. The moon cast misshapen shadows.

'Some of the Old People remembered how the trees were. And those buried there. We had a big ceremony, a few weeks ago now. I brought my boys along,' he said.

'What was it like?'

'Lot of smoke and singing, dancing.'

The hair on her forearms lifted.

'We had to cement them in – not quite the same. But still.'

'It's beautiful.'

'This is only the start, Jay,' he said.

'I've got a list,' she said. 'Of where they're all held. Where they came from. It might help.' Then she smiled, shook her head. This was where the missing trees had gone. He was a step ahead of her again.

'It might.' He struck a match, and the end of his cigarette glowed red as it took. 'Still got your class b?'

'I do.' Work had paid to keep it current; she was one of the few upstairs staff who could operate all of the vehicles. 'Why?'

'I could use another driver,' he said.

The gathering of trees was silvered in the moonlight.

'We'd pay you. Cash. Cover your expenses.'

'Can I let you know?'

'Sure, mate. No hurry.'

It was cold now, and the wine was wearing off. She couldn't help thinking of the others, all those that couldn't be returned. No matter what they did. Ian draped an arm over her shoulder and she leaned into his chest.

NO ONE WE knew went to the new service station but other people must have, because Ian said business was down. The BP cut its prices, and with the new road, passing traffic didn't need to come into town. Then the video shop sold up and Ian's parents started renting out movies, and stocking local fruit and vegetables in baskets out the front. The town got behind them and Ian said he thought they were going to be okay.

He worked for nothing on the weekends and sometimes I would help out if I was staying over. We could eat and drink what we liked and lots of people called in to chat and that was enough for us. I liked restocking the fridges and shelves and we watched some of the best films before anyone else.

Mum and Dad didn't call in to the station anymore, but they still had their fuel delivered to the tanks on the farm. One day Ian's dad had driven the truck, and I had the feeling that our fathers must have spoken at last.

———

Rain kept everyone inside for almost a week. When it finally stopped, I took an afternoon off, at the river. All my major assessment pieces were in, and sometimes field mushrooms grew under the tree where Kieran had fallen. I had a craving for mushrooms on toast. Mum did them up with cream and parsley and pepper, and since I had stopped eating much meat, she was trying hard to come up with new dishes we would all like. Especially leading into exams.

I couldn't have timed it better; some of the mushrooms were just opening out, fresh pink gills beneath the white caps. I soon filled a bucket but left it on the bank. The river was demanding my attention. It was as full as I had ever seen it, creamy, and sliding past rather than flowing. There had been heavy rain upstream, washing a lot of soil into the water.

There was talk of another flood at Forbes. It happened every seven years, some times worse than others. I always thought rivers flowed to the sea, but ours flowed west, into great marshlands and then the Murrumbidgee. They were big on rivers at school, with our houses named after them. I had learned the whole history and course of the Lachlan, the reference to it in 'Clancy of the Overflow', and the building of the dam. But I got its real name from Ian: Calare. He was in Murrumbidgee house, the only one of our rivers still close to its Wiradjuri name, Murrumbidjeri.

I bent to pick up a stick, to stop myself slipping, and realised that it wasn't just silt and muck sliding past. It was a seething crust of shrimp, and yabbies in all sizes and colours poking their claws up through them, as if calling for help. Every now and then a claw would snip a shrimp in half, but perhaps by accident. I couldn't tell if they were feeding or just trying to breathe.

A turtle popped her head up through all that living flotsam and pushed through to the shore, blinking, as if she couldn't quite believe what she was seeing. It was how I felt, too. A water rat scampered up the bank and sat not ten feet downstream. We watched the river together. It was one of those moments when I couldn't turn away, in case I missed something, and in case it was gone when I looked back.

Then the fish started coming up. First just their noses broke the surface, as if sniffing. Then the water boiled and surged and turned an even more awful brown. Hundreds of them breached at once: catfish, gudgeon, perch, fish I didn't recognise. All sizes and shapes swarmed together, from fingerlings to a great old Murray cod, all gasping for air. I could hear them sucking.

Of all the days not to have a camera.

I did what anyone would do, waded in and started grabbing fish. They were slippery, but couldn't get far. I went for the silver perch, glinting like jewels, and threw them up on the bank behind me. I stopped at two plate-sized fish each, but not before I had slipped and fallen in. I was wet through and slimy with mud and filth. I picked shrimp out of my hair, unhooked a crayfish from my sleeve, and threw them back.

Then the water seemed to clear a little and the fish thinned, the yabbies dived, the turtle and water rat disappeared underwater with a plop. The river was back to normal, full and brown, flowing on by as if nothing unusual had happened.

———

The pressure was building, getting closer to exams, and more often than not, I was studying all weekend. Sometimes, during the week, Donna and I stayed back late in the art room, working on our portfolios. She helped me with my printing and I helped her with her canvases. I was turning my lichen photographs into prints, by focusing on one part and enlarging it, developing the shapes and patterns rather than the whole. They were coming out okay, but unlikely to change the world. Donna was in a different league.

'It's your best yet,' I said. She did things with colours and textures that looked like they were going to be disastrous, but when you stood back, once it was all done, it was great. Her final series was farm sheds, which I had thought was going to be dull, but the ones she had finished were good enough for a gallery.

'Thanks,' she said. 'One for the art school portfolio maybe.'

'How's that going?' She was applying for art schools in Sydney, Melbourne and Canberra, but her parents wanted her to have a backup plan.

Donna rolled her eyes. 'They're still on about teaching. It's like they don't believe in me, you know?'

'Yeah.' Mum had really set her sights on me doing law. She saw it as a way for women to empower themselves or something, but it sounded dead boring to me. 'They should believe in you,' I said. 'Show them this one.'

'Maybe,' she said. 'It just shits me that they get all conservative *now*, you know?'

'I guess they don't want you to make the same mistakes they did.'

'True.' She smiled. 'I have to make my own.' She tucked the painting under her arm and dragged her schoolbag off the table. 'What do you want to do?'

'I don't know, but I want to keep studying art and history.' I locked the art room doors behind us. Lambs baaed from the agriculture plot, hoping for an extra feed.

'An art historian, then?'

'Is that a thing?'

'Think so.'

'Cool,' I said. 'Want a lift?'

'That would be great,' she said.

Donna didn't have her licence yet and her family only had one vehicle. It was a little out of the way, at the end of Candalagan Lane, but I liked driving home on the shaded back roads. Donna had made me a mixed tape of all of her favourite songs and I was saving it for the home stretch.

———

Dad was in the kitchen in the middle of the day. I hesitated in the doorway, but needed food to keep me going. 'Where's Mum?'

'Cutting burrs.' Dad looked in the biscuit tin, which I knew was empty. I'd taken the last Anzac midmorning, on a study break.

'Why don't you just spray them?'

'She doesn't like me to use poisons. She's always cut them by hand. Since we were first married. Good for her arms, she says.'

Dad had made her a special tool, kind of a cross between a hoe and a chopper. But I knew perfectly well Mum only went cutting burrs when they'd had an argument. Dad knew I knew, too.

'Got time to run me into town?'

The ute's gearbox had been in pieces on the workshop floor since midweek, Mum said.

The kettle was boiling and Dad slid it off the heat. 'I have to meet with the accountant.'

'Okay,' I said.

I walked barefoot through to the garage while Dad put on his boots and opened the garage doors. The breeze smelled like summer, all warm soil and grass haying off. I backed out the car. Dad shut the doors and climbed in the passenger seat. Neither of us bothered with a seatbelt. The car threw up dust along the driveway, obscuring the house in the rear-view mirror.

'Studying hard?'

'Yeah.' I looked left and right at the road, listened for traffic before pulling out. 'I'm writing a practice essay at the moment.'

'What's it on?'

'Postwar Japan.'

'How they rebuilt their economy?'

'And took up baseball.'

He smiled and looked out over the wheat crops. They were still green but their heads growing heavy with grain. 'Sad, losing so much of their own culture.'

I blew air out my nose and shook my head. *Hypocrite*. History taught us all the lessons we needed, if we bothered to learn.

Dad was still looking out the window. 'What I did was wrong, Jay. A bad decision. But I can't undo it now,' he said. 'I wish I could. But I can't.'

JAYNE SCRAPED THE last of her scrambled eggs, green with fresh parsley, onto a square of toast. They had missed breakfast by several hours and her father was long gone.

Sarah accepted a top-up of coffee. 'Thanks.'

'What time did you girls get in last night?'

Sarah smiled, looked at Jayne.

'Late,' Jayne said.

'Wasn't it a lovely wedding? I like Catherine – I think Matt has done well there.'

'She does seem nice,' Jayne said. She was gorgeous, too. Her last image was of the bride swinging her hair on the dance floor, champagne perfectly still in her left hand.

'You would have met some of Jay's old friends, then, Sarah?'

'I met all the gang, yes.'

Jayne fiddled with the edge of her placemat. 'None of them have changed too much. Except Josh. Big landowner.'

'He's done very well for himself, yes.'

Sarah leaned back to better see out the window. 'Your garden looks lovely, Deidre.'

'Would you like to have a look around?'

'Absolutely,' Sarah said. She stood, gathered up their plates, waitress style, and placed them next to the sink.

Jayne followed them out the back door. Her mother pointed out the tree where Jay had the swing as a child, the shady spot under the acacia where she had built a fairyland, the spiral rock wall garden, and the wattle grove that used to be the soccer oval. She and her father had kicked the ball from their motorbikes. Hitting the underground tank had been a goal at the western end, shooting between the two she-oaks meant scoring at the other. And there was the spot where she had pitched her tent before she was brave enough to go further afield. It was a tour of her childhood as much as of the garden beds.

Sarah stopped at the round bed of daffodils ringed by jonquils and brushed a fly from her face. 'These are wonderful,' she said.

'Jay helped me plant those, when she was little. They just keep on poking their heads up, most years.'

'Sarah's been helping me with my garden,' Jayne said.

Her mother smiled. 'That's nice of you. It's never really been Jay's thing.'

'She's very handy around the house, though,' Sarah said.

'Yes, even her father was impressed with the deck,' Deidre said 'Have you done any more?'

'Just some painting and a feature wall in the dining room.' The brick path took them past a bronze platypus under the deodar, and into a pergola heavy with wisteria. It would be a good spot for a wedding. 'I'll send you some pictures,' Jayne said.

'I'd like that.'

They walked on, through an avenue of young blue gums clotted with red blossom. The lorikeets were already making a racket.

'And this is our orchard, such as it is,' her mother said. 'Some of the old trees have passed away, but the younger ones are coming on.'

'A persimmon,' Sarah said. 'My mother loves those.'

'They're a pretty tree. I don't eat the fruit, but Jay and her father love them.'

'There's a cafe we go to that does a persimmon and custard tart. That changed my mind,' Sarah said.

'Sounds lovely. You grew up on a property, Sarah?'

'In Tasmania,' she said. 'But my mother lives in Hobart now.'

'Tasmania? The perfect climate for gardening,' Deidre said. 'Everything's a bit of a battle here.'

'It's wonderful.'

'And your father?'

'He died a few years ago.'

'I'm sorry. Jay didn't mention that.'

'I *did*, Mum.' It had been half the reason Sarah hadn't been able to move on from her drama queen ex. And her mother always asked about people's parents first.

'You've chosen a lot of hardy plants,' Sarah said.

'I find that anything silver-greyish tends to survive even our worst summers.'

Jayne stood on the edge of the vegetable bed to pluck oranges from the tree. She threw one to Sarah and handed another to her mother. They walked on, past the grapevines and chestnut trees, peeling skin away from flesh.

'What are you girls going to do today?'

'I thought I might show Sarah around the farm.'

'Your old bike's still in the shed,' her mother said.

'Feel like going for a ride?' Jayne grinned.

Sarah laughed. 'Is it big enough for the two of us?'

'We'll manage.'

'You might need to clean it up,' her mother said. 'It hasn't been used for a while. But I believe it's running.'

———

'Do you have a second helmet?'

'You can wear mine.'

'What about you?'

'I was just going to take us for a quick run, down to the cattle yards and back,' she said. 'Feel the wind in our hair.'

'How long since you've ridden?'

'Five or six years.'

'Jay.'

'All right, all right,' she said. 'I'll wear Dad's.' Jayne reached to pull it off the hook in the wall, screwing up her nose at the dust and cobwebs. It looked as if he had given up wearing it now that he didn't have to set a good example. She cleaned it out with a cloth and wiped down the outside, revealing metallic blue paint, and then cleaned her own, as yellow as the bike had once been, and handed it to Sarah. 'Hope it fits.'

Jayne gave the seat, petrol tank and handlebars a quick wipe and hung the cloth on a nail.

'You had a big head, even then,' Sarah said.

Jayne laughed. 'I wouldn't talk. You look like a banana.' She tucked a wisp of Sarah's hair back inside the helmet.

'No visor?'

'We took them off. They soon got scratched.' Jayne straddled the bike, too low for her now, and flicked up the stand. She turned the key, kicked the starter. It turned over but didn't take. She kicked again, and it was alive, but with more of a whimper than a roar. She gave it some throttle.

'It's so loud,' Sarah said, over the engine.

'Climb on.'

Sarah put her arms around Jayne's waist and kicked down the passenger footrests.

'Ready?'

'Hell, yeah,' Sarah said, close to Jayne's face.

'I'll go slow. You just need to make sure your weight follows mine, okay?'

'Got it.'

Jayne took off, giving it a little more throttle than she needed to, overcompensating for the extra weight. She rode downhill, on the track following the fence line, to the cattle yards. When she sped up, heading across to the dam, Sarah whooped.

Jayne turned her head, saw her grinning. The sun was shining, the grass and lucerne paddocks green.

She took the first circuit slow, following a cattle track up and around the banks. Sarah's chin was tucked into Jayne's back, her arms and legs enveloping her. Crows watched from the shaded branches of the willow.

'This is where I used to go crayfishing,' Jayne said, over her shoulder.

Sarah squeezed her tighter, still grinning.

Jayne took the next lap faster, leaning into the curves. Sarah matched her shifts as if she had done it all before. For the third lap Jayne pushed harder, speeding into a hump and launching into the air. She landed perfectly on the track down the steepest side and sped back across the flat.

The shadow of Sarah's raised arms over Jayne's helmeted head moved across the paddock ahead of them.

———

They were buzzing at lunch, talking too loud, as if the wind and engine were still in their ears. Jayne stripped off her jacket, the kitchen warm from the wood stove.

Her mother saw the tattoo and said nothing. Her father took it in and dropped his head.

'It was so fun,' Sarah said. She took the salad from Jayne's mother and set it on the table. 'I had no idea.'

'I would have cleaned up the bike if I'd thought you'd take it out,' Jayne's father said.

'It was fine,' Jayne said.

'She used to ride that thing around and around for hours,' her mother said. 'Buzzing like a bee.'

'The quiche is good, Mum.' She had remembered to leave the bacon out of her pumpkin and sage number, and the homemade wholemeal pastry was a crumbly treat.

Her mother smiled and handed the salad around again.

Her father said nothing. He was probably missing the roast they usually had for Sunday lunch. 'What are you two doing this afternoon?' He addressed Sarah rather than Jayne. Trying hard.

'Jay's going to show me her camping spot, by the river.'

His loaded fork halted. 'Good,' he said. 'There's a lot of water at the moment.'

———

They sat side by side on the bank, watching the slow-moving water.

'I can imagine you brooding here on your own.'

'I did do a bit of that.'

They walked up the rise, hand in hand. The magpies and galahs fell silent. Only the river spoke.

'It's gorgeous,' Sarah said. 'Reminds me of my grandparents' place. Running wild as a kid.'

They stopped at her old fireplace, the stones pale green with lichen – much more than Jayne remembered. Sarah turned away from the river, to the trees behind, and the circle of Cyprus pines, almost mature now. 'Show me where the picture was taken?'

Jayne led the way. 'Mum planted those. That's the other tree the Wiradjuri used to carve. The originals were yellow box, pretty old. They wouldn't have lasted forever, even if left alone.'

'The mound looks higher in the photo.'

'It's settled a lot now,' Jayne said.

'I'm sorry.' Sarah put her arm through hers. 'But you know it's not your fault, right?'

The breeze in the pines made a softer sound than the narrow box leaves had, more of a shushing.

Sarah leaned on her shoulder. 'There's so much sadness here.'

Jayne blinked. 'The man buried up there was a warrior, and would have died nearby. Ian thinks it was at the hand of whites — there are some documented battles not far from here. Maybe you're picking up on that,' she said.

They turned back to the river. Jayne followed a ripple on the surface until it disappeared.

'Do you still have all your gear?'

'I think so. Unless Mum threw it out,' Jayne said. 'Why?'

'I'd like to spend more time here. Could we camp tonight?'

'You'd want to?'

'As long as your mum won't be offended.'

'She will. She's planned every meal. But she'll cope,' Jayne said. 'It will give us all a break. Let's do it.'

MUM WAS TEACHING me to cook. It wasn't like I couldn't feed myself, and I'd been helping her in the kitchen on and off for a few years, but she said I needed to have a repertoire of half-a-dozen meals fit to serve others at uni.

I rolled out wholemeal pastry dough, cut a circle and dropped it in the quiche dish. I flattened it out and pushed the dough into the flutes the way I had seen Mum do it.

'Okay. Now we blind-bake it. The recipe says to use pastry weights but I never bother – the filling flattens it all out anyway.'

I opened the stove, slid the dish onto the middle shelf and set the timer. The rain sounded heavier outside, driving in under the verandah.

I followed the steps to make the egg mixture and sliced leek and feta. It was to be our lunch, so I needed to get a move on. 'Will we have salad with it?' I said.

'I'll do that.' Mum started pulling items out of the crisper. 'How are you going with all your assessment?'

'Okay,' I said.

'What does that mean?'

'It means I'm nearly finished. Just one essay to go. For ancient history. And then my portfolio.'

'When's that due?'

'Next week.'

'Well, you'd better get started!'

'I have started. But I can't cook and study at the same time.'

'True.' She ripped off lettuce leaves and dropped them into one of her raku bowls.

'Donna and I are going to work on our portfolios this weekend,' I said. 'You should see her paintings. They're amazing.'

Mum rinsed her hands under the tap. 'And how are the others going? Kieran and Ian?'

'Okay, I think.' I didn't really know. From the amount of time they were spending at the pub, they didn't seem too concerned. They were not the greatest influences.

'That's good,' she said. 'They're both smart boys.'

They were, but they'd probably left their run too late. The teachers had been too soft on Kieran. He had fallen behind in year eleven and was going to struggle to catch up.

'I can't help thinking Josh should have finished, too,' Mum said.

I shrugged. Josh was happier outside working.

'And what about the graduation dance?' she said. 'Has anyone asked you?'

'*Mum.*' I had been avoiding Liam and Kieran for weeks. It was tempting not to go at all.

'Just asking.'

'Well, don't,' I said.

'It's not far away. I've been thinking about dresses. It's going to be warmish, so—'

'Stop!'

'Okay, okay.'

I filled the sink to start washing up. The dress obsession was irritating, but at least it was distracting Mum from my university choices. Donna had found a new course for me, art history curatorship, at the Australian National University in Canberra. It was perfect. I could do art history as well as ancient history and even archaeology. But Mum thought there was more job security with law.

'What's happening with pottery?'

'Oh, they pretended to be concerned when they got the petition, but there'll be no more classes. Unless we want to go over to Orange every week.'

'Orange? That's a shame.'

'It is. But it's not like I don't have plenty of other things to do.'

I used Mum's oven mitt to pull out the quiche.

'Your father is sick of it anyway,' she said. 'He wants to do something else.'

'Like what?'

'Woodwork, maybe.'

'Something more manly, you mean?' He had been the only adult male at pottery for the last year and a half.

She smiled, watching me pour the mixture into the pastry case.

'Enough?'

'Perfect.'

I carried the dish back to the oven, making sure to keep it flat. 'Plenty of ceramicists are men,' I said. 'Look at Hiroki.'

'True. But they probably weren't farmers first.'

THE TENT WAS musty, and the sleeping-bags, but the fresh air would soon sort them out. The ground was harder, lumpier than she remembered. Or perhaps her body was softer. She should have taken the blow-up mattress her mother had offered.

'What can I do?' Sarah said.

'Maybe gather some kindling? It'll be drier beneath the big trees.'

Sarah strode off, taller outside somehow. Jayne broke up small branches by leaning them against the biggest campfire rock and bringing her boot down. The river burbled, the grass on the banks flat, as if a lot of water had been through. Wind soughed in the wattles behind her.

She got the fire going. That much was still easy – all flames and smoke at first. Sarah had wandered upriver, following the path along the bank. Jayne busied herself with dinner, a styled-down version of what they would have had at home with her parents. One of the latest additions to the town was a trout farm and her mother was keen to show off its wares. Jayne dropped the grilling plate onto the coals and prepared the frying pan for the buttered dill potatoes, a pot for the green beans. Galahs passed overhead, almost the same pink as the fading sky.

Sarah dumped an armload of wood next to the fire. 'Did we bring wine?'

'In the eskybag near the tent.'

'Sunset drinks?'

'Yes, please.' The breeze had dropped, the sky bruising into purple. She tipped the potatoes into the frying pan, placed the foil-wrapped fish on the grill, and took the glass Sarah offered. 'Cheers.'

'This is the life,' Sarah said.

Jayne kept one eye on the river while she shook the pan, looking for the telltale ripple she used to see so often at dusk. The potatoes sizzled, and the smell of dill rose with the steam. She dropped the beans in the boiling water.

'Did you eat this well when you were camping as a kid?'

'Definitely not. Sausages, damper, baked beans.'

'I like damper.'

'I was going to make it for breakfast.'

Jayne served up the trout and potatoes and fished out beans with the tongs. She swapped a plate for her glass, which Sarah had been holding.

'I think this is the most meals we've ever had together,' Sarah said. 'Except for Adelaide.'

'Except for Adelaide.' Hopefully they wouldn't arrive home to a national disaster this time. Drifts of high cloud were pastel pretty, but would obscure the best of the night sky. It was unrealistic to expect perfection but she wanted it all the same.

'Oh, yum,' Sarah said.

The fish was good but the potatoes made it better. The wine, too. Dragonflies flitted over the water, putting on a dinner show.

'Any fish left in this river?'

'Some,' Jayne said. 'Less since the dam.'

'I was hoping one of your silver perch might show itself. They seem to have a thing for you.'

'I thought I had a thing for them,' Jayne said.

Sarah smiled. 'Did you know it's not a true perch, but a member of the grunter family?'

Jayne laughed. 'Really?'

'I know my fish.'

'You do,' she said. 'We could have gone fishing, if we had longer.'

'I wish we could stay.'

'Me, too,' Jayne said. 'But you have something on Monday?'

'A meeting up at the House.'

She meant Parliament House. That was part of how she talked now. 'You have an important job. Enjoy it, you know?'

Sarah tucked her hair behind her ear. 'I do enjoy parts of it.'

Jayne refilled their glasses. 'But . . .'

'I feel compromised,' she said.

'Explain?'

'It was exciting at first. Interesting. And certainly challenging. It's been great for my report writing. And working under pressure. But the more I learn, the less I like.'

'Ethics-wise?'

Sarah nodded. 'How we get some of the information, how it's used. The way it's being used to meet a certain political agenda.'

She meant Iraq. 'We've had spies since ancient Greece. Before, probably,' Jayne said. 'They just didn't have access to satellite imagery. Or the United States of America.'

Sarah smiled. 'True. But that doesn't mean I have to be part of it.'

'What would you do instead?' Jayne took her plate, stacked it on top of her own, and set them down out of the way.

'I can go back to DFAT at the end of my secondment,' she said. 'Where I don't know, but at level.'

Jayne reached under her chair for the marshmallows and handed Sarah one of the two slender sticks she had chosen for toasting. 'Is that what you want?'

'I don't know. I would like an overseas posting. I mean that was the whole point.'

'Where?'

'Anywhere! Asia. The Pacific, maybe.' Sarah's first marshmallow caught fire. She lifted it to her lips and blew it out. 'But you know, it's all part of the same system, isn't it?'

'True.' Most of the Foreign Affairs staff she had met seemed to have their head right up their own butts. They were trained to assess your level and agency, your relative station, your worth to them as a contact – all in a glance. In her case, zip. Except of minor interest as Sarah's partner. Jayne chewed a gooey marshmallow, sucking in air to stop it burning her tongue. 'Do we have to have servants?'

'What?'

'On a posting.'

'It depends where you go,' Sarah said.

Jayne held out her toasting stick, offering a perfectly roasted marshmallow. Sarah took it, popped it in her mouth. 'I have kind of been offered a job.'

'What?'

'With Greenpeace. It's through a friend. I'd have to apply, but it's mine if I want it. An international role, around illegal fishing and whaling.'

'That's perfect!'

'It would be – but it would mean travelling for half the year, and earning half what I am now.' She looked up at the now clear sky. A barn owl swooped across the clearing, its face ghost white. 'Wow,' Sarah said.

Jayne tucked the marshmallow packet in her pocket and shifted her chair closer to Sarah's.

'We could just sell up, become farmers,' Sarah said.

Jayne snorted. 'Hilarious.'

'I like it out here.'

'Me, too,' she said. 'But farming's a lousy way to make a living. And hardly environmental.'

'There are different ways of doing things. We could plant trees, put in an olive grove. Something smaller scale.'

Jayne stared at the dark of the river. She had always wanted an olive grove. To walk, as an older woman, between rows of trees she had grown. That would be her sort of farming.

'What will your parents do? Your dad can't keep going forever.'

'I don't know.' He had tried to hide his limp but she had seen him struggling to bend down to pick up a tyre by the shed. His hip, her mother had said. 'Lease it out, maybe. Can't imagine them moving into town.'

'And you? Have you thought about what you'd like to do?'

'Is it stressing you out?'

'What?'

'I know it bothers you, me not having a plan, but I'll have enough money to live on for a year,' Jayne said. 'I'd like to travel again, get fit, all sorts of things.'

'You're already fit. I just want you to be happy,' Sarah said. 'And hopefully not go to prison.'

'The internal investigation has been closed. The museum just wants it to go away.'

'I know, but what if someone makes the connection between you and Ian?'

'They won't.' Jayne threw another branch on the fire. 'He's not officially affiliated with the land council. Keeps a low profile.' She watched sparks shoot up into the dark. 'I think I will do the masters – if I get a scholarship.'

'You will,' Sarah said. 'Either way, I'm on a good wage.'

'I'll soon pick up some part-time work.'

'Sure, but perhaps we should consolidate. Simplify things.'

'What do you mean?'

Sarah pushed stick ends into the coals with her boot. 'I would be happy to rent out my place, for example. I'm hardly there.'

'Live together?'

'I know you had a bad time with Suzie, but are we going to give this a proper go or not?'

———

There was only a hint of light when she woke. She unzipped the tent, to catch the mist rising off the water and colour creeping into the sky.

It wasn't entirely true that she'd had a bad experience living with Suzie. Or, at least, it hadn't been entirely bad. It was more that she had lost herself in someone else's house and things – someone else's life – before she had figured out much of her own. Now that she had, she was reluctant to give it up.

But Sarah wasn't Suzie – and she didn't want to lose her.

The fire was still alight, a few coals from the log they had dragged on last night smouldering away. She padded out in her boxers and added sticks and leaves until it was flaming, and piled on more fuel. The day was beginning. She stood, arms crossed over her bare chest, and watched the light creep in. The birds started up, and the cicadas. On the other side of the river, a wallaby came down to drink, looking about between sips, as if sensing she was being watched.

When Jayne backed towards the tent, hoping to show Sarah, the wallaby bounded off. She crawled in and kissed Sarah awake, slipping her hand under her T-shirt to cup her breast. 'Morning, beautiful.'

Sarah stirred, smiled.

Jayne lifted the shirt, and took Sarah's nipple in her mouth until it hardened.

'Morning,' Sarah said.

'Come outside?'

'What time is it?'

'One minute off sunrise. I'll put the coffee on.'

Sarah sat up, yawned, and crawled outside in her pyjamas. Jayne pulled on her jeans and Sarah's fleece.

The sun peeked over the tree line, lighting their side of the bank and coppering the water. Swallows and the bigger birds started up, the magpies and galahs, their louder calls the vocals on the soundtrack. Sarah had wandered to the river's edge, rather than the fire. Jayne followed her down and hugged her from behind, chin on her shoulder.

They watched as a sleek head broke the surface and swam right at them, cutting a vee in the river before diving again.

'Was that . . . ?'

Jayne grinned. 'I knew it,' she said.

I WAS ON study-vac, but had agreed to help Dad move the cattle. He asked Mum to ask me, too afraid to knock on my door.

We started early, while it was still cool. I had no fuel in my tank – it had been a while since I had ridden – but Dad tried to hide his impatience while he waited for me to fill up.

I went first, to open the gates. We left them open for the run back. Dad wanted to shift the cattle into the house paddocks, where there was still plenty of grass, and tufts of self-sown wheat.

We worked the cattle out of the trees near the river, then narrowed in at them from each side, funnelling them towards the open double gates, beeping our horns and shouting, 'Hup! Hup!' I just missed a fat goanna sprinting for an ironbark and baulked, almost losing the bike. I had been spending too much time inside.

Once the lead steers were through, we pulled up to let nature run its course.

Dad switched off his bike and folded his arms. 'You ready for these exams?'

'I will be.'

'Not stressing out too much?'

I shrugged. If I was as stressed as some of the other girls, I'd have been studying now rather than stirring up dust. We watched a wallaby thump off on the other side of the fence, put off by all the bellowing.

Dad cleared his throat. 'I know there's a lot of emphasis on final results these days. But you're a very capable young woman, Jay,' he said. 'You can be whatever you want, no matter what marks you get. You'll find a way.'

He only said that because he had no idea – he still called it the Leaving Certificate, and didn't really understand tertiary entry scores, or the handicap the small school gave us under the new system of mean averages. It was a particularly mean system if you were in a small class as well.

Mum was the opposite. She talked about it nonstop, following me into the kitchen whenever I was making a cup of tea. She still thought I should do law just because I could. I had stopped arguing. I had already marked a bachelor of art history curatorship at ANU as my first choice on the university admissions form. If I was offered a place, I'd be one of the first graduates with that qualification.

Cattle flowed through the gate and out the other side, eyeing off the green feed below. Dad didn't race off after them the way he normally would. 'Jay, you've showed a lot of courage. Getting through school the way you have – with everything that's happened.' We watched the cattle picking up speed down the hill. 'We're really proud of you.'

I blinked back tears, focusing on the shrill cry of a plover in the neighbouring paddock. 'Thanks, Dad.'

'This place will all be yours someday. If you want it,' he said. 'I should have thought more about that. I'm sorry.'

'It's okay.' It was and it wasn't – but he was right, there was no going back. And soon I would leave for good, to start my own life.

THEY SET OUT early and for a while it was just them and the trucks hauling food into areas where people had once grown it themselves – and taking up most of the road. Jayne had two wheels over the verge to let a B-double by, sending up a shower of stones.

'Isn't there a railway out here?' Sarah said.

'They don't use it anymore.'

'No wonder the road's so bad.'

'We turn off soon – there should be less traffic.'

'So who did you take to the formal?'

'What?' She could see herself reflected in Sarah's sunglasses.

'You heard.'

'I went with Donna.'

'What?'

'You heard.'

Sarah smiled. 'How did you get away with that?'

They passed green hillocks dotted with new white lambs. Gnarled box and ironbarks clung to the creeks and fence lines. 'Well, she was new, and everyone knew about Kieran, so . . .'

'What did you wear?'

'A dress,' Jayne said. 'We both did.'

'I didn't see any pictures up at the house.'

'As if.'

'I bet your mum has them.'

Jayne pulled a face. 'I'm not so sure about that. She was embarrassed.'

'Seems okay now.'

'Yeah, *now*.' Jayne slowed to sixty as they approached a town. They rattled over the river on a wooden bridge and turned down the main street at the Anzac memorial.

'Did anything happen?'

Jayne laughed. 'No.'

'What about Kieran?'

'He didn't go,' Jayne said. 'He was suspended by then anyway.' He'd got himself suspended – smoking out the front of school – the same day she had turned him down.

'Ah.'

Her mother had pursed her lips as she made the final adjustments to her dress, the night before the dance, but said nothing, although she must have been thinking *poor Kieran*. Just as she had said nothing about the museum theft. Her father had waited until they were alone in the kitchen after dinner, Jayne with her hands in the sink, while he dried a wineglass with great concentration. 'I heard about the carved tree that went missing from your work,' he said.

She rinsed the last glass under the tap.

'You going to be okay?'

'I can handle it, Dad.'

'I'm sure you can.' He took a plate from the dish rack, dried it, and placed it on top of the others in the cupboard in front of him. 'I didn't get to catch up with Ian the other night,' he said. 'How's he going?'

Sarah and her mother were laughing in the lounge room. She washed another of the plates, part of the pale green Japanese dinner set her parents had had since their own wedding. 'Good, I think.'

'They've done great things with the golf club. We wouldn't have even considered it as a wedding venue in my day.'

'It was lovely.' She started on the cutlery.

Her father had put a hand on her shoulder. 'We worry – but we support you, Jay. In whatever you do.'

She slowed for a woman on the pedestrian crossing.

'Oh, look at that cute house,' Sarah said.

It was an original brick cottage behind roses and a picket fence, with bay windows and a sweet verandah. 'They have a good bakery here, too,' Jayne said.

The country opened up, larger paddocks and rolling hills green with wheat, the occasional freshly planted windbreak on the side of a hill. The road, too, was wider. Jayne accelerated, sitting well above the speed limit. She watched the road ahead for police.

Sarah adjusted her sun visor. 'You didn't tell your parents about the redundancy, did you?'

Jayne shook her head. 'There was already so much going on. I thought it would be better when I know what I'll be doing instead.'

'Fair enough,' Sarah said. 'So, last day today. Big.'

'Feels weird.' Everything felt weird, being home, having seen the boys, going back.

'Where's your lunch?'

Jayne swerved to avoid a pothole. 'At Elderflower.'

'At the gallery? Make sure you have the Mr Curly dessert.'

'You know the menu?

'It's famous – it was in *Gourmet Traveller*,' Sarah said. 'Would it be okay if you drop me straight at work?'

'I gathered. From the outfit.' Sarah had more suits than there had been at the wedding. All organised by colour in her walk-in wardrobe.

'I prefer camping attire, you know,' Sarah said.

'You look great in both.'

'Charmer,' she said. 'We should do more of it.'

'Camping?'

Sarah smiled. 'All of it.'

The sun was above the windscreen at last, and the highway coming up. 'I've been thinking,' Jayne said.

'Yes?'

'I think you should take the Greenpeace job.'

'Really?'

'It's using your degree to help the environment. And travel,' she said. 'With . . . what was the word you used? You envied my job's—'

'Clarity.'

'That's it – this is perfect for you.'

'I know. It's about the money.'

Jayne took the turn-off for the highway. 'If you're happy to rent out your place, we could live just as well on a lot less. I have the payout, and hopefully the scholarship.'

Sarah was grinning. 'Are you sure?'

'I could probably even travel with you sometimes.'

'You're right,' Sarah said. 'I'll ring him today. See if it's still available.'

'Okay. And we'll take it from there.' Jayne indicated and pulled into the passing lane. 'There's something else,' she said. 'I've been offered some cash-in-hand work. Something I'd really like to do. But I need to talk to you about it first.'

———

She printed out all of the collection notes relating to Emily and the Gatton collection and slipped them into her bag. Her arborglyph folder was already locked in her desk at home. She forwarded any personal files – mainly old job applications and half-finished project proposals – to her private email address and deleted them from the server. She responded to a few last emails, filed them, and cleared the inbox. Done.

She had thought herself irreplaceable for a time, the work critical. In the end, it took less than an hour to remove all signs of yourself. The machine continued on just fine without you, and you without it. It was an important lesson.

Her coffee cup, plunger, plant and bits and pieces went into a cardboard box, along with her reference books and the pictures she had stuck up on her wall over the years: images of this or that piece, postcards from colleagues when they travelled, the movie ticket stub from her first date with Sarah. *The Quiet American* – that should have been a clue that Sarah would end up working with the spooks.

It was like packing, full of mixed feelings. Endings. She was going to miss the view, looking out over the lake, and seeing the weather hit the Brindabellas. She would miss having an office, too. A job. A title. A place in the world. Who was she without all of this?

Dan knocked on the open door. 'Oh, it looks so empty.'

Jayne pulled a sad face. 'I guess it's really happening.'

'Morning tea is ready,' he said. 'No speeches. Just our team and a few extras.'

'On my way.'

———

They ate their last meal together in the gallery's sculpture garden, mist rising from the ponds, water trickling. Marnie and Dan sat either side of her and were super attentive, keeping her wineglass full. It was nice to think that she would be missed. She didn't really have room for dessert but ordered it anyway. Farewells always involved too much food.

Noni had positioned herself so that her pink and red Marimekko dress was set off perfectly by the reeds and lilies. She stood now, to make the speech. Jayne's full stomach tumbled as her history was recounted. She sipped her wine even though she knew she had already had enough. All ideas for her own speech were fading.

'Apart from being the fittest member of staff, Jayne has many strengths. We're a small family, and Jayne has been a great team player. She is one of the most dedicated and thorough officers I have worked with,' Noni said. 'Many junior staff have benefited from the *rigour* of her training and mentorship.'

Marnie and Dan giggled.

'She has also been a great advocate for the Australian collection during a period when fashions tended elsewhere. Above all, she has been a loyal friend and colleague, and I know I speak for everyone in wishing Jayne well with whatever she does next.' There was a lot of noise, more than was warranted.

Jayne stood to accept the gift. It was large and square, wrapped in silver, like a trophy. Somehow, she took hold of it, and shook Noni's hand in a relatively smooth movement.

She tried swallowing the lump in her throat but it wasn't going down. Then someone made a joke, and she managed to thank everyone and offer a few appropriate, if trite, words. 'Look, I've learned so much from all of you. This has been the best job I've ever had – but it's time for me to try other things,' she said. 'I see our dessert coming, so I should end there. Thank you.'

She made it back to her chair just as Mr Curly was set down. Its Leunig-inspired top was a twisted cone of scorched meringue curling over stewed rhubarb and lemon curd in a pastry shell. It was so perfect, she found herself in tears.

'Oh, sweetie.' Marnie put her arm around her. 'Come on.' She fished a packet of travel tissues from her handbag. 'Here.'

Jayne blew her nose.

'If you don't want Ms Curly there . . .' Dan said.

Jayne laughed. 'Hands off. She's mine.'

———

She took the new bike out early, to catch the mist over the lake. She was now a proud Bianchi owner. Once she had taken it for a test ride, she hadn't been able to resist – it was every bit as good as she had dreamed. The guys had optioned it up with time pedals and the same seat Ullrich had used. If only he had stuck with Bianchi. He had only managed fourth in this year's Tour, his first ever finish below second – but to her, he was still the gentleman of cycling.

Rowers stroked over the still water and wading birds called from beneath greening willows. It was her first official day of freedom, and the world seemed so alive. It was always most alive in the morning, and around water.

She had the masters proposal and scholarship application in her satchel, ready to hand in. It had been harder than she had expected to put her ideas into academic language again. Sometimes describing what you wanted to do was far more difficult than doing it. She was still in two minds, afraid to share her material, given what was at stake. After all those years behind the scenes, and liberating the trees in secret, this was a project she wanted the credit for.

The gears were slick, and the new tyres made a satisfying hum as she picked up speed. The saddle was a little firm, but it would soften. And she was sore from last night. With Sarah. The after-effects of camping still lingered, a little wildness brought home with them somehow.

The sun was out properly now, revealing a beautiful spring morning. She flew past banks of pink and white blossom heralding the cultural institutions up ahead. They were the real heart of the city, not the Parliamentary Triangle – though they shared that space.

She passed the flags of all of the recognised nations, from around the world. Only those from home were missing. She pedalled up and around onto Commonwealth Bridge. A breeze had picked up, off the water, cutting through her scarf. Cars sped past, locked in the rat-race. Once across, she took the spiralling path off the bridge, down to the other side of the lake.

She had to test the brakes to avoid a family of ducks – a mother leading her new brood. Grown men setting down model boats in a calm corner of the lake looked up as she sped past, joggers smiled. It was all about the bike. The colour, the lines – beauty. The machine was perfection.

On campus, she switched to the roads, arcing around to the new humanities centre among white trunks. It overlooked the old Academy of Science, the spaceship dome of a building, which until recently had housed human heads in jars of formaldehyde.

She locked her bike and removed her new helmet. Ullrich-blue, it had been her parting gift from work, with a matching jacket. Sarah must have had a hand in that. Lorikeets chattered in the branches above, blossom debris rained down. She slipped her application out of her satchel and hurried inside, her bike shoes silent on new blue carpet. The office was closed. There was a submissions box, but she still needed a signature, and was set on delivering it by hand. She checked her watch, tapped her fingers. Her first day of freedom, and she was still on a schedule.

Catering staff delivered trays of sandwiches and cakes for a conference: Sustainability and the Humanities, the sign said. The office would have to open before too long.

She took a copy of the *Canberra Times* from a fresh pile and sat on the couch to wait. It was on page two. There was to be a parliamentary inquiry into Indigenous artefacts held in Australian cultural institutions. Sometimes life could surprise you – for the better. Institution heads were supporting the inquiry, offering to open their doors. But it all would take years. In the end there would be a long report with a list of recommendations, some of which a future government might or might not implement. Too little, too late, and all too slow.

She flipped to the sport section and found the overnight cycling results a few pages in.

———

Jayne threaded her way back onto the bike path and sped past Black Mountain, towards the other end of the lake. It was more like flying than riding, the machinery propelling her on and on. She slowed at the little park and dismounted, leaning the bike against a poplar. She wandered down to the bench seat, gazed at the water, and, once she was sure there was no one around, reached into the bin for the yellow envelope. She slipped it down the front of her bike pants and returned to her ride. 'Let's go, baby.'

She reached Scrivener Dam in record time. One of the gates was open, water rushing out with a roar. She paused to watch, grabbing hold of the railing. Spray tickled her face and blurred her sunglasses. She took them off and wiped them dry on her thermal shirt.

Dairy Farmers Hill was bare but green. Local government had announced that the site, over six hundred acres, was to be given over to a national arboretum. An arboretum had been part of Griffin's original concept for the city, one of the flourishes scrapped by the miserly government of the day. Now there was to be a new design competition, incorporating the existing forests of Himalayan cedar and cork oak, planted in the city's early days, most of which had somehow survived the fire.

Meanwhile, the fires inquiry was still going. There were rumblings that Coroner Doogan wasn't the right woman for the job, which was a question that probably wouldn't be asked if the coroner were a man like everyone expected.

She waited for another cyclist to pass and a woman walking her dog to disappear over the next hill before removing the envelope from her pants and tearing it open to retrieve the keys.

The truck was waiting in the car park. A white removals van, in good order. She unlocked it, leaned her bike against a tyre, and opened up the rear doors. She lifted the bike inside and climbed after it, strapping it to the inside frame. 'See you soon, baby.' She removed her helmet, jacket and bike shoes, and hopped down to close up the back, pushing with her shoulder to force the lever into the slot. She jogged to the cab in her socks, threw in her satchel, and scrambled in.

She checked the glove box: two spare sets of plates and a packet of bullets. Not crushed, not past their best-by date, but perfect. She smiled and tucked them in the centre console for later. 'Okay. Let's go.' She started the engine. It was quiet inside the cab, but the thing was a beast, the biggest she had driven for a decade. She adjusted the side mirrors and pulled out slowly, taking the exit road back to the Parkway, towards the city.

Her first job was to move Sarah's furniture and boxes, then wash the truck, strip off the decals – Erica the plumber had taught her how to do that, with a spatula and a hair dryer – and change the plates before heading for Sydney overnight.

She changed lanes and looped up towards Acton. So many circuits, crescents and roundabouts had to have influenced Canberra's character. Its government processes, too.

She and Sarah were outside all of that now. If everything went well, she would be back in time for their first weekend of living together, and Sarah's first day with Greenpeace.

At the lights, she glanced out over the lake. The flags were flapping, and the old Lakeside ferry laboured into the wind, carrying tourists past the museum, the library and gallery. This was just the beginning.

Acknowledgements

THIS ONE TOOK half a village. I hope the result does this story justice, and reflects the energy everyone has put in. Warmest thanks to:

My wonderful publisher, Robert Watkins, for pushing me, his belief in the book, and the life he has given it.

Kate Stevens, Ali Lavau, and Elizabeth Cowell for making the sentences the best they could be. Allison Colpoys for the most beautiful cover. Anna Egelstaff and Jessica Skipper for keeping me on the road. And my extended Hachette family for their ongoing faith and support.

Lawrence Bamblett for reading an early manuscript and providing guidance on representing Wiradjuri burial trees and culture.

Ellen van Neerven for helping me get more of the most important things on the page.

My mother, Barbara, for continuing to make it possible for me to write full time.

Matthew Russell for Tour and Bianchi advice – I hope I did it justice (sorry for giving your name to the little brother in this story, but you *will* always be younger).

Fish 'coming up' is a rare but real phenomena (though probably now confined to the past). My description owes a great deal to Eric Rolls' account of a similar event on the Namoi River many years ago, in *The River*.

I would like to acknowledge the Wiradjuri people, traditional owners of the land on which I was raised – which has shaped who I am and how I see the world – and to pay my respects to Wiradjuri elders past, present, and future.

Author's Note

I AM A descendant of white settlers. I grew up on a property between Grenfell and Young, in central west New South Wales – Wiradjuri country. I first learned about Wiradjuri burial trees, or arborglyphs, in 2012, while researching a nonfiction piece about ironbarks. I found a link to a New South Wales State Library exhibition booklet containing pictures of Wiradjuri and Kamilaroi burial trees, taken in the early twentieth century. There was also a map, showing the location of dozens of 'grave trees' across New South Wales, including several not far from where I lived. I was struck by two things: the beauty of the carvings, and shame at my lack of knowledge of them. That shame only deepened when I found out that today, there are only a few trees left intact in their original locations.

It is my understanding that the arborglyphs mark the graves of significant male elders, and the unique designs both show who they were in life, and the way to the Dreamtime. There were probably hundreds of them when the First Fleet landed.

I came across them again when researching Australian nature writing. Louisa Atkinson, who wrote columns for the *Illustrated Sydney News* and the *Sydney Morning Herald* during the 1850s and 1860s, described and illustrated a grove not unlike the one in this book. Atkinson – who also referred to white settlers as 'invaders' – documented the discontinuing of the tradition. I underlined a particular sentence: 'No more trees were carved.' I don't know if that is true or not – but an idea for a story was seeded.

Many arborglyphs were destroyed as part of the initial dispossession and clearing of Kamilaroi and Wiradjuri land for farming. Some were later cut down and removed for display in gardens, museums and galleries. There were still many in place as late as the 1960s. While some would have been lost to natural causes, as a child of the 1970s and 1980s, I remember some of the conversations around the introduction of Native Title. I can imagine what happened to the rest of those trees.